Plodding along at two or three miles an hour gave Jonathan ample time to think. And his thoughts centred around Louise Vail.

She was an extraordinary woman. He had no idea why she had left home and assumed that foolish disguise. He had expected to have found that out long before now, to have exposed the girl for what she was and marched her back home to be chastised by her papa. Instead all he had learned was that she could use a sword, play whist and had the courage of a lion—and, rather than exposing her, he was going along with the game she was playing.

The trouble was he did not think it was a game; at the back of it all was something deadly serious. Courage she might have in abundance, but she was also afraid. He had seen it in her lovely eyes. He could not wait to get back to her and then, by hook or by crook, he would have it out of her.

Born in Singapore, **Mary Nichols** came to England when she was three, and has spent most of her life in different parts of East Anglia. She has been a radiographer, school secretary, information officer and industrial editor, as well as a writer. She has three grown-up children, and four grandchildren.

Recent titles by the same author:

RAGS-TO-RICHES BRIDE
THE EARL AND THE HOYDEN
CLAIMING THE ASHBROOKE HEIR
  (part of *The Secret Baby Bargain*)
HONOURABLE DOCTOR,
  IMPROPER ARRANGEMENT
THE CAPTAIN'S MYSTERIOUS LADY*

*Part of *The Piccadilly Gentlemen's Club*
  mini-series

THE VISCOUNT'S UNCONVENTIONAL BRIDE

Mary Nichols

First published in Great Britain 2010
Large Print edition 2010
Harlequin Mills & Boon Limited,
Eton House, 18-24 Paradise Road, Richmond, Surrey TW9 1SR

ISBN: 978 0 263 21160 3

Harlequin Mills & Boon policy is to use papers that are natural,
renewable and recyclable products and made from wood grown in
sustainable forests. The logging and manufacturing process conform
to the legal environmental regulations of the country of origin.

Printed and bound in Great Britain
by CPI Antony Rowe, Chippenham, Wiltshire

THE VISCOUNT'S UNCONVENTIONAL BRIDE

Chapter One

May 1760

The Vicarage garden, though not large, was a haven of tranquillity. Its flower beds were bright with the colour of hollyhocks, sunflowers, larkspur and feverfew and redolent of the scent of roses, lavender and pinks. Louise had always loved it and, even as a small girl, she had enjoyed helping the gardener with sowing seeds and nurturing the plants. The old gardener was gone now, replaced by young Alfred Rayment, but she still liked to tend the garden and was never happier than when she was on her knees, clad in a plain round gown covered with a sacking apron, weeding or picking off the dead blooms.

Today was warm and sunny after a little rain the day before, and she had decided it was time to tackle the weeds in the narrow bed beneath

her father's study window. She had been working contentedly for some time when she heard
voices through the open window.

'Elizabeth, Louise will have to be told. She is
no longer a child, she is a woman grown and old
enough to understand.' Louise clearly heard her
father's words, wondering what it was that occa-
sioned them. He sounded unusually grim. Had
she breached his strict code of conduct? Had she
whispered to her brother Luke during his sermon
on Sunday? Had he seen her riding astride which
he did not consider at all ladylike? But if that had
been the case, he would have summoned her to
the study and rung a peal over her. She had never
been in awe of him and could usually wind him
round her thumb, so she would have been peni-
tent and he would have smiled and forgiven her
before letting her go. On so trivial a matter, he
would not have had a discussion with her mother
beforehand.

'No.' This was her mother's voice, unusually
resolute for her. 'We left Moresdale to escape
the past, to make a new beginning and I do not
see why we should rake it up again now.'

'My dear, I know it is distressing for you and
will be for her, but she will soon recover. It is not

as if we are rejecting her, or that we have ceased to love her, but she will want to marry soon and the gentleman she chooses will have to be told the truth.'

Louise had ceased to pull up the weeds; she was sitting back on her heels, her weeding fork idle in her gloved hand, trying desperately to understand what was being said, hardly daring to breathe for fear of betraying her presence. That they were speaking of her, she had no doubt, but the words they were uttering were incomprehensible. What truth? What past did they need to escape from? She had a vague recollection of moving to Chipping Barnet when she was very small, but her memory of where they had lived before that was hazy.

'But why say anything at all?' her mother asked.

'Because it would be fraudulent for her to enter into a marriage with such a secret and aside from that, there is always the possibility of someone discovering it and telling her prospective husband. That would not do at all, you must see that. It would be despicable of us to allow him to learn it through a third party.'

'Who will discover it? No one knows but you and I…'

'And Catherine,' he reminded her.

'Catherine will never breathe a word about it. It is more than she dare do.'

'Surely you do not think she has managed to keep it a secret from her husband all these years? Augustus Fellowes is no fool; he would likely know if Catherine was hiding something from him. And there may be others. I was not present when Louise was born and neither were you, so how do you know no one else knows?'

Louise put her hand over her mouth to stop her cry of distress becoming audible. How could he say her mother was not present at her birth? It was nonsense. Unless… Unless… Oh, no! She would not, could not, believe that, but her mother's next words confirmed her worst fear.

'She has been so happy with us, to learn her parents are not really her parents at all will break her heart,' she was saying. 'I may not have given her birth, but I am as real as any mother. My feelings for her are the feelings of a mother. I am happy when she is happy, sad when she is sad, hurt when she is hurt, and this will undoubtedly hurt her. I don't know how you can even think of doing it to her.'

A cool wind played about Louise's hair, but it was not cold that made her shiver, but shock. She could hardly take it in. Papa, the man who had nurtured her from babyhood, praised her when she had been good, chided her when naughty, given her an education, clothed and fed her, loved her, was not her papa at all. And Mama, to whom she had turned with all her problems, which had somehow always been miraculously solved, was not her mama. It must also mean Matthew, Mark and Luke were not her brothers. They were older than she was. Did they know the truth, that she was… Who *was* she?

'Elizabeth, I am a man of the cloth,' her father went on. 'I am supposed to set an example of honesty and rectitude, but, for your sake, I have harboured this secret all these years, but my conscience will not allow me to let her marry in ignorance. She could marry a nobleman…' He wandered further from the window and Louise did not hear the end of his sentence.

'Oh, Edward, she was never so puffed up as to hope for that. It was only Luke's teasing when he said she should marry a viscount.'

'Well, of course it was. I know that, but the truth…' Again his voice was lost. He was evidently pacing back and forth.

'Then can you not postpone speaking to her until she is ready to marry? Please leave her in ignorance a little longer, I beg of you.'

Louise did not hear his reply. She flung down the gardening fork, ripped off her apron and gloves and scrambled to her feet, her mind in turmoil. She did not know which way to turn and set off at a run down the garden path. But she was not thinking of the garden, not thinking of anything except the conversation she had just heard.

At the end of the path was an arbour of honeysuckle and pink climbing roses and here she flung herself on to a bench, too numb even for tears. She had lived all her life not knowing she was anything other than the beloved daughter of the Reverend Edward Vail and his wife, Elizabeth. And now it seemed that was a lie. She felt as if she had been broken into tiny little pieces, like a smashed vase dropped from a great height, never to be put together again.

She still could not take in what she had heard and wished with all her heart the last half-hour had never happened. If Papa and Mama were not her parents, who were? How did she come to be living with the Reverend? Had she been given away by her true parents? Whatever it was, it seemed it was a stigma that could possibly make a prospective husband reject her. She had often wondered why her own eyes were an unusual hazel flecked with green when all three brothers' eyes were blue and her father's were grey. The boys had fair hair, but hers was dark. Had she, along with her colouring, inherited some bad family trait she might pass on to her children? Even if that were so, how could any mother bring herself to give away her child?

Catherine. Catherine Fellowes. The name had burned itself into her brain. Was she her natural mother? Who was she? Where was she? From what she had heard, the woman was alive and afraid to divulge the truth, even to her husband. Did that mean Louise was not her husband's child? It seemed the most likely explanation. How many people knew she was a…? What was she? A bastard? There, she had thought that dreaded word even if she had not said it aloud. She was a nobody without a name except the one given to her by the Reverend and his wife.

Why had they taken her in? Why keep the secret from her?

Could she go on, living the life she had, helping her father teach the village children, helping her mother with good works, going out riding with Luke, the youngest of her brothers, the only one still living at home, going to social occasions, meeting her friends, looking forward to falling in love and being married one day, just as if she had never heard those words? It was impossible. From now on, she would look at everything and everyone with fresh eyes, as if she had never seen them before. The people around her, the comfortable old rectory, the church where her father preached and where the whole family worshipped, the servants, her friends, the villagers: all would look different.

A cuckoo sang somewhere close at hand, its note repeating itself in her head long after it had flown away and could no longer be heard. 'Cuckoo. Cuckoo.' She was a cuckoo in the comfortable nest of the vicarage. Oh, it hurt; it hurt badly. The tears flowed at last, hot and blinding, streaming down her face unchecked.

She mopped them up until her handkerchief was sodden, but they ceased at last and gave way to anger. It was easier to be angry, anger did not hurt quite so much. She stood up and hurried purposefully back to the house, intent on confronting her parents and demanding an explanation, but they were nowhere to be found. Her father had been summoned to a sickbed and her mother had gone into the village, so she was told by Hetty, the parlourmaid. Even Luke was out, but she did not think she could confide in him, even though they were very close and he was the favourite among her three brothers, perhaps because he was nearest her own age. Apart from the servants, she was alone in the house.

She went up to her room, the pretty little room that had seen her grow from a tiny child to a beautiful woman, had seen her in all her moods, happy and sad, but never as miserable as she felt now. She sat on her bed, staring at the wall opposite her on which hung a picture of Christ surrounded by children and under it the text: *Suffer the little children to come unto me.* As a child she had loved that picture, but today its message seemed especially poignant. Papa had suffered her to come to him, but it seemed now as if he had changed his mind. Who was Catherine Fellowes? Where was she? The unknown woman seemed to be beckoning to her from the past. *Come unto me.*

Viscount Jonathan Leinster rode into London on the Edgware Road in leisurely fashion. It was a warm day and he was in no hurry, which was just as well because the crowds around the Tyburn gibbet were thicker than usual. He had just come from a dutiful visit to the family estate near Barnet and had endured the usual lecture from his father about venturing into matrimony and settling down to raise a brood of children. He would do that when he was good and ready and not before and certainly not with Dorothea Mantle, whom his parents had decided was eminently suitable. By suitable they meant she had the breeding, the social position and the dowry they considered necessary for the heir to an earl, and the Earl of Chastonbury at that. They took no account of her looks, disposition or standard of cleanliness, which, as far as he was concerned, made her eminently *unsuitable*.

He understood, though he did not see eye to eye with, their anxiety to have him married and produce the next heir, but their marriage did not set an example he wanted to follow. His mother had once told him it had been arranged by their respective fathers and she had dutifully accepted it. To everyone outside the family, they were a contented married couple, but they led separate lives with very little in common at all, except their parenthood of himself and his young sister, Arabella. His mother had not said it was a disaster, but he knew it was. His father had had a string of mistresses and his mother in desperation had taken lovers, none of which seemed to bring either of them any happiness. Belle had followed in her mother's footsteps and married the man her father had chosen for her and that had been an even bigger disaster. Henry was fifteen years older than Belle, a cruel man who used his wife ill. Jonathan had advised her to leave him, but she had a horror of the scandal and preferred to endure the misery, especially as their mother had told her it was her duty to do so. Jonathan had sworn it would not happen to him; he would need to be very, very sure before he got himself leg-shackled. The visit had not been a success.

He reined in, not so much because he was interested in what was happening around the gibbet but because the crowds were so thick it was almost impossible to force a way through them. It was then he remembered this was the day Robert Shirley, the second Earl Ferrers, was to be hanged for murder, the first peer ever to suffer that fate; the usual capital punishment for a member of the nobility was to have his head severed from his body with a blow from an axe. His pleas to be sent to the Tower for execution had been in vain; he was to be treated like any other common criminal. Even thinking about it made the hairs on Jonathan's neck stand on end and he felt as if his cravat were choking him. Not that he had ever killed anyone, except once, and that was in a duel and did not count. It was a fair fight and a long time ago, when he was a cabbage-head and had not yet learned to temper conquest with mercy.

Instead of being taken to the gallows in a plain black mourning coach, the noble lord was being allowed to take himself there in his own landau in a macabre procession that was driving the populace wild with excitement. It was headed by five coaches, all belonging to the Earl, so that as each appeared the crowd cheered it to the echo, only to be fooled because it was empty. The sixth, however, did contain the Earl, dressed in a white suit embroidered with silver. He was accompanied by the Sheriff of London and the Tower chaplain, with warders as outriders. Behind them came more coaches bearing the Lord High Steward, Masters in Chancery and twelve judges and behind these the Earl's friends come to give him a good send off. London had never seen anything like it. What, Jonathan asked himself, had James been thinking of to call a meeting of the Club today of all days? It wasn't as if they had had a hand in bringing the Earl to justice; he had needed no searching out and his action in cold-bloodedly shooting his steward had left him no defence.

Jonathan did not wait to see him hang and moved on, turning into Tyburn Lane and thence to Hyde Park Corner and into Piccadilly to the London mansion of Lord Trentham, a member of the government, who had given up a room in his house for the meetings of the Society for the Discovery and Apprehending of Criminals, popularly known as the Piccadilly Gentlemen's Club. Here he found the others of the group gathered in a room set aside for the meeting.

Jonathan breezed into the room, bade everyone good day and made them a brief bow before subsiding into the only empty chair round the table. The place at the head of the table was occupied by Lord Drymore who, as Captain James Drymore, had founded the Society nine years before. On his left was Harry, Lord Portman, immensely rich, who pretended to be a macaroni, but was as astute as any man and whose particular interest was in coiners, men, and women too, who counterfeited coins of all denominations. Their exploits were becoming so widespread they were beginning to threaten the stability of the economy.

On James's right was Sir Ashley Saunders, a one-time naval man and a confirmed bachelor, or so he maintained, whose chief concern was with the security of the realm. Both these men had been with James from the beginning and Jonathan had joined them soon afterwards. A newcomer was Alexander Carstairs, one-time cavalry captain and an expert on weaponry. And lastly, at the foot of the table was Sam Roker, who, though not ranked a gentleman, was admitted to the company on account of being James's devoted servant and friend and very useful to have with you in a tight spot. Besides, he knew his way round the rookeries of the capital where thieves and cutthroats were wont to hole up.

They were all very different men, both in background and temperament, but they worked well as a team and Jonathan was pleased to be counted one of their number. Sometimes they were joined by Sir John Fielding, London's Chief Magistrate. Blind as he was, he had a fearsome reputation and it was said he could recognise any number of thieves by the sound of their voices. Today he had other duties, probably to do with Earl Ferrers.

'I am sorry I am late,' Jonathan said. 'But there's no getting through the traffic today. I never saw such a sight. Ferrers has the whole capital in a ferment. You would never think he was riding to his death.'

'At least that is one more criminal who has received his just deserts,' Ash said. 'And I, for one, am glad to see the law deal even-handedly, no matter what rank the accused holds. There should not be one law for the rich and another for the poor...'

'We all concur in that,' James said. 'But can we get on? I intend to set off for Blackfen Manor tonight. Amy will soon be brought to bed with our fourth and I wish to be there when it happens;

even if it is only pacing the corridors. Now, Ash, what have you to report?'

'The City is quiet again after the latest onslaught of the mob, intent on pulling down the dwellings of the Irish labourers,' Sir Ashley told them. 'It was all stirred up by a building labourer who had been discharged as a troublemaker. He roused them to fury, but once I had him in custody and talked to his followers they dispersed and no real harm done, except a few bloody noses. But I will keep an eye on things.'

'Good. What about you, Harry?' James queried.

Harry stopped examining his beautifully manicured nails to answer him. 'Jed Black has escaped from Newgate again. That man is as slippery as an eel and should have been hanged long ago.'

'What's his crime?' Alex asked. Being new to the group, he did not know the story behind some of their operations.

'He's a notorious coiner and murderer,' Harry explained. 'Head of a gang. I had a hand in his arrest some weeks ago. He has a crafty lawyer who keeps finding reasons to delay his trial and he is not prepared to languish in prison when he has a lucrative operation waiting for him to return to it. He escaped once before and a devil of a job it was to track him down and have him taken up again. Now it's all to do again.'

'Do what you can,' James said. 'The man is dangerous and must be brought to book.'

'Ten to one he had accomplices on the outside and bribed the guard,' Harry went on. 'I plan to go to the gaol and ques-tion the warders and the man's fellow prisoners.'

'He's too fly to go to ground in his usual haunts,' Sam put in. 'Do you want me to help?'

'Yes, if it's agreeable to you, James.'

'By all means.' James turned to Jonathan. 'Jonathan, what about you?'

'Acting on information received, I recovered most of Lord Besthorpe's property and returned it to him and no harm done,' Jonathan reported.

'By that I suppose you mean you did not arrest the perpetrator?'

'No. He was a skinny little urchin. Couldn't bring myself to hand him in.'

James laughed, remembering how he had done the same thing himself years ago and saved Joseph Potton from a life of crime. The lad had grown into a fine upstanding young man who now worked for Jonathan.

'The nipper was used by others to climb into a tiny window at his lordship's house,' Jonathan went on. 'I came up with them while they were dividing the spoils and the men made good their escape, leaving the bratling to carry the can, but I will unearth them. The boy gave me their names in exchange for his freedom…'

It was then Luke Vail interrupted the meeting, having begged the man on the door to let him in. He doffed his hat, bowed to everyone, then addressed himself to Jonathan. 'My lord, I need your help urgently. My sister, Louise, has disappeared. We, that is the family, are beside ourselves with worry. I heard you were a member of the Gentleman's Club that likes to solve mysteries and it seemed to me you might consent to help find her.'

Jonathan studied him carefully. The young man was dressed in the sombre clothes of a cleric, which sat ill on his broad, athletic figure and youthful good looks. 'I know you, do I not?'

'Yes, my lord, I am Luke Vail. We were at the same school, though not in the same year. My father is the vicar of Chipping Barnet, hard by your father's estate. I am to take up a curacy in Bedfordshire in two weeks.'

'Louise, you say,' Jonathan said. 'I seem to remember seeing her once when I attended your father's church. We go to St Saviour's as a rule. She was a pretty little thing.'

'She is not a little thing now, my lord, she is twenty and the apple of my father's eye, being the only girl in the family.'

'When did she disappear?' James asked. 'Under what circumstances?'

'Yesterday afternoon when everyone was out of the house. My mother came home from shopping to find her missing. Her gardening apron and gloves and the little fork she used for weeding had been flung down on the flower bed and abandoned. It is not like her to be so untidy; she usually puts them away in the potting shed before she goes indoors. I questioned all the servants and our young gardener told me he had seen her running down the garden path as if the hounds of hell were after her—his words, not mine. He said she sat in the arbour at the bottom of the garden for some time, then suddenly got up and ran back into the house. Later he saw her leaving with a small portmanteau…'

'She has run away with a lover, perhaps?' Ash put in.

'Certainly not!' Luke was indignant. 'She would not, even if such a person existed, which he does not.'

'Did the gardener speak to her?' Jonathan asked.

'No, he said it was not his place to question the young mistress and she frequently went into the village carrying a basket of provisions or a bag of clothes and such like to be given to the poor families. She is well known for it and he thought nothing of it.'

'Then has she gone visiting friends?' James asked. 'Have you enquired?'

'Certainly I have. No one has seen her.'

'Did you enquire if she had boarded a coach?' James asked.

'Yes, it was one of the first things I did. No one saw her and everyone knows her in the village, so if she had done such a thing it would have been noted. Her horse is still in the stable. I rode to my brother Matthew's house about three miles distant, in case she had taken it into her head to visit him. She was not there nor had been. No one had seen her. I searched the roadside in both directions in case she had met with an accident, but to no avail. She had not been to Mark's either. He is another brother and has a living near Rickmansworth, though how she would have gone to him I have no idea. Someone would have had to take her. He had seen nothing of her. We do not know what to do next. My mother is distraught.'

'I can understand that,' James said. 'And she left no clue as to her intentions?'

'No, though she did leave a note telling our parents not to worry and she would soon be back…'

'There! I said she had run away with a lover,' Ash said.

'No, she has not. I wish you would treat the matter seriously.'

'We are treating it seriously,' James assured him. 'But we exist to track down criminals. If no crime has been committed…'

'Please make an exception in this case. She would not willingly have worried our parents by staying away all night. We think something dreadful must have happened to her. Help us to find her, I beg of you,' Luke said desperately.

'This seems like a job for you, Jonathan,' James said at last. 'But you must lose no time or the trail will have gone cold.'

Jonathan rose to obey. 'How did you arrive here?' he asked Luke.

'I rode.'

'Good. I will ride back with you at once. Let us hope the crowds are not so thick now…'

They could not ride side by side until they had passed the Tyburn gibbet. The hanging had been accomplished and the body taken down, but some of the crowd still milled about, talking about it, buying mementoes, waiting to see if there would be any other convicts to meet the same fate. There was usually more than one dispatched on hanging days. As soon as they were on the open road and the noise behind them had faded to a distant hum, Jonathan questioned Luke more closely about his sister's disappearance. Had anything happened to trigger it off? Had she been unhappy at home? Had she expressed a desire to visit friends or relations? To all of which the young man was non-committal.

And when he asked for a description of Louise, the only reply Luke made was, 'Oh, she is beautiful.'

'That is not much help. What does she look like? Is she tall or short? Fat or thin? What is the colour of her hair and her eyes?' He still had that hazy memory of the little girl in church, in a blue dimity dress with a huge blue bow in her hair. It had been thick, curly hair, he recalled.

'She is tall for a woman, I suppose, and slim. Her hair is brown, but not an ordinary brown. It has a special sheen to it. Her eyes are...' He stopped to think. 'Green, I think. Or perhaps they are brown. Do you know, I cannot be sure.'

'No distinguishing features?'

'She don't wear patches. Nor powder. Nor a wig. Don't need 'em.'

It was as much as he could expect; brothers never were very observant when it came to sisters, though they might describe their mistresses perfectly well.

When they arrived at the Barnet vicarage, he was greeted by a sombre cleric and a woman beside herself with grief. He was of average height and breadth, wearing a bag wig and spectacles. She was approaching fifty, a small, neat woman, with greying hair and pale greeny-grey eyes. The pair appeared to be out of sorts with each other, but endeavoured to set aside their differences to offer him refreshment and answer his questions. They could only repeat what Luke had told him, that Louise intended to go because she had left a note, but that was understandable since everyone was out and would wonder what had become of her; it only said she would not be gone long and would soon be back. They did not, for a moment, believe she meant to worry them to death. She was a madcap, always ready for adventure, her brothers had seen to that, but that did not mean she was unfeeling. She would not hurt a fly, let alone her family, all of whom loved her.

'Might I see the letter?' he asked.

Mrs Vail fetched it for him. It was very creased and tear-stained. *Dearest Mama and Papa, they say eavesdroppers never hear good of themselves, but I could not help listening, so you will understand why I have to make this journey, but I shall not be gone long, so do not worry about me. I promise I will be back as soon as I can. Your very affectionate Louise.*

'What was it she overheard?' he asked.

'It was nothing,' Mrs Vail said. 'My husband and I were talking. The window was open and she was weeding the flower bed. We had no idea she was there.'

'Whatever it was would have made her unhappy?'

Husband and wife looked at each other as if unwilling to answer and it was left to Luke to reply. 'She was always cheerful. She had nothing to be unhappy about.'

Jonathan felt sure they were hiding something; Mrs Vail was particularly uneasy. 'What time did you go out and what time did you return?'

'It was the middle of the morning,' the Reverend said. 'I had to visit a parishioner who was dying and took the gig. I gave my wife a lift into Barnet to do some shopping and arranged to meet her at a friend's house to bring her home. It was about five in the afternoon when we returned.'

'And young Mr Vail?' Jonathan queried, turning to Luke.

'I was out riding. I arrived home just before my parents, but I did not think anything about Louise being missing, until my mother became worried.'

'So the house was empty for five hours. May I question the servants?'

'Certainly, you may,' the Reverend told him. But I have already spoken to them all myself.'

'I am sure you have, but they might have remembered something more.'

Jonathan swallowed the tea he had been given while the servants were summoned. One by one they denied any knowledge of Louise's whereabouts or any intention she might have had to leave home. He asked and was given permission to examine the garden and speak to the outside servants. A young man weeding a flower bed looked up as he approached. He assumed he was the young gardener Luke had mentioned.

'I believe you saw Miss Vail before she left,' he said. 'I have been asked by the Reverend to help find her.'

'Yes. She was acting strange and so I told them, but I never spoke to her. I wish I had, 'cos when I went home I discovered my sister had disappeared too.'

'Your sister? Do you think they are together?'

'I reckon they must be. Miss Vail would never be so foolish as to go anywhere but the village all on her own. An' Betty left a note sayin' she was goin' on an adventure an' it was a great secret and I wasn't to tell a soul, but when I saw 'ow worried Mistress Vail was, o' course I told her. It seemed to ease her mind. It vexes me, that it does. Betty shouldn't never 'ave agreed to go, and I'm worried about her too.'

'You did right to speak out. How many out-door servants are there here?'

'Only me and the coachman, Jaggers. You'll find 'im in the stables.' He pointed in the direction of a group of outbuildings.

Jaggers, it appeared, had been with the family man and boy and he could tell his lordship all about the boys and their little sister. 'Spoiled, she were,' he said, 'though not in bad way. She was the sunniest little thing you could imagine and a welcome daughter after three boys. They treated her like one o' theirselves, always ready for mischief and for a dare.'

'They have not always lived at Chipping Barnet, have they? I seem to remember an earlier incumbent when I was a boy.'

'They come from Yorkshire. I were with them then, came along o' them when they moved. Drove the carriage for them.'

'Whereabouts in Yorkshire?

'Moresdale.'

'Could Miss Vail have gone there?'

The old man shrugged. 'She were askin' me about it earlier in the day, but then she was always full o' questions. I didn't think anything of it.'

'When? What time?'

'About noon, as near as I c'n say.'

'Was she agitated?'

'No, just talking, as if she were interested like, while she groomed her mare.'

'But she didn't take the mare out?'

'No. An' she couldn't 'ave asked for the gig because the Reverend had it out.'

'So, either she was walking or she meant to take the stage.'

'If she have bin so foolish as to attempt the stage, I fear for her, that I do, what with the terrible state of the roads and the chance of being attacked and robbed. I hopes you can fetch her back and no harm done, my lord.'

Jonathan thanked him and returned to the house where he found Mrs Vail alone in the parlour. 'Ma'am, I have just been speaking to your coachman. He tells me that you moved here from Moresdale.'

'Yes, we did. Fifteen years ago now.'

'Do you think your daughter might be attempting to go back there?'

'She does not know where it is. She was only five when we moved down here. I doubt she would remember it. And why would she want to go back there?'

'I do not know, but perhaps you might hazard a guess?' It was said meaningfully. 'Why, for instance, did she abandon her gardening clothes on the flower bed? It seems to me that something startled her. Can you tell me what that could have been?'

'No, my lord.'

'Cannot or *will* not?'

'Cannot. I beg you not to ask.'

The lady was so nervous, Jonathan was sure she was hiding something. 'Madam, I will do what I can to find your daughter, but it is necessary for me to know everything, you understand? I cannot work in the dark.'

'My lord, forgive me, I am not myself.' She seemed to gather herself with an effort of will. 'All I can tell you is that we were talking of the place where Louise was born and that might have aroused her curiosity, but I can hardly believe she would try to go there. She has never travelled anywhere on her own before. It is two hundred miles away and goodness knows what at the end of it—' She stopped suddenly as if conjuring up some dreadful calamity in her mind's eye that she could not put into words.

He decided she was afraid of something else beside the hazards of the journey. 'Nevertheless, you do believe that is where she is heading?'

'Perhaps.' It was said reluctantly.

'Does she have any money? She will not go far without it.'

'The Reverend gives her pin money…'

'How far will that take her?'

'I do not know. She has little reason to spend it. Furbelows and fancy ribbons never appealed to her, so she may have a little saved. And…' She stopped and swallowed hard. 'I fear she sometimes plays cards with Luke and his friends and is always boasting of how much she has won.'

He almost laughed aloud at the thought of a vicar's daughter gambling, but restrained himself. It was not a time for laughter. 'How much has she won?'

'I have no idea. It is only a little fun, but if my husband were to hear of it he would be very angry. I cannot think it amounts to more than a few shillings.' She was unhappy about his questioning and wished to bring it to an end. 'Go after her, my lord, please, bring her safely back to us.'

'I will do what I can to find her, but short of tying her up and carrying her off, I cannot force her to return, you understand.'

'Yes, but do your best to persuade her, I beg you. But whatever you do, please see she comes to no harm.'

He was still not completely satisfied, but he did not think he would get anything more out of her and took his leave. Finding runaway daughters was not the sort of thing the Club took on, but there was no time to go back and consult James, who in any case had gone home to be with his family, so it was up to him to decide whether to proceed. There was a mystery here and if the law had been broken, then that was reason enough. Besides, he was intrigued.

'I don't know why we 'ad to go all the way to Lunnon, only to come straight back ag'in,' Betty said as the coach drew up at the Red Lion in Barnet. 'You changed yer mind, Miss Louise?'

'Shh,' Louise whispered, glancing at the other

passengers to see if they had heard, but the noise of the horses being changed and the ostlers and coachmen shouting to each other had drowned her voice. 'I am not Miss Louise. I am Mr Louis Smith. And you are Mrs Smith. Call me Lou, like I told you. And in answer to your question, no, I have not changed my mind. We could not have boarded the coach here, everyone knows us.'

Betty giggled. 'Not like that, they wouldn'.'

Louise looked down at herself. She was wearing a pair of breeches, which had once belonged to one of her brothers, tucked into her own riding boots, a blue wool coat with enor-mous pockets and pearl buttons, a long matching waistcoat, a white linen shirt and a black neckcloth, all once worn by one or other of her brothers. Her hair was tied back in a queue such as military men adopted and fastened with a slim black ribbon and topped by a tricorne hat. The ensemble was completed with a sword belt into which she had put Matthew's small sword; since becoming a parson he had ceased to carry a weapon. And into the capacious pocket of the coat she had put a pistol, which she had taken from a drawer in Luke's room, along with a pouch containing ball, powder and tinder. She was a good shot, but had never aimed at anything but a target and doubted she would have the courage to use it in any other circumstances. But having it made her feel a little safer, more manly.

The disguise was the result of much soul searching the day before on how best to travel. She felt she would be safer as a man and she knew there were some old clothes of her brothers stored in the vicarage attic, but even in men's clothes the prospect of going alone had daunted her, although not enough to make her turn from her determination to make the journey. And she knew roughly where to go. Jaggers was a talkative man and liked to tell her tales of his boyhood in Yorkshire and how he had been taken on by the Reverend, 'afore he come down south' as he put it. He hardly needed encouragement and she soon had a place name, the one she had heard her mother mention, though he had no idea exactly where it was in relation to Barnet. 'Moresdale is a fair distance,' he said. 'T'other side of York. It were where you were born, Miss Louise.' She wondered if he knew the truth, but she couldn't go round asking everyone she met if they knew she was not her father's daughter.

She had been leaving the house with a portmanteau containing her disguise, together with some feminine clothes she would need when she arrived, when she became aware of Alfred Rayment, their young gardener, watching her. She thought her adventure had been foiled before it began, but he did not seem particularly curious and she supposed it was because she often took items of clothing to the village in a bag and he would think nothing of it if she acted naturally. She smiled and went on her way.

It was then she hit upon the idea of asking his sister if she would accompany her. Alfred and Betty lived in a cottage on the other side of the village. Betty was seventeen, a couple of years younger than Alfred, and acted as his housekeeper. They had no parents. She had a round, rosy face, blue eyes and thin pale hair. She was always clean and neatly dressed. When asked if she would like to go, she had become as excited as a child. 'I ain't ever left home afore,' she had said. 'It'll be summat to tell me children, if'n I was ever to find m'self a husband.'

It solved another problem for Louise—where and how to change into her disguise. Betty thought it was a huge joke and Louise did not tell her it was very far from a joke.

'Perhaps not, but I could not take the risk leaving dressed as a woman,' she said in answer to her friend's comment. 'We would never have got away if someone had recognised me and told the Reverend.'

The girl was in her best dress, the bodice of which was laced across her stays and the neck filled with a cotton fichu. They were an unprepossessing couple, but that suited Louise's purpose. 'Yes, but why did we have to go all the way to Lunnon first,' Betty persisted. 'I never bin in such a frightenin' big place afore.'

Never having travelled by public coach and having little idea where they habitually stopped, they had walked towards London, carrying their bags. It soon became obvious to Louise they must find transport. Their bags, though containing the minimum possible, were heavy and it would not be long before she was missed and being searched for. To be found on foot within half-a-dozen miles of home would be the ultimate humiliation. They had stopped a carrier's cart and asked the driver for a lift. He had taken them right into the heart of the Capital and directed them to the Blue Boar in Holborn where, so he told them, they could pick up a coach to almost any destination they cared to name.

But there had been no coaches leaving for the north until the morning. They had walked about all night, not daring to ask for a room anywhere, and at dawn had made their way to the inn and paid their fare to York. Louise was taken aback by the amount she had to pay; three guineas left little for bed and board on the way and she feared her small savings would not last and she might have to sell what little jewellery she had. She had no idea how to go on after they reached York, but she told Betty, as confidently as she could, they would cross that bridge when they came to it.

She was almost holding her breath in case someone whom she knew boarded the coach at Barnet, but no new passengers claimed seats and the original four were soon on their way again. The die was cast. She was going to find Catherine Fellowes and then she might have her questions answered. It had briefly occurred to her that the lady might no longer live in Moresdale even if she ever had; she could not even be sure of that. She might have moved away, or even died.

Louise hoped not; it would be sad never to have known her. She would never find out if she did not go, would she? Curiosity had always been one of her characteristics, but this was more than curiosity; this was a need to discover her identity. But it did not mean she wanted to leave the loving couple she would always look upon as her parents; she would come back. She had said so in her letter. She hoped they understood that this was something she had to do and it did not mean she loved them any less.

She settled back in her seat, prepared to sleep if she could, and advised Betty to do the same. 'We have been awake all night,' she whispered, with one eye on the couple sitting opposite them. 'And if we are asleep, no one will engage us in conversation, will they?'

Most of the roads close to the metropolis had been turnpiked, but even those had been churned up by heavy wagons in winter and baked into ruts in summer. They were jolted from side to side and sleep was almost impossible. They passed through Hatfield, changed horses at the Duke of York at Ganwick Corner, then again at Stevenage without incident and were approaching Baldock when it happened.

Louise was drowsing, but was jolted fully awake by the shout of the guard and the coach being pulled to a sudden stop, followed by the sound of a gun being fired.

'Highwaymen!' she gasped, as the door was wrenched open and a black cloaked figure wearing a mask and brandishing a pistol ordered them out on to the road.

Chapter Two

Jonathan left the vicarage and rode to Chaston Hall, which was only eight miles distant, where he kept his coach and carriage horses. Finding a standing for them in London was difficult and his father's estate in Barnet was large enough for them to be no trouble to him and near enough to the capital for him to send for them if they were needed.

He told his parents he would be away some time on the Society's business, though he did not explain the nature of the business. And though they decried his secretiveness, they had become used to it. They bemoaned the day he had ever met James Drymore and his band of gentleman thieftakers. If it were not for them, he would be dancing attendance on the year's hopefuls at London's society balls and finding himself a wife. He would not find one chasing all over the countryside after criminals. At twenty-five, it was high time he set up his own establishment; his bachelor rooms in town did not count.

He smiled politely and allowed them to go on for some minutes before excusing himself and hastening out to the stables to tell Joseph Potton to harness up his travelling coach. He might be quicker on horseback, but if and when he caught up with the runaway he would need a vehicle to convey her home. 'You and I are going alone,' he told Joe. 'Take a change of clothes, I do not know how long we will be gone.'

Joe grinned. 'Chase 'em and nab 'em business, m'lord?' he queried, using his own name for the Society. He was a sturdy twenty-year-old, though sometimes he behaved like someone twice his age, which was hardly surprising considering he had been born in poverty without a father and with a mother who turned him out when she was entertaining her men friends. The courts and alleyways of Ely had been his home. He would still be there if James had not rescued him and given him an education to fit him for a life in service. It was on James's recommendation Jonathan had taken him on.

'Yes, now make haste—we have not a moment to lose.' The young lady had a day's start and must be well on her way by now. In Jonathan's favour was the fact that he had a far superior vehicle and was prepared to drive through the night, which the public coach would not do.

He left the boy to do his bidding while he went to his room to supervise his packing and console Hilson, his valet, for not taking him too. He changed swiftly from his silk coat, waistcoat and breeches and his lace-trimmed shirt into something resembling a yeoman farmer: brown stuff breeches tucked into sturdy boots, dark brown wool coat over a long narrow waistcoat and flat-crowned felt hat. He had never worn a wig and his own hair was tied back in a queue. The whole outfit horrified Hilson and though he had seen it before he bewailed that his young master should so far forget his rank and dignity as to dress like one of his father's hired labourers. Jonathan simply laughed and pointed out he would not have the embarrassment of dressing him if he did not accompany him. Even so, he did allow the man to pack some decent clothes for him in case it became necessary to revert to being the Viscount. He heard the coach being brought to the front door and, picking up his bag, raced down and climbed in.

While daylight lasted, they made good time and had passed through Stevenage and were approaching Baldock, in the gathering twilight when Joe pulled the horses to a halt. Jonathan stuck his head out of the door. 'What's up?'

'Something blocking the road ahead, my lord. A coach I think. Oh, lor', it's a hold-up!'

Jonathan left the carriage and climbed up beside Joe, the better to see. There was no doubt of it; the coach ahead of them was being searched by armed robbers. One had his head and half his torso in the coach searching it while its passengers stood on the verge being guarded by a second man with a pistol.

Jonathan, who always travelled with a pair of loaded pistols against such an eventuality, withdrew them from his pocket and urged Joe to spring the horses and make as much noise as he could.

Joe enjoyed doing that and between them they managed to make it sound like a cavalry charge. Joe brought the horses to a shuddering halt only inches from the back of the coach. Jonathan stood up on the box and fired his pistol at the gun hand of the man guarding the passengers. It flew from his hand. He swore and put his injured hand to his mouth. The man who had been searching the coach emerged and stood beside it empty-handed. 'Stand still if you value your life!' Jonathan commanded, aiming his second pistol at him, at the same time handing the first to Joe to be reloaded, which was done in record time. It was a routine they had practised many times and it meant he nearly always had a loaded weapon to hand. The robbers, seeing themselves outmanoeuvred, gave themselves up.

'Thank you, sir,' the coachman said, looking daggers at his guard, whose blunderbuss lay undischarged on the seat. 'A most timely intervention. We are in your debt.'

Joe, the coachman and the guard tied the men securely with spare cord usually used to secure luggage on the roof, and bundled them into Jonathan's carriage, while he turned to see if the passengers had been hurt.

'You are to be congratulated, sir,' a gentleman in the plain black suit of a cleric told him. 'Such presence of mind I have rarely met. I am persuaded you are a military man?'

Jonathan bowed towards him, neither con-

firming nor denying it. 'Is your good lady hurt?'
The lady in question was sagging against him, a
handkerchief held to her face.

'Very shocked, sir, but not hurt. She will be
calmer by and by.'

Jonathan turned to the other couple, a slight
young man and a girl, who was white as paper
and shaking like an aspen. The man had his arm
across her shoulders. 'I must add my thanks to
the others,' he said, in the rather reedy voice of a
youth. It puzzled Jonathan because it was so out
of keeping with the look of him.

Dressed in a coat and breeches of blue
woven silk, well made but not of the high-
est order, he stood erect, his head high, one
hand on the hilt of the sword at his waist, the
other round the young lady, protecting her.
His face looked as though it had never needed
a razor, and his eyes—oh, those eyes! They
were wondrous eyes for a boy: the colour of
a hazelnut, flecked with tiny spots of clear
green. And his hair, for all it was tied back
and crammed under a hat, was like dark, bur-
nished copper; brown, yes, but it only just
escaped being red. He assumed they were
two not-quite-adult youngsters running away

to Scotland to be married against the will of their parents. He smiled at them. It was none of his business.

'I suggest you return to your coach and continue your journey,' he said. 'I will follow in my carriage and make sure you are not waylaid again.'

'You would travel with those two?' the young man asked in surprise, indicating the two prisoners.

'No, I shall ride up beside my driver and take them to the magistrate in Baldock. Have no fear, they will not trouble you again.' He watched as the four passengers climbed in. The coachman inspected the vehicle for damage; having satisfied himself there was none, he climbed up beside the guard and they set off.

Jonathan returned to his own carriage and followed, cursing his luck because he had to drive slowly behind the coach when he would rather be further on his way. He could only hope that Miss Vail did not deviate from the usual route to the north and throw him off the scent. It was unlikely; the Great North Road was the only viable road and even that had not been turnpiked its whole length.

* * *

'He were impressive, don't you think?' Betty murmured to Louise, watching the cleric trying to comfort his sobbing wife.

'Who?'

'Why, our rescuer, o' course. The way he made those two ruffians stand still and allow themselves to be trussed up was summat miraculous.'

'He had a pair of pistols.'

'So he did, and he knew how to use them.'

'You think I should have pulled mine from my pocket and fired it?'

'No, course not. You didn' hev the time.'

'It is not loaded either.'

Betty had a fit of the giggles, which Louise put down to nerves. 'Do leave off, my dear,' she said, managing a gruff voice for the benefit of the other passengers. 'I am sure the Reverend and his wife do not find the situation amusing.'

Betty became serious for a moment, then smiled again. 'Oh, but he was handsome, don' you think?'

'I did not notice,' Louise lied. You would have to be made of stone not to notice a man like that. Their eyes had met and held for a long minute as if each were trying to memorise the features of the other. He had a clean open face and blue eyes, which reminded her a little of Luke, whom she had left behind. His hair, the colour of ripe corn, had been cut short and curled around his face, leaving the back long enough to be secured in a short plait and tied with a narrow ribbon. His clothes were nothing to speak of, but he wore them with distinction. The clerical gentleman was probably correct and he had been a soldier. But she agreed with Betty—he was extraordinarily handsome. She had to remind herself she was supposed to be a man and should not be thinking such thoughts.

She and Betty had rear-facing seats and if she leaned a little towards the door, she could see the other coach, still following them. It was a rather grand equipage and not at all in keeping with the man, which made her curious, curious enough to make her forget, or at least push from her mind, the reason for her journey. She began to wonder if he was all he seemed. Had he stolen the carriage? Had he had designs on their coach himself and been foiled by the highwaymen ahead of him? But if that were the case, he would hardly have arrested them and promised to take them to the magistrate. Of course he could let them go as soon as they were out of sight, but the coach stayed close behind, the young driver matching the pace of his horses to theirs. It did not stop; no one left it.

They were soon in Baldock and passing under the arch into the yard of the Bull. Louise felt some trepidation on entering such an establishment, but stiffened her spine and in her best masculine voice requested a room for himself and his wife, giving their names as Mr and Mrs Smith. If the innkeeper thought that was an alias, he gave no indication of it and conducted them to a tiny room tucked away at the back of the building. If you want a room to y'selves, this is all I've got,' he said. 'It's this or share.'

It was hardly more than a large cupboard with a foot-square window, but sharing was the last thing Louise wanted to do. 'Thank you,' she said. 'It will do. And we should like a meal.'

'Dining room's downstairs,' he said, lighting another candle from the one he held and putting it down on a chest, which, with a bed and a single stool, was the only furniture in the room. There was a jug of water and a bowl on the chest and a rough towel hanging on a hook.

As soon as he had gone, Louise sank on to the bed and looked about her, glad the candle was so feeble; she did not think she would like to see her surroundings any clearer. 'Well, here we are,' she said with an attempt at cheerfulness. 'Our first night.'

Betty stood looking down at her. 'How many other nights like this do you reckon we shall hev?'

'Four or five. I suppose it depends on the state of roads and not having any more hold ups like we had today.'

'I pray we do not, though if we was to be res- cued every time by a couple of handsome strang- ers then I shouldn' mind.'

'Oh, Betty, how can you say that? And re- member you are supposed to be my wife. If you start making eyes at strange men, I shall have to become very jealous.'

'Oh, wouldn' that be fun!'

'I do not want to draw attention to ourselves, Betty,' she said severely. 'I am not sure my dis- guise will bear close scrutiny.'

'Nor I don' neither, 'specially if you was to tek your coat off. That binding you put round y'self ain't tight enough.'

Louise had stripped off her coat in order to wash and could see what Betty meant. As soon as she had completed her ablutions, she tightened the binding that was supposed to flatten her breasts and was not at all comfortable and put the coat on again. 'Let us go down and find the dining room,' she said. 'I am hungry.'

'T'ain't to be wondered at, we had no supper last night, nor breakfast this mornin', and the bread and ham we had at that inn in Welwyn were not enough to feed a sparer,' Betty complained.

'Come along then. And please remember I am Lou, not Miss Louise, not Miss Anything.'

'Yes, m…Lou.'

The dining room was crowded, but the first person Jonathan saw when he entered was Mr Smith sitting on the end of the bench at the refectory table, which all but filled the room. He had taken off his hat and his thick hair seemed to spring out round his face. His nondescript wife sat beside him. Both were tucking into their pork chops as if they had not eaten for a week. He smiled, walked down the length of the table and took the vacant seat at the head of the table next to the young man.

'Good evening,' he said, as a waiter put a plate of food in front of him. 'I trust the rest of your journey was uneventful?'

Louise lifted startled eyes to his. She had been talking about him only a few minutes before and here he was in the flesh. He was searching her face as if puzzled by it and she felt the colour rise in her cheeks. How stupid for a man to blush! 'Yes, uneventful,' she murmured, remembering to lower the timbre of her voice, then turned to look down at her food and concentrate on eating.

'We didn't think we should see you again,' Betty told him, picking up a chicken leg in her fingers and gnawing at it. 'What happened to those two highpads?'

'They are safely locked up,' he said, and though he was addressing Betty it was at Louise he was looking.

She knew that if she continued to behave like a nervous schoolgirl he would soon penetrate her disguise and she must do something to assert herself as masculine. She started by taking a long pull at the quart of ale which stood at her elbow and was glad her brothers had dared her to try theirs so she was not as shocked as she might have been by its bitter taste.

'Glad you turned up when you did, sir,' she said, putting the pot down again. 'We were taken aback by the suddenness of the attack and I did not have time to draw my own weapon…'

'Your weapon?' Jonathan queried, smiling faintly.

'Yes. One of Mantle's best.' She thrust her hand into the pocket of her coat and pulled out the pistol.

'Good Lord! I never thought you meant it. Can you fire it?'

'It would not be much use to me if I could not, would it?' It was put back in her pocket before he could pick it up and realise it was unloaded. Mark, who was the best marksman of her brothers, had always said it was dangerous to carry a loaded pistol; it might go off in one's pocket, and the sight of an unloaded one was often enough to save one's life. The gentleman's arrival on the scene had saved her from having to put that theory to the test. 'I fear highpads are the scourge of travellers and one needs to defend oneself.'

'True,' he murmured, endeavouring not to smile. 'And the sword?'

'Given me by my fencing master,' she said. That was partly true. Matthew had taught her to fence and it had been his sword, one she practised with until Papa had told her it was not a suitable accomplishment for a young lady.

'And no doubt you can use it?'

'Oh, you need have no fear on that score.'

He was amused. No doubt the young shaver was boasting to impress his young lady, though to look at her she seemed singularly unimpressed. At that moment she was making eyes at Joe, who had seated himself opposite her. He would have to have words with that young man.

'Let us introduce ourselves,' he said. 'My name is Jonathan Linton.' It was a name he used when on Society business. It left him free to assume whatever pose he chose; sometimes a title could be a hindrance.

'Louis Smith. This is my wife. We are on our way to York to visit relatives.'

'What a coincidence, so am I, travelling to York, I mean.'

She stifled her dismay; he was altogether too perspicacious for her peace of mind. 'I hope you have not been too delayed by having to come to our rescue.'

He smiled. 'I could not have gone past, could I? Your coach was blocking the road. Besides it would have been unchivalrous and it behoves all of us to maintain law and order where we can.'

'You are never a Bow Street Runner!' gasped Betty.

'No, I am not. I am simply a private citizen doing his duty as he sees it, and glad I am that I did. I have learned those two men are wanted for other crimes in London and will be sent back there to stand trial. I am happy to have been instrumental in bringing them to justice.' He smiled as he spoke. The two men had seen no reason to hide their real names when asked for them at the Baldock magistrate's office and he had been surprised and delighted to discover they were the two he wanted in connection with Lord Besthorpe's burglary, fleeing London. His journey had not been a wasted one, even if he never caught up with Miss Louise Vail.

He ought to have driven on through the night in an effort to catch her, but had decided not to risk his horses on the roads which, north of

Baldock, were not always kept in good repair, in spite of the tolls. If his own horses were given a night's rest, he could take them on the next day instead of hiring post horses. Besides, he was intrigued by the young whippersnapper who faced him now. There was something smoky going on and he hated unsolved mysteries.

The meal was finished and the cloth removed. A jug of ale, a bottle of Madeira wine and another of cognac were put on the table alongside glasses and a pack of cards. Jonathan, still amused by the boy, decided to test him further. He picked up the cards and began to shuffle them. 'Do you play, Mr Smith?'

Louise hesitated. She could play a good hand of whist, but no doubt the man expected to play for money and she did not know if she dare risk it. But dare she refuse? She was sure he was already suspicious of her. And supposing she were to win, how much easier it would make their journey to have a few extra guineas in her pocket. 'Yes, I like a game, sir, but I do not play deep. To risk more than one can spare seems to me irresponsible in the extreme.' This was a long speech for her and was said in the deepest voice she could manage, which made her cough. She took another long pull of ale to clear her throat.

'We are in agreement, Mr Smith,' Jonathan said, pouring more ale for himself. 'But one must do something to wile away the rest of the evening.' He paused and again scrutinised her face. 'Unless you prefer conversation?'

'No, let us play a hand or two of whist,' Louise said quickly. At least playing cards she would not need to talk much and the men might not notice she drank very little.

Jonathan turned to two men who sat on the other side of Louise. They were dressed in fustian coats and leather breeches and wore black bag wigs. 'Gentlemen, will you make up a four?'

They agreed and moved to join Jonathan and Louise at the head of the table, introducing themselves as Bill Williams and Charlie Burrows. Betty moved away to talk to Joe. Louise did her best to concentrate on the cards at the same time as she kept an ear for what Betty was saying. She was not sure the girl would not inadvertently give the game away. She lost the first hand and reluctantly added a half guinea to the pot. 'Betty, my dear, I think you should go to bed,' she suggested. 'I am sure you are tired and we have a long day ahead of us tomorrow.'

Betty scowled but obeyed. Louise realised everyone was grinning. She laughed. 'Must keep one's hand on the mare's bridle, don't you think? Shall we go on? Your deal, I believe, Mr Burrows.'

The evening wore on. Without having to worry about Betty, Louise was able to concentrate and luckily for her the cards fell well. She put them to good use and soon had a small pile of coins at her elbow. But the strain of maintaining her role and her previous sleepless night were beginning to tell. This was nothing like making up a fourth with her brothers, even though they had taught her well. This was fraught with tension. And Mr Jonathan Linton seemed not to be able to take his eyes off her. Was he studying her face in order to intimidate her into playing badly? She began to feel more and more uncomfortable.

'I think this must be my last hand.' she said, putting her hand to her mouth to stifle a yarn.

'But the night is young,' Williams protested.

'Nevertheless I am for my bed.'

'Ain't anyone ever told you, 'tis not done to go off

with the winnings without giving a body a chance to win some of it back?' Burrows added.

'There is no sense in going on if one is going to lose everything one has gained,' she said, putting her hand over the coins she had won and drawing them towards her, intending to put them in her pocket. Before she could do so Jonathan put his hand over hers and stopped her.

'You can't do that, Mr Smith.' He was enjoying himself hugely. Those wide eyes, the unruly hair, the delicate hands with their neatly manicured nails, the voice that wavered from a squeak to a rumble, the delicate colour in his cheeks, all proclaimed a young lad barely out of puberty, trying to act like a grown man. Burrows and Williams had undoubtedly come to the same conclusion and had determined having some sport with him.

Not that he would be an easy victim. Jonathan had watched him closely; the young man seemed to know which cards each of his opponents held, had played his own hand judiciously and won. Had he cheated? If he had, he had not detected how it had been done. But what if he were not the innocent, but an accomplished confidence trickster? His apparent innocence would deceive most people.

Solving mysteries was the *raison d'être* of the

Club; as long as they were travelling in the required direction, he would to stick with his mission and have a little fun, at the same time. He still had his hand over the young man's, imprisoning both it and the coins beneath it. 'You have to prove your success was not beginner's luck.'

She longed for her bed and the feel of his warm, strong hand over hers was having a very strange effect on her. It made her feel weak and womanly and that would never do. She pulled her hand free. 'I have to prove nothing, Mr Linton. It was a little game to wile away the evening. They were your words. The evening has sped by and now I am for bed. My wife will be waiting for me.'

'We must not keep the little lady waiting, must we?' Williams said with a laugh. 'Whose hand is on the reins now?' Then everyone laughed. Jonathan's own lips twitched, but he refrained from joining in; he did not like to see the boy humiliated. Why that was, he did not know.

Furious Louise snatched up her winnings and left the room with all the dignity she could muster.

Betty woke as she was taking off her coat. 'Did you win?'

'Yes.'

'Good. We can eat well tomorrow then.'

They could, but what it had cost her in nervous tension was only now beginning to make itself felt. She was shaking with relief to have escaped so lightly. Those men could easily have detained her and taken her winnings from her—Burrows and Williams, in particular, frightened her. She did not include Mr Linton in her condemnation, though why she did not she was not so sure. He was not like the other two, being more of a gentleman, but what difference did that make? Gentlemen could also be rogues.

She put the extra guineas in her purse and slipped it under her pillow before climbing into bed beside Betty. If her study of the timetables of the York coach had informed her correctly, she had three more nights to endure like this one. At least, they might not be so bad. She put her hand under the pillow and felt the comforting presence of the purse. Betty was right; they would travel in more comfort the rest of the way.

Before he undressed for bed himself, Jonathan sat down to write his daily log, which was required of him when on the business of the Society. He stated the facts without embroidery.

Mrs Vail's attitude had led him to believe there was something suspicious about her daughter's disappearance and after questioning everyone at the vicarage, he had come to the conclusion she was travelling to Yorkshire, probably accompanied by a young girl, the sister of her father's gardener. He had followed in his own carriage and come upon a coach being held up by highwaymen, whom he had apprehended. The Society would be pleased to hear that the two men involved had turned out to be Lord Besthorpe's burglars. He had handed them over to the Baldock magistrate and was continuing his pursuit of Miss Vail.

Louise did not see Mr Linton at the breakfast table next morning, even though, to her shame, she looked for him. He had probably set off much earlier. She and Betty ate a hearty breakfast to prepare them for the day ahead and, having paid their dues, boarded the coach to continue their bone-shaking journey. She was disconcerted to discover the cleric and his wife were no longer with them and they were joined by a very fat lady with a kitten in a basket and the two card players of the evening before. It meant she had to be doubly on her guard and speak as little as possible.

It was not long before she became aware that Mr Linton's rather splendid carriage was behind them again. Sometimes it stopped when they stopped, sometimes it overtook them and disappeared in a cloud of dust, but then it must have stopped to change horses somewhere else because it was soon behind them again. They were on a turnpike road which was better than most and made good progress, though sometimes they were held up by lumbering wagons and sometimes they had to squeeze themselves to one side to allow a carriage to go past at breakneck speed.

On they went, up and down hills, through woods, alongside fields of growing corn, past cows grazing in meadows, through tiny hamlets where women at their doors stopped to stare as they passed and children, playing in the road scampered to one side. Through Ware they went, then Wadesmill and Puckeridge to Buntingford, where they stopped at the George and Dragon for a whole hour instead of the two or three minutes allowed for a change of horses. Jonathan and his man followed them in, much to the delight of

Betty, who was convinced Joe had taken a shine to her.

'Mr Linton, it is strange, is it not, that we keep bumping into each other?' Louise ventured. 'Are you following us?'

'Not strange at all, Mr Smith,' Jonathan said. 'This is the Great North Road; in truth, it is the only road worthy of the name going north from London and even then it is very bad in parts. It seems reasonable to assume that anyone beginning a journey at about the same time, will arrive at stopping places on route at about the same time. That is why the coaching inns are where they are.' He ignored her question that he might be following them. 'I am about to leave, but I have no doubt somewhere along the way we shall meet again. I shall look forward to it.' He swept her a bow. 'Your obedient, sir.' And with that he strode out to the yard and climbed into his carriage, now sporting a fresh set of horses. Joe was on the driving seat.

Louise watched it go, half-relieved, half-disappointed. Was he right, would they see him on the road again? In spite of herself she liked him; she liked his good looks, his captivating smile, his teasing good humour. Above all she liked to know he was close at hand in case they had any more frightening adventures and especially now when she was forced into the company of Burrows and Williams.

They heard the passengers being called to the coach and left the remains of their dinner and went out to it. It was becoming a familiar routine, this bumping along and then stopping to change horses and then bumping along again, sometimes at a canter, sometimes no more than a walk, but whatever speed they went, it made her whole body ache.

They passed through Huntingdon, a quaint little town with narrow twisting streets, once the home of Oliver Cromwell and Samuel Pepys, so she was informed by Burrows, who was the more talkative of the two men. Somewhere they must have passed Mr Linton without knowing it, because soon afterwards he was behind them again.

'What is the man about?' Williams demanded. 'He comes and he goes. It is almost as if he were following us.'

'I asked him that,' Louise told him. 'His answer was that if two coaches set out at the same time to go to the same place, they are bound to come across each other from time to time.'

'That might be true if they were equal in weight and horseflesh, but that vehicle is lighter than this, carries only two passengers and is pulled by four of the finest cattle I have seen for an age. He must be very high in the instep to be able to command the best the posting inn can procure. He could outrun us easily if he had a mind to.' All of which, Louise realised, was true.

'He's keeping an eye on his money,' Burrows said with a laugh, nodding towards Louise. 'Wants the chance to win it back.'

'He is only watching out for us,' Betty said, relieving Louise of the need to comment. 'We were held up afore and he's making sure it don' happen again.'

'When were you held up?' Burrows asked.

'Yesterday. Two vicious-looking men with pistols tried to rob us. Mr Linton shot the gun out o' the hand of one o' them, cool as you like. Then he tied 'em up and took 'em to the beak.'

'Why would he do that?'

'What else was he to do with them? Couldn' leave 'em there, could he?'

'No, I meant why take it into his head to keep pace with this coach?'

'I dunno, do I? Mayhap he's one o' them thief-takers. I reckon he's done that sort of thing afore.'

'Do you think so?' Louise queried. It seemed the most logical conclusion and she wondered why she had not thought of it herself.

'Yes, an' glad I am he's there,' Betty said.

From Huntingdon they progressed to Stilton, a hilly village which had given its name to a cheese, where they stopped at the Bell only long enough to change the horses and see to their comfort and that enabled Mr Linton to pass them again. They approached Stamford through woods that made Louise wonder if that might be a place to expect more highwaymen, but they continued without incident and found themselves in a beautiful town rising from the banks of a slow-moving river. It had narrow streets, grey limestone buildings and a proliferation of churches. They stopped at the George for the night.

Louise had hardly left the coach and stretched her cramped limbs than the Linton carriage hove into view and pulled up in the yard. Mr Linton, as cheerful as ever, jumped down and greeted them with a sweeping bow before accompanying them into the inn. It really did seem as if they were stuck with him.

'Mr Linton, are there no other inns in this town?' Louise asked.

'Oh, very many, but I like this one,' he said, smiling broadly. 'The company is so congenial.'

Chapter Three

The inn was an extremely busy one and Louise wondered if she and Betty would be able to obtain a room to themselves, but while she was trying to persuade the innkeeper to find one for her, Jonathan stepped in and offered his room, which a few sovereigns had already procured. 'I will take whatever mine host can find for me,' he told her. 'I can sleep anywhere.'

She hesitated—she did not like being beholden to this man. It was not just pride, but the feeling that before long he would penetrate her disguise and know her for what she was and then he would have his fun with her and everyone would know she was a female and she would look foolish and vulnerable. She did not want that, but on the other hand, sharing a room with men was something she most certainly could not do. 'Thank you, sir,' she said. 'I would not mind for myself, but my wife is nervous of being alone, you see…' She looked at Betty, who was once again chattering to Joe and not looking at all nervous.

'I understand.' he said, assuming the young man was jealous and not inclined to let his wife out of his sight. If she really was his wife. 'You are welcome.'

Louise and Betty were conducted upstairs to a spacious room that looked out on to the busy yard. Water was brought for them to wash. Louise stripped off and sponged herself down, but the clothes had to be put on again. The only others she had were feminine garments. She smiled suddenly, wondering what Mr Linton would say if he could see the contents of her bag. It might be fun to change and appear as Miss Louise Vail. She imagined him staring at her in disbelief and then smiling and kissing her hand and saying he liked her much better as a woman. She suddenly became cross with herself for thinking like that. It was pure fantasy and she was doing herself no favours indulging in it.

They went down to the dining room for supper and found themselves again sitting with Jonathan

Linton and Joe Potton. Burrows and Williams were a little further down the table. Louise was beginning to perfect her masculine voice, but she did not use it any more than she had to. Mr Linton's attempts to engage her in conversation were met with little more than polite monosyllables. When he offered her a dish, she took some from it and said, 'Thank you, sir', and when he commented on the fine weather, she said, 'Very fine, sir.' She thought she was doing well until the meal ended and Burrows suggested they continue the game of cards abandoned the night before. 'You must give us the opportunity to recoup some of our losses, Smith,' he said.

'I did not win so much,' she said, pretending indifference. ''Twas only a trifling amount.'

'A trifling amount,' he repeated. 'Then let us put up the stakes.' He turned to Jonathan. 'Will you join us in a game for trifling stakes?'

Jonathan considered declining, but they would only ask someone else, and he wanted to be near the boy, if only to protect him if his losses became too great and he found himself at odds with his playing partners. He accepted, cards were called for, the seal broken and the game began.

Louise was careful, very careful, especially as the half-guinea stake was now a guinea. If she lost all her money, what, in heaven's name would she do, stranded miles from her objective and with home so far behind her it seemed like another life? Some way must be devised to end the game before that happened. They would not allow her to plead tiredness as she had the evening before.

They played several hands in which she won a little and lost a little, mainly due to inattention. 'Mr Linton, I could have sworn you held no more trumps,' she said after he had trumped her winning hand.

'Are you accusing me of cheating?' It was said angrily.

Now what to say? She had not meant to accuse him, simply to point out that her concentration had momentarily lapsed. Admit it and let them walk all over her? Tell them she was too tired to go on? She shrugged. 'If the cap fits, Mr Linton...'

The boy had nerve, more than he would have dared under the circumstances, Jonathan conceded. 'I have no cap, Mr Smith. Nor anything up my sleeve.' He shook his sleeves out one by one to prove it.

'God's truth, the young shaver's bold as brass,' Bill Williams put in. 'Call him out, Linton. You can't let him get away with calling you a cheat. I'll stand second for you.'

The whole thing was getting out of hand and Jonathan wanted to bring it to a speedy conclusion, but he had been insulted and he was not in the habit of letting anyone, least of all a green bantling, get away with that. He hesitated. 'Go on,' Charlie Burrows urged him, while Louise held her breath. 'You are not afraid of that skinny young cub, are you?'

Frowning inwardly, Jonathan took a deep breath and addressed Louise. 'You give me no choice, sir. I must call you out.' It was either that or be accused of cowardice, which was unacceptable to him.

How on earth had she got into such a pickle? Louise asked herself. She wanted to turn and run all the way back to Barnet. Never, in her wildest dreams, had she imagined something like this. The teasing and banter that went on when she played her brothers for pennies and shillings had not schooled her for such a situation. She should never have started to play either yesterday or today. Now what was she to do? Admit herself in the wrong and take the ridicule of everyone in the room, not only the other players but everyone else who had stopped whatever they were doing, to listen and wait. And she would have to abandon her winnings. She had been counting on those.

'You give me no choice either, sir,' she said. 'I accept.'

'You accept?' he asked in astonishment, then to give the boy a way out, added, 'I will take a simple apology in lieu.'

She was nothing if not stubborn. 'Would that not be tantamount to admitting I am in the wrong?' she asked.

'Yes, but you are.'

'Stop beatin' about the bush, Linton,' Williams said. 'Mr Smith, as Mr Linton's representative, I ask you to name your second and choose your weapon.'

'Swords,' she said without hesitation. Unless Mr Linton was particularly cruel and determined, he would not deal more than a glancing blow, just enough to draw blood, before saying he was satisfied. A pistol shot could kill without him meaning it to. Why she thought he did not want to kill her, she did not know. And in the last few days she had become more than a little reckless. As for a second… She looked round the room. 'Will anyone here stand by me?'

'I will,' Joe said, at a nod from Jonathan.

'I'm not having duels on my premises,' the innkeeper said. 'If you must fight, take yourselves off somewhere else. There is a field on the other side of the river just outside town. Go there.'

'It's too dark now,' Bill Williams said. 'We will meet there at dawn.'

'I will take charge of the pot,' the innkeeper said, scooping it up. 'You can have it back tomorrow.'

Louise went up to her room to find Betty taking up most of the bed and snoring her head off. Should she wake her and insist they leave at once? Where would they go if she did? And did she really want to be branded a coward? Would they come after her and exact their pound of flesh anyway? Why, oh, why had she been so foolish as to start this escapade in the first place? If her parents had not been out when she returned to the house after the shock of hearing what she had, if she had been able to speak to them there and then instead of being alone to stew over it, she might not have done what she had. Now it was too late.

She sat on the edge of the bed and let the tears roll down her cheeks. They were the first tears she had shed since sitting alone in the arbour. She had been so determined to find her lost mother, she had given herself no time for tears, no time for reflection or considering where it was all going to lead. If only she could have confided in Luke, he might have come with her, kept her safe, let her be herself, not some mythical Mr Smith. And on top of all that she felt responsible for Betty.

In a few hours the sun would come up and everyone would gather in the field on the outskirts of the town to wait for her and Mr Linton to appear. To the onlookers it would be an entertainment, like a play, to be watched and applauded. She dreaded it and wondered how to get out of it without making a complete cake of herself. She could say her sword was broken, but they would find her another and she needed a weapon she was familiar with. She rose and went to the hook on the back of the door where she had hung her belt before going down to supper. She withdrew the sword and made a few practice moves. It felt comfortable and balanced in her hand and reminded her that she had always enjoyed fencing and been good at it. She had to go through with this charade of a duel or lose all credibility as a man of honour.

Jonathan had no intention whatever of killing the lad. He would not hurt a hair of his head. He had killed once before in a duel and the sight of the man's bloodied body being carried away had been a terrible shock and one he would never forget. Ever since then he had avoided getting into situations that called upon him to defend his honour. So how had it happened this time? He was annoyed with himself for handling things so badly. He had only to declare he did not fight children and everyone would have laughed and there would have been no challenge.

But how could he have done that? The boy would have been humiliated, made a laughing stock and he did not want to subject him to that, but he was of a mind to teach him a lesson. One simply did not go about accusing people of cheating at cards without a shred of evidence.

He wondered why the pair had embarked on the adventure in the first place—could it have been for a jest, or a wager? Or was there something deadly serious behind it all? Once or twice he had caught an expression on the young man's face that hinted at sadness, and a softness to those extraordinary eyes that belied his confident strutting. Jonathan found himself changing from being an-noyed, to sympathising and wanting to help. But that did not extend to failing to appear at the duel himself. Honour had to be satisfied.

He thanked his fencing master that he was proficient enough to pretend to be fighting with a will, to defend himself while holding back from dealing a fatal blow. He wished he had learned it before he had killed that last time. He did not know why he was thinking like this; his adversary would not show up. He would be gone by dawn. Sighing, he sat down to write his log, making it sound dull and uneventful; he certainly did not mention he was to fight a duel.

Louise watched the dawn come up, heard the ostlers and grooms busying themselves in the yard and wished herself anywhere but where she was. There was a knock at the door and Joe's voice called, 'Time to get up, Mr Smith. You have half an hour. Shall I order breakfast for you?'

'No, thank you,' she called back. Food would choke her. 'No breakfast. I shall join you directly.'

She heard him move away and his footsteps going down the stairs. She left the bed and dressed herself. It occurred to her that if her coat were to be torn, she did not have another. She was shaking with nerves as she pulled on her boots and buckled on her sword belt. She turned, intending to shake Betty awake, but changed her mind and left her sleeping.

Downstairs the dining room was empty; there was no one eating breakfast, nor even any waiters. She went outside. The yard was deserted; the people who had been working there earlier had disappeared, but Joe came from round the side of the building to join her. 'Where is everyone?' she asked.

'They're all at the field, waitin' for you.'

Her heart sank. There would be a huge crowd to witness her humiliation. Would they be baying for blood? She wanted to dawdle and delay her arrival, but what would that avail her? Putting her hand on the hilt of her sword, she fell into step beside Joe, their footsteps echoing on the cobbles. In her mind she rehearsed all the moves she had been taught and wondered if she would be given the opportunity to execute them or whether Mr Linton would pierce her defence before she could make any move at all.

The field was crowded, but they made way for her and some cheered. 'Go to it, young shaver. Show the bully he can't walk all over you.' Others laughed, calling her a bratling who wouldn't have the strength to lift a sword, let along wield it. The gibes hardened her resolve; she put her chin in the air and made her way to where an arena had been roped off. Mr Linton and his second, together with the innkeeper, who was acting as referee, stood waiting. Mr Linton was in breeches and shirt sleeves and she became uncomfortably aware of his powerful physique, his masculinity, so very different from her own slim figure and lack of muscle. But here she was and there was no going back.

Jonathan watched as she drew her sword from its scabbard and tested its blade with her thumb. And then Joe was helping her off with her coat and cravat and she was obeying the beckoning hand of the innkeeper and joining him in the middle of the arena. Jonathan was a bag of nerves himself, but only on the boy's behalf. He must not hurt him, he told himself, remembering that other duel so many years before, when he had dealt that fatal blow for which he had never forgiven himself.

The formalities were gone through and then they were alone, facing each other, the flat of their swords held point up against their lips in salute before taking their stance. They were given the command and the duel began.

They sparred a little, feinting, moving backwards and forwards and once Smith lunged and nearly had him. He parried with a riposte, which the boy easily avoided, and suddenly Jonathan realised the lad did know what he was doing and really could put on a good show. He began to be a little less diffident and made one or two real moves, which his opponent answered with moves of his own.

Louise found herself enjoying the cut and thrust and was annoyed when she realised he was holding back. She renewed her attack, making him defend himself. They danced back and forth, lunged and parried while the crowd cheered. Wanting to finish it quickly, Jonathan lunged a little wildly and the boy came back with a high outside riposte that nicked his upper arm, drawing a pinpoint of blood.

If she had been the challenger, Louise could have said she was satisfied with first blood and put an end to it there and then, but as she was the one who had been challenged, it was left to her opponent to admit defeat. The crowd roared their appreciation; they were in no mood to agree that honour had been satisfied. The duel went on, though Jonathan had to use all his skill to defend himself, let alone try not to hurt his adversary. It was this that made him momentarily lose his concentration. His weapon was suddenly knocked from his grasp. Louise stood back and waited for him to pick it up.

He hesitated. Where was this all going to end? He was a man of the law, the Society required him to uphold it at all times and what was he doing breaking it? Having a game? Did Louis Smith think it was a game? He had to end it, but not in this ignominious way. He bent to pick up his sword.

It was then, as he straightened up, he noticed

her gently heaving breasts from which the binding had slipped and was confronted with the fact that he had been crossing swords with a woman. What a fool he had been! Why had he not seen it before? Those magnificent eyes, the unruly hair, the sensitive hands with their neatly manicured nails, the delicate colour in her cheeks, all proclaimed he was facing a member of the gentler sex. Why had he not realised it before? The signs had all been there. What did she think she was playing at? He could not fight a woman. His sword arm dropped.

She noted his reluctance and wondered at it; he was a long way from defeat. 'You hesitate,' she said, pointing her sword at him. 'Do you concede?'

The crowd roared their disapproval. 'Fight on,' they shouted. 'You can't let a stripling like that best you.'

They saluted each other formally and began again. He danced about her, parrying her advances and watching for his opportunity to bring it to an end without betraying her for what she was.

She was beginning to tire chasing after an illusive target, who seemed not to abide by the usual rules, but kept moving back. His defensive tactics did not please the crowd, who began cheering the boy. Jonathan saw his chance, knocked her sword aside and went in to the chest, his blade hovering half an inch from the material of her shirt. He pricked it just enough to put a tiny tear in the cloth, but not enough to pierce her skin. A sharp downward stroke would have had the shirt off her back. He saw her eyes widen in horror. 'Give in?' he murmured, knowing she would never risk being exposed.

She dropped her sword, all the fight gone out of her. The crowd turned away, a few of them muttering with disappointment that the youth had given in when none of his blood had been spilled, but most praising him for the show he had put on. It had been a fair fight between skilled opponents and most had no complaints. Louise turned to Jonathan, who was dabbing at the cut on his arm. 'Are you hurt, Mr Linton?'

'A scratch, nothing more. You fight well, Mr Smith.' Did she imagine it or did he put unusual emphasis on her name?

'Thank you, Mr Linton. So do you.'

They walked side by side, the tall muscular man and the slight, effeminate youth, to where their seconds held their coats. Betty had joined Joe and was watching them approach, her eyes alive with excitement. As Jonathan reached out to take his coat from Joe, his arm accidentally knocked against Louise who was reaching out for her own garment. Already more than a little shaken by her ordeal, it took her off balance and she would have gone down if he had not reached out and grabbed her.

The contact of his hands on her shoulders was only momentary, but it was enough for him to feel the soft feminine flesh beneath his hands and for her to shudder at the sensation his touch caused. She felt so weak with the shock of it, she was afraid her knees would give way. This man was so strong, so masculine, so…so *physical*. The feeling was different from anything she had experienced before. Her brothers often grabbed hold of her, especially when she was younger and joining in their rough and tumble; her father sometimes took her shoulders in his hands to emphasise some point to her, but it had not felt like this. This made her tremble all over.

Pulling herself together, she stepped away from him. 'Thank you, sir.'

'My pleasure.' Her masculine attire was off-

putting and alluring at the same time and made
him feel ill at ease. He could not smile at her as
a man would smile at a woman, he could not
take her hand, certainly he could not kiss her,
which he had been very tempted to do as they
stood so close, facing each other.

Betty came forwards to help her on with her
coat. 'Let's get out of here,' she whispered. 'You
shouldn't hev took your coat off. The binding's
slipped.'

'I could not have fought in a coat, could I?'
Resisting the temptation to put her hand to her
breasts, she hurriedly did up the buttons, picked
up her sword and strolled off arm in arm with
Betty, as casually as she could manage.

Jonathan watched them go. Here was the missing Miss Louise Vail, he was sure of it, though
why she was not miles ahead he had no idea. She
had not been abducted and as far as he could see,
no crime had been committed. She was simply a
spoiled young lady looking for adventure. It annoyed him to think he had been sent on a wild
goose chase. The Piccadilly Gentleman's Club
was never founded to investigate such a paltry
affair. He would return to Barnet and make his
report to her parents and then wash his hands of

her. But could he leave her where she was, prey to whoever decided to have some sport with her? Besides, the memory of those lustrous eyes, appealing to him not to tear her shirt off, could not be cast aside. And had not Mrs Vail entreated him to see no harm came to her? And had he not promised to do his best to return her to the bosom of her family?

'Do you think anyone else noticed the slipped bindings?' Louise asked when they were out of earshot and making their way back to the George.

'Don' know. I reckon Mr Linton did. He was closest.'

Too close, she realised. 'We will stay in our room until the coach is ready to leave. Perhaps we will not see him again.' It was said more in regret than hope, she realised. But now was not the time to be mooning over a handsome man; she was on a mission, a most important mission, one that would probably dictate how the rest of her life would evolve. It was certainly not the time to get involved with cards and duels and handsome young men, whose touch excited her. She must hold herself aloof.

'Much hope of that,' Betty said. 'He's bin with us all the way so far, so I don' reckon he'll stop now.'

The coach was in the yard, the horses harnessed and the driver and guard inspecting the vehicle, tackle and horses, making sure all was well before taking his passengers on board. A woman with a young child, a young man escorting a schoolboy, and a man in a black coat, green with age, were waiting to board it. Louise and Betty just had time to go to their room, rebind her breasts, collect their bags and pay their bill before hurrying out to take their seats.

They were about to set off when Jonathan opened the door again and handed Louise a purse. 'Your winnings, Mr Smith. It would be a pity to leave it behind when you fought so hard to keep it.' And before she could utter a word, he had shut the door and was gone.

Louise sank back in her seat, utterly exhausted. The journey that she had expected to be boring and uneventful was certainly not that. It had been one of terrible tension, made worse by her own inability to turn her back on a challenge. She supposed that was why she had come in the first place, to answer the challenge to find her mother, the one who had given her birth, not the one left behind in Barnet. If she had known how difficult it would be, would she have come? Could she have gone on living at the vicarage knowing that out in the wider world was a mother who might have regretted giving her away? And even if she had no regrets, Louise wanted to know. There was in her a deep need to understand. It cancelled out the bouts of homesickness and guilt that crept up on her when things went wrong. They still had a long way to go and she must take more care. She could not expect Mr Linton to go on extricating her from the pits into which she kept falling.

He had done that when they had been duelling. Any other man would have had no compunction about ripping off her shirt. Only Jonathan Linton would have let his blade hover and ask in an undertone if she was ready to give in, knowing she could not go on much longer. He had not wanted to hurt her. And then to hand over the purse. As the winning duellist, he would have been justified in keeping it, but how grateful she was for it. She must stop thinking about him. She shut her eyes, trying to sleep, but it was not easy. Even if she could have slept through the jolting of the coach and Betty's constant chatter with Mrs Slater who had the child on her lap, she could not shake off the vision of a broad expanse of chest and two strong arms holding her upright. And now she could hear rain drumming on the roof.

'Why don't the fool pass us?' the man in the shiny old coat complained. He had introduced himself as Greg Turner when they first set out. He had a ruddy complexion as if he spent long hours out of doors. 'He's been on our tail for miles.'

Louise opened her eyes and twisted round to look behind, knowing perfectly well what she would see through the sheets of rain, which were turning the dusty road to claggy mud.

''Tis only Mr Linton,' Betty said. 'He's always behind us.'

'Why?' The man seemed decidedly nervous and kept putting his finger in his cravat to loosen it. He had, Louise noticed, lost the forefinger and the top joint of his thumb from his right hand.

'He's watchin' over us,' Betty giggled. 'Our guardian angel.'

They had been late setting off on account of the coachman and guard being intent on watching the duel. Louise had been glad of that or they might have been left behind. They stopped at the Angel in Grantham for a meal, but were not allowed to dawdle over it because the coachman wanted to make up for lost time. Louise, sitting near the window trying to spoon scalding hot soup into her mouth, saw Jonathan's carriage go past, rainwater spraying out from under its wheels, and would not admit, even to herself, that seeing him go without so much as looking her way had sent her spirits into her boots. Was that the last she would see of him? Had he gone from her life for good?

'Some guardian angel,' she murmured to Betty. 'He's gone straight past.'

'We'll pass him again, I'll stake my oath. An' if we don't, he'll be wherever we stop for the night.'

'How do you know?'

'Joe said he had business with the coach.'

'With us?' she asked in alarm. 'What business could he possibly have with us?'

'He didn't say with us. Only the coach.'

'Do you think he might be a highwayman? We've nothing worth taking except my purse. And the others look even poorer than we are.'

'I asked Joe that and he were right crabby. He said his master was on the side of the law.'

'Oh.' She was thoughtful, thinking of Betty's guess that he was a thieftaker, a man who earned his living tracking down criminals. They had had a bad reputation in years gone by when Jonathan Wilde was the most notorious of them. He would tell thieves where there were good pickings and then arrange to return the stolen goods to their owners for a fee, which he shared with the thieves. It had been a very lucrative racket until he had been brought to book and hanged like the criminal he was. Since Henry Fielding had formed the Bow Street Runners nine years before, now under the direction of his brother, Sir John, one did not hear so much about them. Could Jonathan Linton be one of those? Although they operated in London they had been known to pursue criminals into the country. 'Is it against the law to impersonate a man?' she queried.

'I dunno, do I? But you did steal the clothes and the sword and pistol.'

'I didn't steal them.'

'You sure as eggs didn't get give 'em.'

'You are overreaching yourself, Betty,' she said

angrily, though the girl's words had hit home and made her feel guilty. 'I only borrowed them and my father would never set the law on me. Now let us go back to the coach and remember who you are supposed to be.'

'Your timid little wife,' Betty said, following her. 'I'm tired of that. I like Joe…'

Louise sighed heavily. She had enough to contend with, without Betty becoming mutinous. 'Have patience, Betty. One more night and a day and we will be in York and then we can drop the pretence.' She said it confidently, but she did not feel confident. Perhaps when they reached York, her troubles would not be over, they might only just be beginning. Catherine Fellowes might not be all that easy to find. She might have died.

The rain had made them reduce their speed until Louise felt they could have walked faster. Mr Linton would be miles and miles ahead by now. Why did she keep thinking of him? Why could she not put him from her mind? Had he really guessed that she was not the man she pretended to be? If he had, it obviously amused him to keep up the pretence. Perhaps she was not the object of his interest after all, perhaps it was Mr Turner. The man was obviously afraid of something and his agitation had certainly been heightened when he saw Mr Linton's coach following them. He was sitting opposite her now, looking morosely out on to the rain-sodden landscape and cursing the delay.

The fields either side of the road were a grey expanse of water, with little mounds of turf sticking up here and there. Turnpikes had not yet reached this part of the country and water spilled on to the unsurfaced road from the overflowing ditches and made a quagmire of it. The coachman, in an effort to take the higher ground, had the two inside wheels on the verge and the outside wheels on the hump that ran down the middle of the road, a difficult feat at the best of times. Occasionally they slipped off it and one wheel sank into the mud and they all fell against each other. They went slower and slower and the passengers, Louise included, feared they would come to a standstill at any moment. They were supposed to reach Doncaster by nightfall, but at the rate they were going they would never make it.

'I wish I'd gone by boat,' Greg Turner said, irritably. 'It could not be any slower than this. And it's more reliable.'

'Is that possible?' Louise asked, remembering to lower the timbre of her voice.

'Yes, there's barges goin' up and down the rivers all the time. It's how everyone travelled in the old days, afore the turnpikes, not that turnpikes seem to have done any good hereabouts.'

A bigger-than-usual lurch told them they were in trouble, and though the coachman struggled, he could not hold the coach upright. A wheel sank deep into mud and stuck, leaving the coach tipped at an alarming angle. Everyone gripped their seats as the coach hovered halfway over, then went over, slowly at first and then, with a crunching sound, toppled on its side, depositing them all in a heap on the floor, only it was not the floor but the near side. The horses were neighing in distress, still trying to drag the stricken coach along.

They could hear the coachman shouting to them. They were pulled along in this fashion for some yards before they stopped. Louise just managed to prevent herself from crying out like the woman she was. The schoolboy was lying on top of his escort, with his hat over his eyes and his legs in the air; Betty was moaning and Greg Turner uttering oaths. The little boy was screaming, but his mother was so dazed, she did not seem to know where she was. Her presence of mind had undoubtedly saved him from injury at the expense of a nasty bang on her own head. Louise scrambled to a sitting position and took the child from her and hugged him, making soothing noises. Greg Turner stood up, not caring who he was treading on, and pushed at the off-side door, now above their heads. It was opened from outside and the guard's head appeared in the opening. Rain dripped off the brim of his hat. 'Anyone hurt?'

'I've broke me wrist,' Betty moaned.

Louise, though shaken, was unhurt, for which she was thankful; having to be treated for injuries would almost certainly have exposed her for the woman she was. For the same reason she could not indulge in panic. Taking a firm hold of herself, she handed the child up to the guard. The schoolboy, who had managed to get to his feet, hauled himself out without any help, leaving his escort to help Mrs Slater. Louise turned to assist Betty. She pushed her from behind while the guard leaned in and took hold of her arms to pull her out, making her shriek with pain. Left alone in the stricken coach, Louise made a determined effort to haul herself out before anyone could lay hands on her to help her.

Incongruously and unjustifiably, she felt angry. Not at the coachman, not at the horses, nor her fellow passengers, but at Jonathan Linton. He had dogged them all the way and now, just when she needed him most, he chose to absent himself. It was irrational she knew, but she could not help wondering where he was.

It seemed to Jonathan he had been sitting in this lane for hours. It was nothing but a cart track with hedges on each side and trees screening it from the road, which was why he had chosen it. But already the water was rising over the rim of the coach wheels and if he did not move soon, that would be stuck fast. 'Something must have happened to them,' he said to Joe who had joined him in the coach, where at least it was dry. 'They should have passed us long ago. You don't think we've missed them, do you?'

'Shouldn't think so, my lord. But if I'd stayed on the box, I could have seen anyone on the road…'

'And have you catch your death? 'Even inside the coach, Jonathan was becoming chilled to the marrow. Joe, who had been driving through the rain hunched in a greatcoat with the collar turned up about his ears, must be feeling ten times worse. 'Fine summer this is turning out to be.'

Joe put his head out of the door and looked at the ground. 'The track looks more like a river,' he said. 'If we don't get moving, my lord, we'll be stuck here 'til doomsday.' He glanced up at the four horses; he had thrown a blanket over the back of each, but they looked thoroughly miserable, snorting and throwing their heads to shake off the rain.

'You are right. Off we go.'

'Which way, my lord?'

'Good question. Back, I think. I am sure they have not come past.'

Joe jumped down, splashed through the mud, removed the blankets, folded them and put them in the boot, then he went to the leader's head and took hold of the bridle. 'Come on, me beauties, give a good pull for old Joe and we shall soon be on the road again.' It grieved him to be turning away from the comfort of a room at the inn somewhere not so many miles ahead of them, and warm stables for the horses, but he could hardly blame his master for being worried about the girls. Oh, he knew they were both girls; his lordship would not be chasing all over the countryside, worrying himself over a young shaver. Besides, Betty had hinted as much.

As soon as the carriage was on the road again, he climbed back on the box. 'Call it a road,' he muttered. 'I ha' seen better farm tracks in Barnet.'

Jonathan heard him and smiled. He was a good lad, but he liked to grumble and, not having been brought up to be subservient, did not think it necessary to endure in silence.

They found the overturned coach less than twenty minutes later. The passengers were all out on the road, the horses had been freed and everyone was standing surveying the vehicle as if looking at it would miraculously make it right itself.

Jonathan jumped down and went quickly to Louise who was standing beside Betty. The girl was holding her left hand against herself with her right. 'Anyone hurt?'

It was on the tip of Louise's tongue to say,

'Where have you been all this time?', but stopped herself in time. 'Betty seems to have hurt her wrist. Mrs Slater was knocked out for a time but she is conscious now. She has a nasty bump on her head. The baby was frightened, which is hardly surprising, but he is not hurt. Everyone else seems to have sustained only bruises and a scratch or two.'

'And you?' he asked.

'Right as ninepence.'

He smiled. Did nothing disturb that young woman? Cool as a cucumber, she was. He called to Joe to come and help the ladies and children into his carriage, then turned to inspect the coach. The axles seemed unbroken, but he could not see the nearside wheels, which were deep in the mud. 'Let us see if we can lift it,' he said. 'If we all heave together, we might be able to get a branch or a rock under it to prop it up. If we can get it upright on its wheels, it might not be too much damaged and be possible for it to be driven to the next village.' He stripped off his coat and turned to put it into his carriage. Louise was standing watching him. He smiled. 'Why not get into my carriage out of the rain?'

'With the women and children sir?' she

queried. 'I collect you said we should all heave together.'

He chuckled. She was nothing if not determined and he could not argue with her without giving her and himself away. 'Then find something to wedge under the wheels when we lift it.' He went back to the stricken coach. The coachman, guard, Joe and the young man joined him and together they bent to take a hold of the coach.

Louise, looking about for a thick branch to use as a lever, saw Greg Turner pick up a rock from a small heap beside the road, probably put there to help fill potholes. The coach was a few inches out of the mud and Louise pushed the end of the branch under the gap at Jonathan's direction. He took hold of the branch and put his weight on it, bringing the coach a little higher. 'Get something else under it,' he ordered.

Louise looked round as Turner came forwards with the rock. It was moment or two before she realised he was not bringing it to put under the body of the coach. He was holding it too high. And the expression on his face was one of pure venom. He was going to bring it down on Mr Linton's head! Joe saw him and, too far away to do anything, yelled a warning just as Louise sprang forwards with a rock in her own hand. The next second the dreadful man was lying on the floor, out to the world. Jonathan let go of the branch and turned in surprise. Louise, unsure whether she had killed the man, was staring down at him in dismay.

'He was going to kill you,' she said, throwing the rock to the ground.

'Oh, Lou,' he murmured. She was trembling and he wanted to take her into his arms and soothe her, tell her not to worry, that she was the most courageous woman he had ever come across, but he held himself in check. Now was not the time or the place, with everyone tired and irritable, soaked to the skin and only wanting to find somewhere in the warm.

'Why?' she asked, as Joe bent over the man to examine him. 'Why did he want to kill you?'

'I have no idea, but I cannot think I have lived all my life without making an enemy or two. I am in your debt, Mr Smith. I owe you my life.'

'Then we are quits,' she said with an attempt at a jocularity. 'You spared mine, I saved yours.'

'He ain't dead,' Joe said. 'But he's got a nasty cut on 'is 'ead.' He turned the man over. The rain had washed his mud-spattered face, washed the ruddy makeup from his face in patches, revealing a pasty complexion, and his dark hair streaked with grey. 'I know him,' Joe said suddenly.

'So do I,' Jonathan murmured. 'It's Jed Black. This is turning out to be quite an eventful journey.'

'Who is Jed Black?' Louise asked.

'He is a convicted felon, a dangerous man. He escaped from Newgate ten days since. The authorities will be thankful to have him safely back under lock and key.'

His words convinced Louise that Betty was right—he was a thieftaker. First there had been those two highwaymen whom he had arrested. He knew they were wanted by the law and now this man whom he had also recognised as a law-breaker. He was not her guardian angel, not her anything. His interest in their coach had nothing to do with her. She felt crushed, which, she scolded herself, was foolish in the extreme. She ought to feel relief. 'What was he convicted of?' she asked

'Murder and counterfeiting coins of the realm. That's treason, you know.'

'Murder!' she repeated, shocked to think she

and the others had spent hours in his company. He could have killed them all.

'Yes. Tie him up, Joe. Then we had better make a move. I think we shall have to abandon the coach.'

The coachman was reluctant to do that, being responsible for it, but it had become evident that one of the wheels was broken and it could not be driven on three, even if they righted it. It was quickly arranged for the coachman and guard to ride two of the horses and lead the other two. There was room in Jonathan's coach for Mrs Slater and her child, Louise, Betty and Jonathan himself. The schoolboy and his escort climbed up beside Joe. The luggage was strapped on the roof and the trussed-up convict they bundled into the boot along with the wet blankets. He had regained his senses and swore revenge on the whippersnapper who had felled him, but Jonathan threatened to hit him over the head again if he did not shut up and he lapsed into silence.

Compared with the public coach this was luxurious, Louise realised. It had more headroom and bigger windows and its seats were padded. And it had steel springs; that, more than anything, contributed to its comfort. It did not mean they could bowl along at any sort of speed; the heavy load combined with the rain and the state of the roads precluded that, but suddenly she was in no hurry to arrive at their destination.

He had called her Lou, which could have been used to mean Louis or Louise and no doubt he had heard Betty use it. But the way he had said it! Softly, almost tenderly. He was sitting beside her now, his arm pressing against hers, his leg very close to hers, the only thing separating them was the material of two pairs of breeches, his and hers.

Not for the first time, she wondered what madness had sent her on this expedition, masquerading as a man. She did not make a very good man. If, as Betty suspected, Mr Linton knew her for a woman, she was not surprised. She was too small and her curves were in all the wrong places. And sometimes she forgot to lower her voice as well as letting him see how horrified she had been at felling that man. She had never hurt another human being in her life and she might have killed him. Even thinking about it made her shake.

He noticed it and smiled to himself. He would

have her out of that coat and breeches and back in skirts before he was done. He wanted to treat her as a woman, with kindness and gentleness and compassion, to put his arms about her and calm her nerves, to taste those warm inviting lips and tell her how brave and lovely she was.

'What are you smiling at, Mr Linton?' Her voice penetrated his reverie.

'Was I smiling?'

'Indeed you were. Pray, share the joke with us.'

'I was smiling at the little boy. See, he is laughing now.'

Why didn't she believe him? He was laughing at her, she knew it and it infuriated her. Now, far from wanting the journey to last forever, she wished it over with. The humiliation was more than she could bear.

Chapter Four

It was dark by the time they arrived in Tuxford and they saw nothing of the village as Joe pulled the carriage up in the yard of the Crown, where they all tumbled out, tired, wet and dishevelled, not to mention hungry. The young man and the schoolboy left them, and in no time at all Jonathan had organised rooms for everyone else and for fires to be lit to help them dry themselves. He ordered a substantial meal and sent for the village wise woman to tend those who had been hurt. She bathed Mrs Slater's head with a soothing balm and bound up Betty's wrist. It was not broken, she assured them, the young lady had simply twisted it and in a day or two the swelling would go down and she would be as good as new. Betty was given a good dose of Godfrey's cordial, which served to make her drowsy. She said she did not want any supper, so

Louise left her sleeping in their room while she went down to the dining room.

She had barely begun her meal when Jonathan joined her. He had changed out of his wet coat and was now sporting a forest-green one with leather buttons. 'How are the invalids?' he asked, noticing she had not changed her coat, probably because she did not have another one.

'They are recovering.' She wished he would not look at her like that, studying her face as if there was something strange about it. He was always doing that and she found it most disconcerting. 'I left my wife sleeping.'

This, he knew, was to reinforce her masculine charade. 'And you, how are you?'

'I am perfectly well, I thank you.'

'Is your coat not wet?'

'No, I dried it by the fire in my room.'

'Then let us hope you do not catch a cold.'

'I am as fit as a fiddle,' she said. 'I cannot remember the last time I took a cold.' She hoped she was right. In her present circumstances it would not do to be ill. She changed the subject hurriedly. 'What have you done with your prisoner?'

'I have taken him to the local constabulary.

He has been securely locked in the round house with a guard put on him until the morning when he will have to be conveyed back to Newgate.'

'How?'

It was a question that had been exercising his mind ever since the man had been trussed up. He did not want to abandon Louise to take him back to London himself and yet he could not leave him where he was. The fellow was notorious for escaping from prisons and he would be out of the round house in no time. 'He must be conveyed in shackles to the nearest sizeable town and handed over to the magistrate who will arrange his onward journey in a guarded prison van,' he said.

'And will you take him yourself?'

He understood she was worried about the rest of her journey. Could it be that he was becoming of some use to her? She certainly needed someone to look out for her. She seemed to have a penchant for attracting trouble and he was reluctant to leave her, ought not to, considering bringing her home to her parents was the task he had been set, and not dealing with other criminals he met along the way. But they had to be dealt with, whatever his personal inclinations might be. 'I shall go with the escort as far as Lincoln. The town is sure to have facilities for sending him on.'

'Oh.' She was more than ever convinced he was a thieftaker. In ordinary circumstances this would not have bothered her; she might even have been curious about the kind of life he led and talked to him about it, but these were not ordinary circumstances. She was plagued by guilt for taking the clothes and the weapons, especially the pistol. Luke might have reported it stolen, not realising she had it. This man, whom she had come to rely upon so much and for whom she had come to have a high regard, might be intent on arresting her.

The thought of being taken up and conveyed to prison as Jed Black was being conveyed terrified her. If that happened, her father, by whom she meant the Reverend Vail, the man of God, would wash his hands of her and she would be without a friend in the world. And she would never find her real mother. On the other hand, if Mr Linton went off to Lincoln, she could go on without him and lose herself once they arrived in York. He did not know exactly where she was bound. Come to that, neither did she.

'I wonder how long it will take to repair the coach,' she said.

'I am persuaded it cannot be mended here. I believe a flat cart is being sent to take it to a coachbuilder.'

'You mean we are stuck here?'

'I have been informed by mine host that another coach will arrive the day after tomorrow and with luck there will be spare seats.'

'Oh.' Two days. Could he go to Lincoln and back in two days?

He could almost read her thoughts and smiled. She would not escape from him so easily. 'I have another solution,' he said. 'You are welcome to use my carriage. I shall not need it going to Lincoln. I have hired a mount…'

'But, sir…'

'Oh, do not tell me you cannot accept,' he put in. 'I have already spoken to Mrs Slater and she is very happy to avail herself of my offer. Her husband is to meet her in Doncaster and she is already behindhand. She does not wish to worry him any more than can be helped.' He paused to give her his most winning smile. 'She will not like going on alone, you know, and you will be a fitting escort for her. And to be sure, Mrs Smith will be able to have her wrist properly looked at in Doncaster.'

All of which was true. 'But are you not afraid to entrust so splendid a vehicle to me?' she queried. 'I know nothing of carriages and how they should be looked after.'

'Now, you do surprise me,' he said laconically. 'A more than fair duellist, an intrepid traveller who turns not a hair when being held up by highwaymen and is swift to act in a crisis, must be master of all manly talents, including tooling a coach.'

He was teasing her. Did that mean he had penetrated her disguise? She must not let him see how dismayed she was by this. She assumed her deepest voice. 'Now you are roasting me, sir. And I shall perhaps have to be the one to call you out this time.'

'No, I beg you not to do anything of the sort,' he said, laughing. 'I ask your pardon.'

'Granted,' she said with relief.

'Going back to the matter of the carriage,' he said. 'I do not expect you to drive it, you know. Joe will do that. Young he may be, but I would trust him with my life.'

'And with the lives of the rest of us,' she said tartly.

'That is for you to say, but if you do not, he will be sorely hurt, I promise you.'

'I never said that!' She had dug another pit for herself, she realised. 'Naturally, I shall be very grateful for the use of your carriage and coachman as far as Doncaster.'

'That is settled then. Do try some of this pudding, it is delicious.' And he offered her the dish.

Later he sat in his room and wrote up his report to send on to the Gentleman's Club. He told of the arrest of Jed Black and the arrangements he had made for him to be conveyed back to Newgate, nothing about a girl dressed as a man, nothing about wonderful hazel eyes with green flecks, nothing about copper-coloured hair and pale hands, nothing about warm red lips and a squeaky voice that made him want to laugh, made him want to grab hold of her, feel her soft body in his arms and kiss the truth out of her. Nothing about Louise Vail at all.

The next morning Louise woke early to find the rain had stopped and the sun was shining.

She rose and went to the window. She could see part of the main street as far as the bend in the road, but it seemed every other building was an inn and they were not old ones either; the place looked newly built. But that was all it had to recommend it. The road was awash with mud and when she looked beyond the buildings, the fields that surrounded the village were waterlogged. Looking after the traveller appeared to be the only means of livelihood for most of its inhabitants.

As she stood there, she saw Mr Linton leave the building and cross the yard to where a horse stood ready saddled. He turned and looked back as he reached it and, seeing her, put his hand to the brim of his hat in salute, before picking up the reins, springing easily into the saddle and cantering off.

She stood a moment, staring out of the window, her mind in turmoil. How had she let herself become so dependent on him, not only for practical things like making sure they were well received at the inns, rescuing them from criminals and lending them his coach, but in more subtle ways, that had more to do with her feelings? She realised she leaned on him as a woman might lean on a man. Her dependency was to do with her senses, her emotions, her confidence, her very real need for someone to support her when she felt alone and weak. He fulfilled those needs. In any other circumstances, she could easily fall in love with him. The thought shocked her and she gave herself a severe scolding. Nothing and no one must divert her from her purpose.

He could not possibly know what she thought of him and yet he had helped her and apparently expected to continue to do so or he would never have put his coach and horses at her disposal. Why? The question plagued her as she turned to wake Betty and help her dress, before climbing back into her own, now hated, male garments. 'Mr Linton is to lend us his coach to go on to Doncaster,' she told the girl. 'Joe is going to drive it.'

'Oh, good,' Betty said complacently. 'It's a hundred times more comfortable than the public coach. Travel in style, we will.'

That was true. The carriage was luxurious and not in keeping with Mr Linton's plain clothes and easy-going manner. It was more like a vehicle for a nobleman and a fastidious one at that. Perhaps the rewards the man received for arresting thieves were enough to buy fancy carriages. But if that were so, why did he not also buy himself a fitting ward-robe? And why was he not going all the way back to London with Black to claim his reward? Why lend them his carriage and say he would see them later? He was a real mystery and yet it occurred to her that although she did not know anything about him, he seemed to be the one constant thing in her constantly moving world. Was he, like her, using an alias? Was he, like her, in disguise? Was that why they were drawn towards each other?

'I sometimes wonder how a man like that, who is not dressed anything out of the ordinary, can have a carriage as grand as that,' Louise murmured as they went down to breakfast.

'Oh, he is not any ordinary man,' Betty said.

'What do you mean?'

'Joe said he was a real gentleman.'

'Well, of course he is,' Louise said sharply. 'I never thought anything else.'

Joe was waiting for them at the breakfast table. He had ordered ham and eggs and toast and coffee, he told them, after bidding them good morning. While they were eating he went out to see that the carriage was ready and their bags safely stowed in the boot.

Betty was right about the journey being more comfortable, even though the roads were as bad as ever. Louise suspected Betty had taken a good dose of some restorative before setting out; she was determined to chatter, but, receiving little more than monosyllables from Louise, turned her attention to Mrs Slater and the little boy, whose name they had discovered was Will, tickling him and making him giggle. Louise smiled at them, but her thoughts were with Mr Jonathan Linton. His presence seemed almost a tangible thing. It was almost as if he were sitting beside her, his knee brushing against hers, his head bent, murmuring in her ear. And what she liked to imagine he was saying made her blush.

As they approached Doncaster, the traffic increased. There were coaches, carriages and wagons converging on the town, along with a great many horses. 'Horse racing!' Betty said in excitement. 'We have come in time for the races.'

'Doncaster is famed for its horse racing,' Mrs Slater put in. 'On race days the town is packed.'

That did not bode well for their accommodation. Joe was obliged to slow the horses to a walk as they passed the racecourse, and entered the town, which was a fair size, Louise realised, with a well-paved high street and several inns, which she hoped would not be too full to accommodate them.

She was becoming used to the routine of staying in inns and though they did not have Mr Linton to smooth their way, it clearly amused Joe to act the gallant in place of his master. He had money given him to ensure they were found respectable rooms, but Louise had the winnings from the card games and it pleased her to insist on paying her way. After bidding Mrs Slater and little Will goodbye, they found accommodation at the Angel, where they were shown to a room at the very top of the house, all the others being taken by racegoers. It was expensive too, more than Louise had expected, but she was determined not to go cap in hand to Joe.

She used some of the hot water with which they had been provided to wash the grime of travel from her hands and face and then helped Betty, who was still suffering from her sprained wrist. They were beginning to look more than somewhat travel worn and that worried Louise. 'I think we will have a light supper in our room,' she said, brushing out her hair and trying to get it neatly back into its queue. 'It will be easier for you.'

'Oh, no, Lou, I want to go to the dining parlour. Joe is expecting us to join him.'

'Betty, I am afraid you are becoming far too fond of that young man. Remember you are supposed to be married to me.'

'I am tired of that masquerade,' Betty said mutinously. 'I wish you would bring it to an end. There is no point in it when we know perfectly well that Joe and Mr Linton, too, know we are two women.'

'How do you know they do?' Louise asked sharply.

'From things Joe has said. The way he always says "Mr Smith", or "your husband" as if he did not believe it and then he laughs. He likes me, I know he does, and—'

'Oh, Betty, we cannot simply change our story now. It will show us up for fraudsters and if Mr Linton should really be something like a Bow Street Runner…'

'He is not. Joe said he is not.'

'What else did Joe say about his master?' She was pandering to her curiosity to know, but she could not help herself.

'Nothing. Only he's a gentleman, the best master anyone could have. Joe said he'd do anythin' for him. He wouldn't do anythin' to displease him and bein' too friendly with me would displease him on account of I am married to you.'

'Betty, I am confused. A minute ago, you said they both knew I was not a man.' Louise laughed.

'Yes, but don't you see? They have to keep pretendin' while you do. If you was to stop pretendin', so could they. Let me tell Joe…'

'No, Betty. Tomorrow I will make enquiries about coaches going to York and we will continue our journey as planned. It is safer for both of us if we travel as man and wife. Let me hear no more of it.'

It was all very well to issue orders, but Betty had come with her as a friend, not a servant, and apart from having all the expenses of the journey paid for her, she drew no wage. 'If you want to have supper downstairs, then we had better go before all the food is eaten,' Louise added by way of an olive branch.

It became clear, during the course of the meal, that Betty had set her heart on going to the races the following day and Joe agreed to take them both. After the roasting she had given the girl, Louise did not feel able to forbid it. 'When will Mr Linton arrive, do you think?' she asked Joe.

'Not tomorrow, that's for certain,' he said, cutting up Betty's food for her, something Louise realised she should be doing. 'Might come the next day, though it's more than likely it will be the day after. We might as well amuse ourselves while we wait for him.'

Louise, who was every bit as tired of travelling as Betty and would dearly love a day staying in one place, gave in. They would go to the races, after Betty had been taken to see an apothecary and had the wise woman's diagnosis confirmed. And then they would resume their journey. Before Mr Linton returned.

Jonathan fretted at the slowness of their progress. The wagon in which Black was confined was heavy; it had to be to withstand a prisoner's determination to break out. It was drawn by six horses. There were two men on the driver's seat and two men riding alongside besides Jonathan himself, all armed. The Tuxford magistrate had laughed at the precautions Jonathan requested to convey one man twenty miles, but when told of the man's past history and been shown the poster Jonathan carried with him, he had realised that here was no petty thief, but a brutal and unrepentant murderer and had issued the requisite orders.

Plodding along at two or three miles an hour gave Jonathan ample time to think. And his thoughts centred around Louise Vail. She was an extraordinary woman. He had no idea why she had left home and assumed that foolish disguise. He had expected to have found that out long before now, to have exposed the girl for what she was and marched her back home to be chastised by her papa. Instead all he had learned was that she could use a sword, play whist and had the courage of a lion, and instead of exposing her, he was going along with the game she was playing. The trouble was he did not think it was a game; that at the back of it all, was something deadly serious. Courage she might have in abundance, but she was also afraid. He had seen it in her lovely eyes. He could not wait to get back to her and then, by hook or by crook, he would have it out of her.

It grew dark before they reached their objective and so the whole cavalcade put up at a hedge tavern just short of Lincoln where they spent an uncomfortable night crowded into a tiny parlour, sleeping on settles, the table and the floor, taking turns to guard the prison wagon where Black remained confined. He was let out only for a few minutes to stretch his legs and use the necessary, with two men guarding him.

Jonathan took his turn on guard, which he was glad to do. The air in the parlour was stuffy and malodorous and the others snored and snorted like a load of pigs. He paced up and down beside the wagon, his mind, as always, on Louise and the mystery of her journey. He had never met a more obstinate and secretive woman. The ladies he had come across before would have swooned clean away at what she had gone through without turning a hair. He supposed it was the influence of her brothers that had made her like that. But he was sure there was a softer side to her that he had yet to discover.

He did not welcome the interruption of Black calling out to him through the tiny slit in the vehicle, which served as a window. 'Hey, thief-taker, how much do you think you'll get for me, hey? A hundred pounds? A thousand? I could better it.'

'I am sure you could,' Jonathan answered evenly. 'I am not interested.'

'Every man has his price,' came the cynical response.

Jonathan wondered how far the man would go and whether any of the guards he had with him might be tempted by offers like that. He would have to keep an eye on them as well as the prisoner. 'Why don't you go to sleep and give us all some peace?'

'If I let you take me back to Newgate, I will have plenty of sleep, don't you think? A long, long sleep. My time now is best spent thinking of a way to get myself out of here.'

'You will be wasting it. I suggest you use it in repentance.'

His answer was a harsh laugh and then silence. When Jonathan's stint on guard came to an end and he let the next man take over, he did not return to the tavern. Instead he paced up and down the road. It was a clear night and he stood and looked up at the stars as if seeing them for the first time. His old nurse used to believe the stars could tell the future and would often expound on what they held for her, and sometimes, in order to make him behave, had said they foretold a terrible end if he did not learn his lessons.

What lesson was he being taught now? he wondered. That it was dangerous for his peace of mind to continue this charade with this wayward girl? What was she up to right now, for instance? Was she playing cards and accusing people of cheating? Was she wearing that sword, her hand on its hilt, as if to say she would draw it on the least provocation? Was that pistol she had in her coat pocket loaded? He did not doubt Joe would look after her and her so-called wife to the best of his ability, but was he up to curbing her wilder ideas?

For the first time he found himself regretting his involvement with the Piccadilly Gentlemen's Club and the necessity of always turning aside from private concerns to bring a wrongdoer to justice. But it was the Club that had given him the task of finding and fetching Louise back to her parents. He had accomplished the first and should have told her at once that he knew who she was and taken her home, mission accomplished. But he doubted very much if she would have let him do that without a fight and, as he had said to her mother, short of tying her up and carrying her bodily, he could not make her go home. He could only stay by her and look after her until the time came to persuade her to return.

Having stuck to her like a leech until she reached her destination, what would he discover? Something so terrible that it would condemn her for ever in the eyes of polite society? Did he really wish to know? The answer was yes, he must know the worst. In any case, it might be something and nothing, a whim, some flimsy excuse for an adventure she knew her mama and papa would forbid. Somehow he did not believe that. Madcap she might be, but he was sure she would never deliberately hurt her parents.

Pacing up and down and looking at the night sky would not bring him answers; he ought to find somewhere to sleep or he would not be alert come the morning. He returned to the tavern and stretched out on a settle, but that was so hard and uncomfortable, he did no more than doze.

* * *

Louise accompanied Betty to the apothecary, who prescribed some medicine and bound her wrist to her chest so that she could not use it, but assured her it would be better in a day or two and then she could discard the binding. She was so thrilled at the prospect of going to the races, she hardly complained at all.

In spite of her qualms, Louise was caught up in some of Betty's excitement as they made their way from the town to the race course, which, even early in the morning, was crowded with owners, jockeys and onlookers who arrived by carriage, cart, horseback and on foot. Food and drink was being sold at booths set up for the purpose and little crowds gathered round the men who were taking bets. It was noisy with music, shouting and laughter. Louise had never been to a racecourse before; it was something her father would almost certainly have forbidden.

With Joe between them, the girls strolled over to look at the horses gathering at the start for the first of four heats. Not so long ago, their owners would have ridden them, but now, in order to give the horses a better chance, they employed boys or very light men, who were dressed in colourful shirts and caps. 'I like the look of the bay,' Joe said. 'He looks to be a stayer. I think I'll venture half a crown on him.'

'Me, too,' Betty said, delving into her purse. 'Put a shilling on him for me, Joe.'

Joe looked at Louise. 'Mr Smith?'

Had Betty been right—did he pronounce the name as if it were a joke? 'Not the bay. I like the big black stallion. What is his name?'

'Black Knight.'

'Then I shall put half a guinea on him to win.'

'You will lose it,' Joe said complacently. 'That animal is little more than a cart horse. Look at his hind quarters.'

'I am,' she said. 'And his shoulders. And the depth of his chest. He will still be standing when your bay has run out of wind.' She delved into her pocket for her purse, noticing as she did so, that it was becoming lighter with every day that passed. She really ought not to gamble. But she could hardly back down now. It was the same when she had accepted that challenge from Mr Linton. Backing down was a feminine thing to do and she was supposed to be a man. She handed half a guinea to Joe. 'Here, put it on for me.'

He took it and disappeared and came back just as the horses lined up for the first heat. There would be three more to follow, the ultimate winner being the one who won most heats. Stamina was every bit as important as speed. It was no good going all out in the first heat and having nothing left for the others. Louise had spied stamina in the black horse.

In a field of twenty, the bay won the first heat, came second in the next and nowhere in the last two, much to Joe's disgust. Black Knight, lumbered home fourth in the first, third behind the bay in the second, won the third by a head and the last by three lengths. Louise pocketed her winnings with a huge grin of triumph. Even as she did so, she remembered Mr Linton. The more she won, the less dependent she was on him. And, she told herself, that was important.

She went to the ropes to watch the second race and it was only at the end of the first heat when she turned to speak to Betty that she realised the girl was nowhere to be seen. Neither was Joe. For a moment she was seized with blind panic. The crowds were hemming her in and it took all her resolve to calm herself and push her way through to look for them. They had never run off together, had they? The thought of spending days looking for them and then having to go back to Alfred and tell him she had lost his sister, was not one she cared to think about. Neither was the prospect of telling Mr Linton his servant had taken off. Joe was not as reliable as Mr Linton had said he would be. She was anxious, frightened and very angry, as she paced up and down, scanning the crowds and peering into booths.

She was becoming desperate and about to leave the ground to look for them in the town, when she saw them coming towards her and Joe was leading one of Mr Linton's horses on which he had put a saddle. 'Joe is going to ride in one of the races,' Betty called out to her. 'He reckons if a cart horse like Black Knight can win, so can Linton's Quarter.'

'Linton's Quarter, what sort of a name is that?' Louise was so relieved to see them, she forgot to scold.

'One fourth of the team that brought us here,' Joe said, grinning. 'He's the best of the four.'

'And what do you think Mr Linton will say? The horse is not used to being mounted.'

'Course he is. Carriage horses often have pillion riders. And he needs exercise. That slow plod we had yesterday was nothing.'

'I am going to put a wager on him,' Betty said. 'What about you, Lou?'

'All right, half a guinea, but, Joe, you are not, under any circumstances, to push the animal beyond his limits. Mr Linton will have your hide for it. I am sure he will not want to delay his journey for an injured horse.' It was not that she had any idea what his destination might be. Mr Linton had been less than open about it. But then so had she, so they were as bad as one another.

Joe did win and hurried off afterwards to rub the horse down and return him to the stables. It was while he was gone and the girls had collected their winnings and were on the way back to the inn, that Betty decided to speak her mind. 'Miss Louise,' she said. 'I don' want to go any further like this. I want to be Betty Rayment, I want to be me, not Mrs Smith. I don' see why we can't be ourselves.'

'I suppose this is all because of Joe Potton.'

'Well, it seem all wrong to me. We've took advantage of Mr Linton and Joe and it ain't fair on them, nor to me. I never realised when we set out that we'd come so far. I'm tired of travelling, always being on the move. I want to be settled.'

Louise sighed. 'You do not want it any more than I do, Betty, but it is not possible.'

'Why not? All you have to do is tell Mr Linton the truth.'

'It is none of Mr Linton's business.'

'There's a fine thing! He hev looked after us, seen to our comfort, lent us his fine carriage and you say what we do ain't none o' his business! I don' know about you, Miss Louise, but it makes me feel real guilty, that it does.'

Louise looked round hastily, but there was no one within earshot to hear her thus addressed. 'Do you think I don't feel guilty?' she hissed. 'Do you think I am so unfeeling that I can take all he has to give and not offer a crumb in return?'

'Seems to me tha's what just you hev been doin',' Betty accused.

Oh, how true that was! 'I have had no choice. Mr Linton is a thieftaker, even if he calls it something else, and I am guilty of more than just deceiving him. I took the clothes, the sword and the pistol and that makes me a thief in the eyes of the law.' She was not sure about that at all, but she wanted Betty to believe it. It was the only way she could be sure she would stay with her and not confide in Joe.

'Oh, I wish I'd never said I'd come,' Betty wailed. 'An adventure, you said, a jaunt, you said, no harm in it at all. You didn't tell me about stealin' things. An' when it all comes out, I'll be blamed for aidin' you.'

'Very likely,' Louise told her. How hard she was becoming, almost like the man she pretended to be, but she could not let Betty go off on her own. 'That is why we must be on our way before Mr Linton returns from Lincoln. If it had not been for that man trying to kill him and having to be taken to gaol, he would still be with us, so we should be thankful for that.'

Betty laughed. 'You don't really mean that.'

'I most certainly do! Now let us say no more about giving up. There will be a coach tomorrow and we shall be on it.' She gave the girl a hug. 'Don't worry. When we get home I will explain everything and we will both be let off.'

'Can't we go home now?'

'No, not until I have done what I came for.'

'And what might that be?'

'To visit the place of my birth. I told you that from the start.'

'Why? Why is it so important? And why do you have to do it secretly?'

'Because I do,' she said. 'Please do not let me down, Betty, I beg you. We are not so very far from York now.'

'And will that be an end of it?'

'Almost,' Louise answered without having any idea if it was. The end of travelling did not necessarily mean the end of the journey, which might continue in another form: the journey for knowledge. How long that would take she had no idea.

They dined with Joe. Betty was unusually quiet and afterwards said she was tired and wished to go to bed. Louise, who had been half-hoping, half-afraid Mr Linton would arrive before the evening was over, was disappointed when he did not put in an appearance. 'I think an early bed will suit me very well,' she said, rising. 'Goodnight, Mr Potton.'

'Goodnight, *Mr* Smith. *Mrs* Smith.' He was grinning from ear to ear. He would laugh on the other side of his face tomorrow when he discovered he had been left to face his master alone, Louise thought grimly.

Her plan was thwarted when she discovered the only coach leaving early the next morning was full with race goers making their way back to wherever they came from. Carrying their bags, she and Betty walked up and down the main street where they hoped to find another coaching company, but the result was the same. No seats. 'We'll have to go back and wait for Mr Linton,' Betty said, hopefully.

It had become a battle between Louise's stubbornness and her longing to be looked after and the stubbornness won. She could not give in now she was so near her destination and, she hoped, the answer to the questions that plagued her, had plagued her ever since her father had dropped that bombshell, had been with her all along the way. If she had not been born in wedlock, if she were a bastard, then there was no hope for her—she would be condemned to the fringe of polite society, she would be unmarriageable, just as her papa had hinted. It was strange that the need to know had assumed an extra significance since she had met Mr Linton.

'No, we'll find a carrier to take us a little further along the road and perhaps pick up another coach somewhere not quite so busy.' They were approaching a building that appeared to be an open stables, where a covered wagon was being loaded. 'Are you going north?' she asked the old man who was heaving a sack of flour over the tail of it. 'We need a ride.'

'I can take you as far as Barnby.'

'Where's that?'

'Five mile up the road, on the way to Selby.'

'The name of the place meant nothing to Louise. 'Is it on the way to York?'

'To be sure it is.'

'Then we will come with you as far as that, if we may.'

He helped Betty up and Louise remembered just in time, that, as a man, she would be expected to get up on her own, which she did, settling herself beside Betty on the flour sacks, just behind the driver's seat.

They took the main street and crossed the river at the north end of the town before continuing up the Great North Road. Louise, looking back the way they had come, half-expected to see Mr Linton's carriage hard on their heels. She had become so accustomed to it being there, it seemed strange without it. But they had not gone far, when they left the main road, branching off eastwards. They were soon bumping along on a very bad road.

'Where are you taking us?' she twisted round to ask the driver, trying not to sound alarmed.

'To Barnby, like I said. I take supplies to the villages and bring back whatever they want brought back.'

'Oh.'

It was soon apparent that the roads that joined these villages were little more than cart tracks and she realised it was unlikely Mr Linton would think of pursuing them this way. They had lost him, which was a good thing, she told herself without much conviction.

But what if something happened? What if they got stuck in the mud which, given the state of the lanes, would not at all surprise her? It had happened before on a road much better than this one. Supposing, when they were set down, they could not find their way? She looked at Betty and realised the same thought had crossed her mind.

She turned back to the carrier. 'How will we go on from Barnby? Is there a coaching inn?'

'There's a tavern, but I never saw a coach there. If people want a coach, they get me to take them to Doncaster.'

'But we have just left there. We do not want to go back.'

'We could,' Betty ventured.

'No. Our way is north.' She resumed her questioning of the carrier. 'You said we could get to York this way.'

'So you can, if'n you walk.'

'Walk!' shrieked Betty.

He gave a grunt of laughter. 'There's always the river. That do join up with the River Ouse. You can get all the way to York on that.'

Louise had noticed that the lane sometimes ran alongside the river, sometimes veered away from it, and then returned. There were barges and sailing boats on it and she remembered that dreadful criminal talking about using the waterways. 'Then set us down by the river,' she said.

'What do you mean, disappeared?' Jonathan demanded of Joe. 'I told you to look after them.'

'I did, my lord, but I never thought they'd

creep away afore anyone was up. I've searched high and low for them and not a sign of them anywhere. They didn't get on a coach neither. I asked at every inn in the town. All the seats were taken on account of the races.'

'Did they take their bags?' Jonathan asked.

'Yes, and paid their dues to the innkeeper.'

Jonathan, still wearing the grubby clothes in which he had arrived, swore roundly and cursed that murdering Black for the trouble he had caused. The man, true to his reputation, had slipped his manacles and made a hole in the floorboards of his prison and when the man on guard went into the tavern to call out his replacement, still fast asleep on the floor, he had slipped through it and was away across the fields. It had taken them all morning to round him up and it was late afternoon when they had rolled into Lincoln and alerted the magistrate, during which he fumed with impatience, but at last the man had been sent on his way in a second heavy wagon with a new set of guards. Now Black was no longer his responsibility, he could rejoin Louise. It had surprised him how joyful that made him feel and though he would have liked to gallop through the night he had more sense than to ride his mount into the ground. He had ridden as long as daylight lasted and then found a haystack in which to sleep and at daybreak set off again, riding across the hills instead of taking the road, which had cut several miles off the journey. But it had not been enough.

He was furious with Joe and made him tell him exactly what had occurred from the time he left until the boy discovered they had gone. 'When they didn't come down to breakfast,' Joe said. 'I asked the innkeeper's wife and she told me they had left. I've been searching for them ever since.'

'Well, you had better go and harness the horses while I go and clean myself up and change my coat. And then we must go after them.'

He dashed into the inn, demanded hot water and some food packed to eat on the way. He had to find Louise. If anything happened to her, he did not know what he would do. She could be lying in a ditch somewhere, set upon by thieves, made sport of by any of the careless fellows who followed the races. She might have been kidnapped for real. He was beside himself with anxiety. And knowing that, more often than not, she brought her troubles on herself, did not help one bit. 'Louise, where are you?' he muttered as he shrugged himself into a fresh coat. 'Why, oh, why could you not trust me?'

Chapter Five

The carrier set Louise and Betty down close to a landing stage and there they stood with their bags beside them, waiting for a barge to come along. 'You've got us in a fine pickle now,' Betty said morosely, staring across the water at some cows in a field. 'We've no idea where we are. We should have stayed and waited for Mr Linton.'

Worry made Louise snap. 'And be arrested! Be carted off in a closed wagon with no windows and flung into a stinking cell...'

'Mr Linton would never do that.'

'How do you know?'

'Because he knows you are a foolish woman and he likes you.'

'Nonsense!' Louise exclaimed.

'I reckon you like him too. I reckon tha's half the trouble. You won't admit it.'

This was too close to the truth to be borne. 'We cannot go back. For a start, I have no idea where we are; secondly, there will be a barge along any minute and we can ask for a ride.'

'And then he'll never find us.'

'I cannot think why you should want him to.'

'Joe will get into awful trouble for not stopping us and tha's not fair. An' I shan't ever see 'im again.'

Louise managed a smile. So, it was of Joe she was thinking. 'Haven't you told him where you live?'

'Course I have.'

'Then if he thinks anything of you at all he will find you.' And me too, she realised with a start, since they both lived at Chipping Barnet. The thought cheered her because when she went home and everything was explained, Mr Linton might come calling and they could get to know each other properly. He was not a nobleman, not someone who would look down at her humble origins. But if she were a bastard, even he would turn his nose up at her. Everyone would. Her cheerfulness lasted exactly thirty seconds.

'Well?' Betty demanded. 'What do we do now?'

Louise pointed to a barge being pulled along

the towpath by a plodding horse and it was going in the right direction according to the flow of the current. 'Sir!' she called to the man whose hand was on the tiller. 'Will you take on passengers?'

He steered the craft to the bank and called 'Whoa, Beauty!' to the horse. Then he turned towards the girls. He was a powerfully built man dressed in leather breeches and a leather jerkin. His dark hair was pulled back and tied with a cord. 'What is it you want?'

'A ride, if you would be so good. We want to go to York.'

'Aren't going all that way. I can take you some of the way if you work your passage.'

'Work?' queried Louise, almost forgetting to deepen her voice.

'Yes. Help look after the horse and take the tiller now and again. The little lady can cook our meals and keep the cabin clean.'

Louise looked at Betty. 'Well, my dear, what do you say?'

'Hev we got a choice?' Betty asked morosely.

'We could stand here until doomsday.'

'Then let us go aboard. The sooner we get going the sooner we'll arrive. An' I don' suppose we'll

get stuck in the mud like we did on the road.'
For some reason this made the man laugh. He
held out his hand to help Betty aboard, ignoring
Louise, just as the carrier had done. She looked
down at the green water, swirling with weeds; it
would be no fun falling into that. She threw their
bags on board, took a deep breath and jumped
across, landing with a thump.

'Now, sir,' she said, relieved to find herself
safely on board. 'What would you have me
do?'

'Go down and stoke up the fire so your missus
can cook us dinner. There's a side of bacon, some
eggs and plenty o' bread. And fish. You like to
fish, do you? We can do some of that as we go.'

Louise had fished with her brothers, but most
of their catch and had been too small to be eaten
and had been thrown back to grow bigger. 'Yes,
sir.'

'Stop calling me "sir". Makes me feel uncomfortable, it does. I'm Josh Cottle.'

'Mr Cottle, how do you do?' Louise extended
her hand. 'I am Lou Smith.'

He ignored the hand and pointed to a super-
structure at the stern of the barge. 'There's
the galley.'

It was reached by a walkway running round the side of the barge; the rest of the vessel, apart from the small amount of decking on which they stood, was loaded with timber. Louise and Betty inched their way tentatively round the narrow planking and went into the cabin. 'I hope we don' have to stay on this boat all night,' Betty said, looking round the tiny room. There was a table and two narrow bunks with rough blankets, a cupboard or two and a potbellied fire. Wood was piled beside it. 'There's nowhere to sleep.'

'Perhaps Mr Cottle will allow us the bunks and sleep on deck himself.' She looked with distaste at the bunks and shuddered; she did not doubt they were infested with livestock. 'Or perhaps he will tie up at a riverside inn.'

'Well, if he don' I'm not stoppin' and I don' care what you say.'

Louise was inclined to agree with her; the air in the cabin was hot and stale. They set to doing the tasks allotted to them as the horse pulled them gently along. They shared a meal with Mr Cottle and afterwards, while Betty cleaned the cabin, Louise took her hand at the tiller under Mr Cottle's direction. Although the slowness irked her at first, she had to admit that the scenery was beautiful and the fresh air invigorating. She had left the muddy potholed roads behind her, had left Mr Linton behind too and she was ambivalent about that. For all she was trying to escape from him, she was obliged to admit that if he had been there to share the experience with her, she would have enjoyed the change of scene.

If it were true he knew she was not a man, he had never hinted at it. He had gone on treating her like a man, a somewhat youthful, naïve man, but a man nevertheless. He had shown no interest in her as woman. But why would he? A hoyden dressed in male clothes and one who indulged in duels and played cards and hit men over the head with rocks was hardly likely to appeal to him. Besides, she should not be thinking of him in those terms. She was on a mission to find her mother and until she knew the truth about herself, she should not be thinking of anything else but how to achieve her goal. But, oh, how she missed him! And that was an admission she never thought she would make.

The recent rains had made the river overflow in some places and the poor horse was wading in sticky mud and, because the edge was not clear, was in danger of walking into deeper water. Mr Cottle took the tiller from Louise to guide the barge into the bank and left her and Betty on it while he went to help the horse. Left to use a pole to stop the vessel bumping into the side, Louise felt her lack of muscle. She was soon aching in every joint and Mr Cottle had no patience with her.

'Useless you are!' he shouted, when the barge thumped against the bank, sending ripples of water out over his feet. 'I knew you were too puny to be any good.'

'Then why take us on?' she demanded breathlessly.

'Didn' have no choice. My mate was took ill with the belly ache and I needed someone. And your missus looked as though she'd be more use than you.'

Louise did not disagree with that. Betty had been working in a cloud of dust and now had the cabin looking spick and span.

As soon as they had passed the floods and the land became visible again, Cottle came back on board. He looked at Betty's handiwork. 'Good little housemate you are, m'dear. If you feel like a change, we can send him away.' He nodded towards Louise. 'You and me will do very nicely on our own.'

'No, thank you,' Betty said.

'You don't mean you'd rather have that spidershanks than a fine big man like me?' He grinned at her. 'Do he even know what to do with it?'

'With what?'

'You mean you don't know?' He slapped his thigh and roared with laughter. 'Then I reckon I oughta give you a taste.' He reached out to grab her. His intention was clear and she backed away. Ignoring Louise, he went after her.

Louise could not stand and watch her friend being assaulted. 'Let her be!' She grabbed the man by the shoulders and tried to pull him away. 'She is my wife.'

'I don't reckon she is. Even if you have stood up in front o' the parson, which give me leave to doubt, it takes more than that to make a wife. Go and take the tiller.'

'No, I will not.'

He went to push her away. She came back at him, clawing at his face in the manner of an irate termagant, not a young man. He laughed and grabbed her upper arms and his eyes widened as he realised what he had hold of. She jerked herself away, lost her footing, tried to regain her balance and the next minute was in the river.

Betty screamed and went for the man, who grabbed her and flung her after Louise. 'Go and join the bitch.' He laughed. 'I ha' heard of two men being inclined that way, but I've never come across two women like it. I hope the cold water cools your ardour.'

Louise was treading water, which was thick with weeds, but Betty was weighed down by her skirts and in danger of drowning. Louise went to her aid and grabbed her shoulders from behind. 'Don't struggle. I've got you. Just lie back on me and kick your legs a bit.'

'I can't. Me petticoats…'

'Try, please.' Louise turned on her back and with both of them kicking out, they managed to reach the bank and haul themselves out. The lay on their backs on the grass, exhausted, cold, wet and humiliated. And what was worse, everything they owned was on the barge, now a hundred yards further down stream.

Having ascertained that Joe was right and the girls were not to be found in Doncaster, Jonathan climbed in the carriage and they set out northwards, assuming that was the direction they would take. They had just crossed the bridge and were heading up the Great North Road, when they passed a carrier's wagon coming into the town. Jonathan called to Joe to stop and, before the wheels had stopped turning, was out and chasing up the road after the wagon.

'Have you seen a young couple on the road?' he asked, when he managed to attract the driver's attention and he pulled up. 'A young man in a blue coat and a young lady in a pink striped skirt?'

'Yes, I reckon I have. Run away, have they?'

'Yes. They must be found.' He took his purse from his pocket and extracted a guinea. 'Where did you see them?'

'I gave them a ride. Set them down in Barnby.'

'Barnby?' he queried in surprise. Had he been wrong—had she lied when she said she was going to York?

'Yes, when I told her there were no coaches to York from there, she said they would go by the river.'

'Thank you,' He offered the man the guinea.

'And would you be kind enough to give us directions?'

Jonathan returned to Joe and climbed up beside him. He could see better from that vantage point. 'Take the right fork up here,' he said. 'I am told the road is bad, but that is nothing new. Drive carefully and let us pray they have not gone far.'

Arriving in Barnby, it was soon apparent the fugitives had left. A housewife sweeping the path to her door told him she had seen a couple standing on the staithe. They must have boarded a river craft, probably a barge. He returned to the carriage. 'Keep going,' he told Joe.

The road sometimes veered away from the river and when that happened he left Joe to take the carriage on and walked along the towpath, meeting him again further along. He had no idea how far the runaways had gone and wondered if he ought to try to get ahead of them to wait for their arrival. But if anything should happen to delay them, an accident or something even worse, he knew he would never forgive himself. 'I wonder why I bother with them,' he said, returning to Joe, whose whole attention was on driving the carriage without mishap.

'I reckon you couldn't just leave 'em, my lord. You ain't that kind o' man.'

Jonathan smiled. 'Yes, you are right. But you would not want to abandon Mrs Smith either, would you?'

'Mrs Smith.' Joe laughed. 'You don' think tha's really her name, do you?'

'No, any more than Mr Smith is Mr Smith. The name of that baggage is Miss Louise Vail. But you knew that, did you not?'

'Not her name. Betty never told me it. Is Miss Vail the chase 'em and nab 'em business, my lord?'

'Yes, she is, and a fair dance she is leading us. If it hadn't been for that scoundrel, Black, I'd never have lost them.'

'Oh, I don' know,' Joe said, stung by the implication his master would have done better than he had. 'They'd have still crept away.'

'You are probably right,' he agreed morosely.

'What are they supposed to have done, asides from run away, I mean?'

'It is not what they have done, Joe, it is what

Miss Vail intends to do next that is occupying me at the moment.'

As they had been speaking they covered a little more ground, going through a small copse and, coming out on the other side, Jonathan glimpsed the river again. He asked Joe to pull up. 'Wait here,' he said. 'I'll have one more search and then we'll have to give up. If they make their way to York, we shall have to go there and hope to come up with them again.'

He jumped down and made his way across a meadow to the river bank and began to walk along it. The river had overflowed in many places and he had to watch his step. The sun was moving round to the west and throwing long shadows. His sleepless nights were beginning to tell and he longed for a good meal and his bed. But while those two were out here somewhere, he could not have either.

Looking up from picking his way to avoid the puddles, he saw two bedraggled creatures making their way towards him. He stopped and stared. They were soaked to the skin, their clothes festooned in weeds from the river. Betty's gown clung to her legs and Louise's coat and breeches did nothing to hide her feminine curves.

He could not help it; he put his hands on his hips and laughed.

Louise was at the end of her tether. She was cold, wet and miserable and mourning the loss of her baggage. She would have given anything for a knight in shining armour to ride to her rescue or, failing that, Jonathan Linton and his carriage. But to be greeted by laughter was the outside of enough. 'I suppose you would think it amusing,' she snapped.

He stopped laughing. 'I beg your pardon. But you do present a rare sight. How did it come about?' He had approached a little closer and realised both girls were shaking and their teeth chattering. 'Never mind, no need to tell me now. Let us get you back to the carriage and some warmth.' He took an arm of each and marched them back to where he had left Joe.

The young man jumped down on seeing them. 'Betty, you look half-drowned,' he said anxiously. 'What happened?'

'Explanations later,' Jonathan said. 'Did you dry off those horse blankets?'

'Yes, and brushed them clean.' He went to the boot and pulled them out. One was wrapped around each of the girls and they were helped into the carriage and another tucked over their legs. 'Turn round in the nearest field gate,' Jonathan commanded Joe. 'Back to Doncaster, quick as you like. We shall be lucky if these two do not take a chill. But don't take any risks.' Then he climbed in opposite Louise and they set off.

When she had first seen him coming towards them, Louise had felt such relief she wanted to run into his arms and feel the comfort and warmth of his embrace, to feel safe and cared for, but his laughter had angered her, which had saved her from making a complete cake of herself. The blankets smelled strongly of horse, but they were warm and before long the shivering subsided a little and she felt able to speak. 'Were you looking for us?'

'Of course.'

'How did you find us?'

'By asking questions, my dear. You are not very clever at covering your tracks.' Muffled in blankets, she looked like nothing so much as a bedraggled child. He wanted to hug her.

She looked sharply at him. The endearment had shaken her. 'You know?' she whispered.

'That you are not who you pretend to be? Of

course I know. You have a delightful figure, but it is certainly not that of a man, nor even a boy.'

'Oh. When?'

'When did I tumble to it? Why, when we fought that duel. Once your coat was off, your delightful curves gave you away.' He smiled.

'And yet you fought with me!'

'I had no choice. Dishonour myself or denounce you, and I found I could not do either. We should both have looked ninnies.'

'I felt you were holding back.'

'Oh, not so very much. You swordsmanship is exceptional…'

'…for a woman,' she finished for him.

'For anyone, man or woman. And you play a sweet game of whist. Tell me, who taught you these accomplishments?'

'My brothers.' He was getting too inquisitive for her peace of mind. 'Tell me, sir,' she went on, 'is it against the law to impersonate a man?'

He was amused by the question. 'I suppose it depends why it is done. If it is done with the intention to deceive, it might very well be. And if the clothes have been stolen…' He let the sentence hang in the air.

'I told you so,' Betty put in. 'You had best come clean.'

Louise ignored her and continued to speak to Jonathan. 'And you would know all about the law.'

'No, I would not be so presumptuous as to say that. Why do you ask?'

'But you are a thieftaker?'

'What makes you say that?'

'You took those two highwaymen and that man—what was his name?'

'Jed Black.'

'Yes, a murderer, you said. You knew who they were and exactly what had to be done with them,' she pointed out.

'What else should I have done with them? It was no more than common sense and if you had not seen the man heaving a rock over my head and felled him, I would not have known who he was.'

'I was sorry I did that. I did not stop to think.'

'If you had done so, I would not be here to tell the tale. I am in your debt,' he replied.

'But you have been following us all the way, haven't you?'

'It was unbridled curiosity, my dear, at least in

the beginning,' he said. For some reason he did not want to divulge that he had set out on the journey expressly to track her down. The little rapport they had established would be blown away on the wind if he did that. And she would wonder why he had not said so in the first place and taken her straight back to Barnet. He was not even sure of the reason himself. 'I wondered what you were about. And then when I realised you have a penchant for falling into scrapes, I felt you needed someone to pull you out of them. Today has been a case in point. What would you have done, if I had not come along?'

She shuddered. 'I dare not think.'

'Tell me what happened. It is plain to see you took an unplanned swim. I suppose you count swimming among your other talents.'

'I can swim.'

'But you did not go into the river on purpose, I'll wager,' he said.

'No. We were on a barge. The bargeman said he would take us if we worked our passage. He took a fancy to Betty and...'

'He were 'orrible,' Betty said. 'He had his hands on me and Miss...Lou went for him. He grabbed her and then he saw she weren't a man.'

He stifled his horror and turned back to Louise. 'What did he do to you?'

'Nothing. I pushed him away and then over-balanced and went into the river.'

'He threw me in,' Betty said. 'I thought I were goin' to drown.'

'Attempted murder,' he murmured.

'Oh, you would turn it round to the legality of it,' Louise snapped. 'What is more to the point is that we made it to the bank and did not drown. But our baggage was on the barge and the dreadful man did not stop. We have lost everything, all our baggage and Lu—my sword.'

'That is, indeed, a loss,' he said, trying not to smile. In spite of the tangled hair and pale face, she was still extraordinarily lovely and her attempt at bravado made her even more so.

She delved under her blanket into the pocket of her coat and withdrew her purse and the pistol, both wet. 'But I've still got these.'

'That's something,' he said. He did not doubt she had saved Betty, not only from the bargeman but from drowning too. She never ceased to amaze him. 'Though I am not sure the pistol can still be fired.'

'Oh, I would never have fired it,' she said complacently. 'It was only meant to scare.'

It was dark by the time they drew up at the George. Was it only that morning they had left it? It seemed an age ago. 'You cannot be seen like that,' Jonathan told Louise. 'Wait here, a moment.'

Without waiting for Joe to open the carriage door and let down the step, he jumped down and hurried into the inn. Louise watched him go, realising he had evaded answering her question about being a thieftaker and she still did not know what his intentions were. But she felt strangely untroubled. After what had happened today, she was ready to admit she was not such a doughty traveller as she had expected to be and she dreaded to think of their fate if he had not come looking for them.

He came striding out again two minutes later and conferred with Joe. Then he climbed in and Joe drove them out of the yard again. 'Where are we going?' Louise asked in dismay. She had been looking forward to a room with a fire and a chance to dry her clothes, not to mention a hot meal.

'I do not think you should be paraded through the public rooms of an inn,' he said. 'I have obtained Mrs Slater's direction. I am sure she will help you both.'

'But we cannot impose on her unannounced.'

'I shall announce you,' he said. 'And I heard her say if she could ever do anything for you, you have only to ask…'

'But that was only politeness,' she protested.

'No, I think she meant it. We shall soon find out. But before we approach her, I require a solemn promise from you. Two promises.'

'And what are they?' She was wary.

'Firstly, no more hiding behind breeches. From now on you are to be a woman. I shall explain to Mrs Slater you did it to be safe, but as from now, I shall be looking after you, so there is no need to go on with the charade.'

'That is all very well, but I have no other clothes.'

'I know that, but I am sure some feminine garments can be procured for you. So, do you agree?'

'Yes,' she said, perfectly willing to give the up undertaking. She was sick of trying to be a man; it had turned out to be no safer, perhaps less so, because her masculine guise had got her into all sorts of scrapes.

'Thank goodness for that,' Betty murmured from her corner. Louise had almost forgotten she was there, being more concerned with her conversation with Mr Linton and what he was asking of her.

'But I do not understand why you need to tell Mrs Slater that you are going to look after me,' she said.

'Because I am.'

'Why?'

He shrugged. 'Someone has to. And do not get on your high horse over it. If you are honest with yourself, you will admit I am right.'

She was too stubborn to answer that. 'You said two promises.'

'The other is not to run away again. Not under any circumstances. If Mrs Slater agrees to put you up until we can dress you properly again and continue our journey, it would be prodigiously ungrateful to rush off.'

'I am to be your prisoner,' she said dolefully.

He smiled, though in the gloom of the carriage she did not see it. 'Would that be so very dreadful?' he asked softly.

'It depends what you intend to do with me. Are you going to send me back to Newgate in a prison van?'

He laughed aloud. 'Whatever made you think I would?'

'You are a thieftaker.'

'And are you a thief?'

'I stole my brothers' clothes.'

'And do you think he might not forgive you?'

'Of course he will, but…'

'Louise. That is your name, is it not?'

'How did you know?'

'Louis and Louise are almost the same. It was a simple deduction and as you have not told me your surname I cannot address you formerly. Besides, that would be somewhat stiff under our present circumstances. You may call me Jonathan.'

'Mr Linton. Jonathan. You are very good at evading questions you do not wish to answer…'

'What questions, my dear?'

'What do you intend to do with me?'

'Nothing but escort you to your destination,' he promised.

'But you do not know it.'

'No, but you will tell me, won't you?'

'And then?'

'It depends what we find when we get there.'

'I am going to visit a relative I have not seen for a long time. I am sure you will be utterly bored.'

'My dear, nothing you do bores me,' he said, laughing. 'Infuriates me, amuses me, fills me anxiety, yes, all of those, but you do not nor, I suspect, ever will bore me.'

'But what about your own business in Yorkshire?'

'Oh, that can wait. Have I your word?'

'Oh, yes, if you must.' It sounded ungrateful, but her pride was doing battle with her very real need to be looked after and feel secure.

'Good.' Joe was drawing the carriage up outside a villa in a row of such houses. 'Now, before I speak to Mrs Slater, I need to know your surname. It is not Smith, is it?'

'No.' She paused. What to tell him? The name she had lived with for the past twenty years was the one that came most readily to her lips. 'It is Vail.'

He smiled with relief that she had trusted him with the truth. 'Well, Miss Vail, we shall see what Mrs Slater says. Wait here until I come back.'

After he had gone, Louise sank back in her seat, exhausted by everything that had happened, not only the adventure on the river and the near drowning, but by Jonathan's gentle but insistent questions. She had told him all he wanted to know except the reason for her journey. She could hardly tell him she was going to find a mother who had given her away and to find out if she were a bastard. And if he was still with her when she discovered that, then she would have to find some way of making him leave her, if her promise meant she could not leave him.

He came back to the carriage followed by Mrs Slater. 'Oh, you poor dears,' she said, seeing the two girls wrapped in horse blankets. 'Come into the house, do. We shall soon have you warm and comfortable.'

Jonathan handed the girls out and followed them into the house. It was only a small villa, but it shone with cleanliness. Mr Slater, wearing buckskin breeches and a fustian waistcoat, came from one of the rooms and bowed to the girls, both of whom were glad he could not see their bedraggled clothes for the horse blankets which they clasped about themselves. 'Ladies, you are welcome to my humble abode. I will leave you in my wife's capable hands, but if there is anything I can do…'

'You can have Sadie bring hot water up to the guest room,' his wife told him. 'A hot bath is what is called for. And then some hot broth. Mr Linton, you can safely leave the ladies with me. Come along,' she said, ushering Louise and Betty up a flight of stairs.

'A glass of something?' Arthur Slater asked Jonathan, who had stopped to watch them climbing the stairs.

'Thank you, but no. I have left my carriage and driver out side and we all, men and horses alike, need to find our beds. With your permission, I will call in the morning and we will decide how to go on.'

'Yes, of course. Rest assured, your ward and her friend will be safe with us. My wife will find them some clothes until you can recover their belongings.'

'I am indebted to you, sir.' He had told Mr and Mrs Slater he was Louise's guardian, which in a way he considered himself to be, so it was not exactly a lie, and if they chose to interpret that in a legal sense, he would not disillusion them. The pickle the girls had got themselves in was the result of a prank that had gone wrong, he had explained. Louise had taken it into her head to visit a relative in York, but had not understood the pitfalls of travelling unescorted.

'The debt is mine. My wife has told me how well you looked after her and our Will when the coach turned over. She had been to visit her sister, who has just been delivered of a daughter. If I had known how bad the weather was going to turn out, I would have insisted she postpone her trip.'

Jonathan took his leave with some reluctance. He hoped sincerely that Miss Louise Vail always honoured her promises and she would be there and suitably dressed when he arrived next morning. But before he did so, he had letters to write and shopping to do.

Louise woke to find herself in a comfortable bed, wearing a white linen nightrail that clothed her from head to foot. The curtains of the room had been pulled back and it was broad daylight. Outside the sun shone and she could hear birds singing. For a moment she wondered where she was. And then it came back to her—the journey north, accompanied all the way by Mr Jonathan

Linton, except when he went off with his prisoner and left her to fall into yet another scrape, from which he had still managed to rescue her. It seemed she was to be for ever in his debt. It did not sit well with her pride.

She moved her head sideways and realised that it hurt to do so. Mrs Slater was sitting in a chair by her bed watching her. 'Oh, I did not know you were there,' she murmured. 'Is it very late?'

'Noon, my dear, but no matter…'

'Noon! Oh, I cannot lie here…' She struggled to sit up, but had to lie down again when the room seemed to whirl about her. 'Oh, I am suddenly dizzy.'

'It is not to be wondered at after the ducking you took yesterday. And then to walk about in wet clothes…'

'Betty?' Her friend had been just as wet.

'Betty is perfectly well. She has had her breakfast and gone out with Mr Linton. I have lent her a dress…'

What were Betty and Mr Linton doing going out together? she wondered. Where had they gone? Why had they not woken her and suggested she should go with them? She felt abandoned and desperate to regain her dignity and determination, both of which seemed to have deserted her. 'It is very kind in you. I must get up.' She tried once more to sit and the same thing happened: she was dizzy and her head hurt. In fact, all her muscles ached. 'It must be trying to work that barge,' she said, then smiled wanly. 'Did Mr Linton tell you about that too?'

'Yes, and that you had lost all your belongings. I have said I will find some garments for you, until he can bring you some more.' She smiled suddenly. 'I wonder what his taste will be.'

'I have no idea. I cannot think why he should bother. I had better wear my breeches again.'

'I do not think that men's clothes suit you, my dear. And to be sure they were torn and muddy. I have disposed of them. Mr Linton said you would not need them any more,' Mrs Slater said.

'Oh.' She felt too weak to argue about Jonathan's high-handedness; besides, she had promised Jonathan not to wear the breeches again. She sank back on the pillow, wishing she felt strong enough to exert her independence.

'You have taken a chill, Miss Vail, and must stay in bed a little longer.'

'Oh, please, I am Louise. And I cannot impose on you.'

'It is not an imposition, Louise, but a pleasure. We should all help each other through life, do you not agree? It is what our Saviour taught us.'

'You sound like my father.'

'Your father? I understood you were without a father. Mr Linton said he was your guardian,' the older woman commented.

She was annoyed and inclined to deny the man was anything of the sort, but realised he had probably done it to save her reputation. And truly the Reverend Vail was not her father. She could not tell the good lady that, it would lead to a roasting, a roasting about who she was and where she came from and where she was going. And it was all too much to explain. 'So he is, but that has only come about quite recently. My papa was a devout Christian.'

'I am glad to hear it.' The good lady seemed to accept this ambiguous statement at face value. 'I felt sure you were not the hoyden you appeared to be. A hoyden would not have been so caring and helpful when that coach turned over and that dreadful man…' She shuddered. 'You were very brave and so was Mr Linton.'

'Thank you.' If she had any idea of confiding the truth, she discarded it. The woman obviously lived by her religious principles and they would not include giving house room to a runaway, especially one who was probably the result of an illicit liaison. Mr Linton had been kind to shield her from that. But how had he explained what she was doing in a public coach while he came behind in his own carriage?

'I will have some broth sent up to you, and then you must sleep some more. Nourishment and sleep are the best cures for your ailment. And when you are quite well, we will talk some more.' She stood up, patted the covers and left Louise to her thoughts. But her head was so muzzy she could not think straight, let alone formulate a plan. Nor did she think sleep and nourishment were the cure for her ills. She wished she had not promised Mr Linton she would not leave Mrs Slater. Why had he gone off with Betty? Betty was a little turncoat; she would have something to say to her when she put in an appearance. But supposing she did not? She had said she wanted to go home. Is that where she was, on the way back to Barnet, escorted by Mr Linton, leaving her to stew here, too weak to move…?

* * *

Jonathan had taken Betty to help him choose suitable clothes for Louise. They had visited several shops where ready-made gowns could be obtained. His mother and sister had all their gowns made for them and a fine penny they cost, but there was no time to have gowns made for Louise and he did not think sumptuous clothing and hooped petticoats were appropriate under the circumstances. He smiled to himself as he turned over readymade muslins, gingham and jaconet in pinks and blues and greens, open gowns, silk petticoats, closed gowns, quilted stomachers, laced stays, flimsy scarves, ladies' shoes. 'What do you think?' he asked Betty. The girl was wide-eyed and giggly.

'They are all very fine, sir. I am sure M…Lou will be happy with whatever you choose, but…'

'But what? And why can you not refer to her as Louise?'

'She said I was to call her Lou until she gave me leave to say her real name.'

'But that is Louise?'

She nodded, looking at the ground where some puddles still remained from the downpour of two days before, picking her way round them.

He knew she was uncomfortable about the quiz-zing and though he had intended to pursue it relentlessly, believing she would tell him more than Miss Vail would, he could not go on with it. It would be making the poor girl into a sneak and that was not fair. Louise Vail must tell him herself. And until she did he would stick to her side.

He was perfectly aware that was not what he had been commissioned to do—find her and bring her back was all that had been asked of him—but he could not help wondering what was behind her flight. It was something that had turned her from a happy madcap into a rather sad and lonely traveller and he could empathise with that. He could not force her to go back, would not if he could, and he had a feeling, which he could not explain, that she was going to need him. 'But what?' he said, going back to the dis-cussion about clothes. 'You said Miss Louise would be happy with anything but…'

'She will insist on paying for them herself and her purse is all but empty, so please, sir, do not be too extravagant.'

'I shall be as extravagant as I choose to be. You may safely leave Miss Louise's scruples to me.' Discarding the idea of pink and lemon, he picked up a taffeta gown in a clear green, the green in her oh-so-expressive eyes. 'What about this? Will it fit her, do you think? She is a little taller than you, but your figures are similar. You could try it on and we shall see if the size is right.'

Betty was shown into a room at the rear of the establishment and a few minutes later emerged in the green gown. The vibrant colour did nothing for Betty, but he knew it would be just right on Louise. 'Yes, it will do nicely,' he said, handing her a deep blue silk. 'Now try this one.'

And so it went on, from shop to shop. Picking gowns, none intended to be worn with hoops; he hated the cumbersome fashion and chose those which only needed lightly padded petticoats. Selecting jackets and mantles, gloves and scarves, hats and shoes was one thing, but picking hose and underwear had Betty blushing to the roots of her fair hair. He did not seem to notice, but at least he did not ask her to try them on and parade before him! When he was satisfied he had bought a wardrobe sufficient for the remainder of her journey, he then bought dresses, shoes and underwear for Betty, who blissfully stammered delighted thanks, and having paid for everything and arranged for it to be delivered, he escorted her back to the Slaters' villa, only to discover Louise was far from well.

'She has taken a chill,' Mrs Slater told him. 'But it is hardly to be wondered at, is it? I have dosed her with Godfrey's cordial. It always helps my little Will.'

He was surprised at how alarmed he was, how anxious to be of help. He wanted to rush straight up to her room and see for himself how she was. 'What can I do to help?' he asked, as Betty slipped away. 'Have you sent for a doctor?'

'Yes. He has just left.'

'What did he say?'

She smiled at the young man. Guardian or not, he obviously felt a great deal more for the young lady than he had told her. 'It is a chill, but if she is kept warm and nourished, she will take no harm'

'Thank goodness for that,' he said with feeling. 'I am grateful for your help, Mrs Slater.'

'It is the least I can do. The doctor advised three days in bed and both young ladies are welcome to stay here until Miss Vail is fully recovered.'

'Are you sure it is not too much for you? Shall I engage a nurse for her?' he asked.

'There is no need. I can nurse her with Betty's help. What will you do?'

'I shall stay at the inn until we resume our journey. May I go up and see her?'

Her hesitation was only momentary. Mr Linton was Miss Vail's guardian and a gentleman in the very best sense. 'Yes, but do not tire her, sir. She needs to sleep. It is the best cure, do you not think?'

'Indeed. I will not stay long.' And with that he bounded up the stairs, leaving her smiling.

Chapter Six

He tapped lightly on the bedroom door expecting Betty to answer it, but when she did not, lifted the latch and peeped inside. Louise was alone in the room, lying in bed, propped up with pillows. She appeared to be asleep. He knew he ought not to go in, but she looked so wan, so vulnerable, he could not make himself turn away. He crept across the room and sat in a chair beside the bed to watch her.

She was lovely; her thick curly hair was spread across the pillow and formed a coppery halo. Her long, dark lashes lay on cheeks that were paler than they ought to be. Her mouth was ever-so-slightly ajar, because her cold made breathing difficult. She had thrown back the covers, revealing her nightrail half off one white shoulder. Her bosom rose and fell and he caught a glimpse of the top of one breast. An arm was flung out towards him, palm uppermost. He felt his breath catch in his throat and a strong wave of desire coursed through him. He ought to go, put temptation well out of reach, remember who he was and what he was supposed to be doing on this strange journey. Instead he reached out and put his hand over hers and continued to study her features as if in thrall.

She stirred sleepily and opened her eyes. Amazing hazel eyes flecked with green met his blue gaze. 'You came back,' she murmured.

'Of course I came back.' He smiled. 'There is no being rid of me, my sweet, not until all is resolved. You are stuck with me.'

'Oh.' She tried to sit up, realised she was only half-covered and lay back again, drawing the sheet up to her chin. 'And that extends to my bedchamber, does it?' She smiled as she said it, because she was so happy and relieved to see him.

'If you cannot leave it, yes.' He understood her; it was surprising how well he understood her.

'You do not trust me. You think I might pretend to be ill in order to escape.'

'But you gave me your promise. I assumed you meant it,' he said.

'I do not break my word.'

'I am glad to hear that. But why must you escape? Is my presence so disagreeable?' It was asked gently, as if he really wanted to know the answer.

'You know it is not. I have had cause to thank God for it on several occasions in the last few days.'

'Few days,' he repeated. 'Is that all it is? It seems like a lifetime.'

It was like that for her too. The life before this journey seemed a distant dream, the life after it was full of uncertainty. He was the one who held the two together. There was an unseen bond that drew them together, getting tighter with every day, every minute that passed. It was a bond she had to break, if she was to fulfil her errand. But not now. Not yet. Not until… 'Why did you tell Mrs Slater you were my guardian?'

'Would you have me say I had never met you until a few days ago, that I had picked you up on the road? I wanted her to welcome you as a gentlewoman.'

'Oh. What else did you tell her?'

'That you had embarked on the journey as prank and as soon as I heard of it, I set out after you and glad I am that I did, because the trip has certainly not been uneventful. Of course I did not say anything about playing cards and fighting duels, that would have condemned you for ever in her eyes.'

'Thank you for that. Where was I going on this prank of mine?'

'To visit relations in York.'

'But that is the truth,' she pointed out.

'There is no point in lying if you do not have to, is there?' It was said with a smile.

'No, but you are not my guardian. That was an untruth.'

'No. Until we reach the end of this voyage of discovery, I am *in loco parentis*, so it was no lie.'

It was strange that he should use the phrase voyage of discovery—it exactly described how she felt about it. But he did not know what she was set on discovering, so what was his objective? More searching out of thieves and murderers? Her head was too confused to sort it all out. 'The whole of life is a journey of discovery,' she murmured. She was having trouble keeping her eyes open. 'But why do you want to share mine?'

'Now do you know, I have been asking myself that question and I do not know the answer.' He stood up, still holding her hand. 'But you are tired. Today, you rest and tomorrow too, and perhaps the day after that we will resume our discourse on life and fate and what makes us do the things we do. I shall leave you now.' He lifted her hand to his lips and kissed the inside of the palm. 'But I will be back.'

She watched him walk across the room and disappear, then shut her eyes. She felt tired beyond imagining, but even in the midst of that, her senses registered that kiss, the butterfly pressure of his lips on the inside of her hand and the strange sensations it aroused in the pit of her stomach. She was too tired to analyse it now, but it left her feeling at peace with herself for the first time for days. She fell asleep with a half-smile on her lips.

She had a robust constitution and recovered quickly and was soon itching to be up and dressed, but Mrs Slater insisted on keeping her in bed the three days the doctor had ordered and after that allowed her to come downstairs in a dressing gown, one of the many items of clothing Jonathan had procured for her. She had been dismayed when she learned from Betty how much he had bought. It was more than she could ever repay. He told her he did not want repaying; it was little enough to make her respectable again. If he could spend so much, he must be very plump in the pocket. Did it come from his thieftaking exploits? What was behind it all? Why bother with her? She could certainly not bring him a reward.

It was not only the clothes; he came every day, bringing little presents of flowers, sweetmeats and sugar plums. He was as attentive as any lover, Mrs Slater said, which made Louise smile. The good lady did not know the truth, that he had appointed himself her escort, the reason for which escaped her. And Betty was enjoying herself hugely being squired about by Joe; she did not care if they did not take another step. But Louise did. Mrs Slater had been kindness itself and she appreciated it, but the woman who had beckoned her to 'come unto me' still beckoned. The journey had already taken far longer than she had ever anticipated and Mama and Papa back in Barnet would be worrying about her.

While she had been ill, she had found herself thinking more and more of her life in Chipping Barnet with the loving couple who had brought her up. She remembered happy family occasions, her lessons with her brothers, picnics, learning to ride and shoot and fish and her impatience with sewing and drawing and her mama's insistence that she should persevere. She remembered especially how she had always been cared for when she had childish ailments, rare occurrences because she was well nourished. How coddled she had been, and her brothers invading her sick room and jollying her along. She missed them all.

And suddenly she wanted Jonathan to know them and for them to know him, to know how he had looked after her *in loco parentis*, to use his own words. Not that he felt a bit like a parent to her, he was far too young for a start, probably little older than Luke, but he didn't feel like a brother either. She did not know what he was, could not even be sure Jonathan Linton was his real name. All she knew was that he had become part of her life and she would miss him when he had gone. At the end of their voyage of discovery, he had said, and perhaps they would both discover more than they had bargained for.

At the end of the week, Louise dressed properly for the first time to go down to dinner to which Jonathan had been invited. She wore the green dress he had bought for her. It fitted so well it might have been especially made for her. The stomacher was quilted brocade in a lighter green than the taffeta gown itself. The green of that was as vibrant as newly cut grass and fitted closely into her waist, its open panel revealing a ruched petticoat, edged with cream lace. It had small false hips to accommodate a little padding in her petticoat, which served to emphasise her slim waist and hint at the round curves beneath it. The sleeves were narrow to the elbow and then widened to a cascade of cream lace. The outfit was finished off with green satin slippers, a chicken-skin fan and her only piece of real jewellery, a pearl necklace, brought with her in case she needed to sell it for funds to continue her journey. Her unpowdered hair had been piled up and arranged in curls on top of her head with a few corkscrew curls nestling in her neck.

Jonathan, who was waiting in the drawing room with Mr and Mrs Slater, was bowled over by this apparition of loveliness. Could this be the stripling he had crossed swords with, the hoyden dripping river water, the wan child who lay sick in bed needing comfort? She was all of these and much, much more. Something very strange was happening to him; he was losing his wits. It was better to lose your wits than your heart, he decided. But until he came to his senses, it was a pleasurable state to be in. He smiled and bowed over her hand. 'My dear, you look lovely. I knew that green would suit you.'

'I thank you for it,' she said, pleased by his compliment. He was changing, she decided. The impatient man trying to deal with a troublesome pest was acting the gallant. If she did not know him better, she would have said he was coming round to liking her a little. He certainly seemed to know her taste in clothes.

Betty arrived in one of her new gowns, with a spruced-up Joe at her side, feeling big and important to be dining with his betters, just as Sadie, the maid of all work, came to tell them dinner was served and they moved into the dining room. It was a convivial gathering over a simple meal, but all the better for that. They talked about everything: music, art, the dreadful weather, the state of the roads and the growing problem of highway robbery and violence. 'At least one of the miscreants is behind bars now, thanks to you, Mr Linton.' Mrs Slater said.

'And Louise,' he added, smiling at her. 'She was the one who laid him out.'

'I did not stop to think,' Louise said.

'No, my dear, we know that,' he said. 'Thinking before you act is something you have yet to learn.'

'Sometimes there is no time for such niceties,' Mr Slater put in before Louise could flare up at that. 'Sometimes our instincts serve us best.'

'I sincerely hope I do not have to call upon my instincts in that manner again,' Louise said. 'And I am glad Mr Linton was able to identify him.'

'If I remember correctly, it was Joe who first did that,' Jonathan said, looking across at Joe who was whispering with Betty, not paying any attention to the conversation. He put out his toe and gave him a sharp kick. The young man looked startled for a moment, then sheepish. 'We were speaking of Jed Black,' Jonathan told him.

'What about him?' Joe asked.

'How did you know him?' Louise asked.

'He's not the handsomest of men, is he?' Joe said. 'And he has a finger and half a thumb missing.'

'Do you know how that came about?'

'No, it could have been in a fight, or shut in a door, or an injury at work.'

'Work!' Jonathan laughed. 'The man does not know the meaning of honest work.'

Louise shuddered. 'Let us not talk of him. He is safely put away, and there are more pleasant subjects of conversation.' She turned to Mrs Slater. 'Did you know Mr Potton took us to the races the day after we arrived in Doncaster? We enjoyed it very much. I put a modest wager on Black Knight and won. It was exciting.'

'The races are an important part of Doncaster's attraction,' Mr Slater said. 'People flock to the town from miles around; some even come from London.'

'Yes, it was why we could not find a seat on a coach to continue our journey and ended up on a carrier's wagon and a barge.'

'Why did you not wait for Mr Linton?'

Louise coloured. 'I am afraid we were out of sorts with each other at the time.'

Jonathan laughed. 'I do believe Louise has now learned not to turn her nose up at my efforts to help her. We go on together. Is that not so, my dear?'

'Yes,' she said. 'When?'

'It depends how you are feeling. When you are well enough.'

'I am perfectly well now, and though I am very grateful to Mr and Mrs Slater for all they have done, I think we have imposed on their good nature long enough.'

'We have been glad to have you,' Mrs Slater said. 'You are welcome to stay.'

'I know, ma'am,' Louise said gratefully. 'But I feel we must be on our way.'

'Tomorrow, then.' Jonathan said. 'If we set off early we should make York in a day. I believe the roads have been improved over that section.'

And so it was arranged.

At eight o'clock the following morning, Jonathan's carriage was at the door. Goodbyes were said and promises to write were made. Louise, dressed in an amber gown that heightened the colour of her hair, climbed in, expecting Betty to follow her, but that young lady clambered up beside Joe, saying she meant to bear him company.

'Do you think it is quite proper for her to do that?' Louise asked as Jonathan took his seat beside her and they moved off.

'Proper, Louise?' he teased. 'How can *you* talk of proper? Are you so very proper yourself?' He was inordinately cheerful. She had accepted his escort and now he could keep her safe and enjoy her company and perhaps she would at last confide in him.

'No, but I feel responsible for her.'

'You, responsible?' He pretended incredulity.

'Why not? I asked her to come with me. I did not know I was going to lead her into scrapes.'

'Why did you ask her?'

'I did not want to travel alone. I thought a husband and wife would attract less attention.'

'My dear, you cannot fail to attract attention, whatever you do. It is the way you are.'

'How do you know the way I am? You know nothing of me, just as I know nothing of you. I might be shy and retiring, afraid of my own shadow, trying to be brave when I am really a coward,' she retorted crossly.

'You might, but give me leave to doubt it. A coward would not have accepted a challenge to a duel, nor felled that ox of a man, nor fought a bargee and saved her friend from drowning. A coward would have died of fright long before now. I can only surmise your upbringing was out of the ordinary.'

'No, it was very ordinary.'

'Will you tell me about it?'

'Why?'

'I am interested. Do you have a father and mother, brothers, sisters, people who care for you?'

'Yes, parents and three brothers, no sisters.' As she said it, she wondered if that might not be true. How did she know she did not have sisters? Or that she did have brothers? Questions like that brought her quandary back to her full force. She was a woman without a place in society.

'Then why abandon them to go travelling? It must have been something very compelling. A lover, perhaps.'

She looked sharply at him. It had not occurred to her that anyone would think that. 'No, it is not,' she snapped. 'Just because I want to visit a relative, does not mean you may jump to conclusions about my morals.'

'I beg your pardon.' The astonishment in her eyes when he made the suggestion would have given him his answer even if she had not denied it and he was surprised at how relieved he felt.

'And I have not abandoned my family. They know where I am.'

'Do they?' he asked softly.

'Yes.'

'And they gave their blessing to this escapade? Oh, Louise, you do not expect me to believe that, do you?'

'I left them a letter explaining where I was going and that I would soon be back. I did not expect we should be gone so long. When we arrive in York, I will write and tell them what has happened to delay my return.'

'And after that?'

'Why, I will go my way and you will go yours,' she said with a lightness she did not feel.

'Supposing I will not agree to that?'

'Why should you not? You have business in Yorkshire, you told me so.'

'I also told you it could wait. I will see you to your destination.'

'But you do not know where that is.'

'True, but if I stick by you long enough, I shall find out, shan't I?'

'I cannot think why you want to. I have been nothing but trouble to you.'

'True,' he said, grinning wickedly. 'But such delightful trouble. I shall be very sorry when this voyage of discovery comes to an end and would prolong it as long as I can.'

She turned to stare at him. Why did he rail at her one minute and pay her compliments the next? He was having fun with her. 'Well, I would not. We will part in York.'

He did not contradict her because the coach was drawing into Ferrybridge. It was a very busy place, being on a crossroads where coaches branched off on to several routes, York and Edinburgh, Glasgow and Carlisle, and Leeds, besides being the crossing point over the River Aire. There seemed to be coaches, carriages and horses everywhere and several inns. Joe drew up in the yard of the Angel for the horses to be changed and Jonathan helped Louise down to stretch her legs and go inside for refreshment.

He was still musing on her determination to be rid of him. For the first time in his life he was being rejected by a personable young lady and instead of making him shrug his shoulders and let her go, as it would have done not so long before, it had made him all the more determined to hang on to her. His own feelings puzzled him. He wanted to shake her, make her confide in him, be angry, at the same time as he felt her unhappiness, the front of self-confidence she put up to hide it. He wanted to protect her, probably from herself. If it was not a lover, who was it she was so set on visiting? She had said her parents knew where she was going and a phrase of her letter came into his mind: *you know I have to make this journey.* He was sure that Mrs Vail, at least, had been hiding something from him. He wished now he had insisted on knowing the whole. Would he then have taken the commission? He smiled to himself as he watched Louise picking up a chicken leg and gnawing it; it would have been his loss if he hadn't.

Louise looked up and saw him watching her. He had a way of doing that which made her feel transparent, as if all her bones and sinews and nerve ends were in full view, especially the nerve ends. Did he understand that her reason for wanting to be rid of him was not that she disliked his presence, but quite the opposite? She liked him too much, and if in the end she was revealed as the daughter of a mother who had to keep her birth from her husband, then she would be too ashamed for him to know it. How did a woman keep a pregnancy from her spouse, unless he was often away from home for long periods? Perhaps that was it. Or perhaps she was never married at all. It was getting closer now, this revelation, and she was suddenly very nervous.

They finished their meal and were soon back on the road, making for Tadcaster, where they would have another change of horses. Jonathan seemed to have no difficulty obtaining the best there was to be had and they fairly bowled along in good weather.

'We shall make York today,' he said. 'What then? Is your destination close enough to be reached by nightfall?'

'I am not sure. I must make enquiries. If it is not, I must put up somewhere. What about you?'

'Me?'

'Yes. You have quizzed me about my destination, but have said never a word about yours. In truth, you have told me nothing about yourself at all. You could be the worst rogue in the kingdom for all I know.'

He smiled. 'You do not believe that, do you?'

'No. You have proved you are not. You could have taken advantage of me over and over again, but you have not. I wonder why. Is it because my rackety ways give you a disgust of me?'

'No. They are part of your charm.' He paused. 'Do you wish I had taken advantage of you?'

'Certainly not! I was simply curious. Other men might have.'

'I am not other men, Louise.'

'Then are you married?'

'Married? No, I am not.'

'Betrothed, perhaps?'

'Not that either. Marriage is not something that I am in any hurry to undertake. It is too serious to be entered into lightly. It is for life and choosing the wrong lady for a spouse can end in a lifetime of regret for both. It is too much of a lottery.'

'You sound bitter.'

'Not bitter, Louise, cautious.'

'Then have you never been in love?'

He laughed. 'Dozens of times in my green days, though I was never foolish enough to propose and the feeling did not last, for which I give thanks.'

'Then you were never truly in love. Real love lasts,' she said simply.

'No doubt you are right.'

'And the ladies in question?'

'I do not think their hearts were broken.'

'You make yourself sound callous and I cannot believe you are like that. Something must have given you an aversion to marriage.'

'I am not averse to marriage, simply against rushing headlong into a union just because it is expected of me.'

'Who expects it?'

'I was speaking generally,' he said hastily.

'Is that why you chase all over the country tracking down criminals, simply to escape what is expected of you?'

Her questions were hitting home a little too uncomfortably. 'No. I am not the one running away. You are.'

'I am *not* running away.'

'No,' he murmured. 'I take that back. I cannot imagine you running away from anything.

Exactly the opposite. You are more likely to confront your fears, even when it would be wiser to withdraw.'

'Now you are roasting me,' she accused.

'No, I am being serious. Those brothers of yours have a great deal to answer for.'

'What do you mean?'

'They have made you too intrepid, too independent, blind to the risks you are taking. Why not give up and go home? It will be my pleasure to escort you.'

'No, I am nearly there now.' She looked out of the window, wondering, not for the first time, whether it would be better to give up the quest, especially now, when she knew she must part from the man at her side, who had protected her so ably. That would come to an end when they reached York because she could not allow him to learn the truth about her.

The countryside had given way to houses and they were soon drawing into the yard of the White Horse to change horses, the last time they would do so before reaching York, nine miles away, a mere nothing compared to the miles behind them.

They were soon on their way again, but they

seemed to have exhausted their conversation. Both were silent, each wondering what the future might bring.

An hour and a half later, they found themselves passing under the archway of a tower that guarded the entrance to the walled city of York, then over a bridge, between houses and businesses. A little later they turned sharp left and a little way along the street, stopped at an inn which, according to its sign was the Black Swan. Joe jumped down and came to the door, just as Jonathan opened it. 'Shall we rack up here for the night, my…sir?' He hurriedly corrected his slip of the tongue.

'Yes, if there is room for us all. Miss Vail and I have unfinished business.'

A purse full of sovereigns and his winning smile obtained rooms for them and Louise and Betty were soon being conducted up the staircase with its dark oak panelling to a comfortable bedchamber. Jugs of hot water were brought up to them, so that they could wash off the grime of travel and change into fresh clothes before going down to the dining room to have dinner.

'We are here at last,' Betty said, sprawling across the bed. 'Tha's what you wanted, ain't it?'

'Yes. I am sorry it has taken so long. I am afraid our folks at home will be worried about us. I shall write and tell my parents we have arrived safely. I will include a note from you, if you like. No doubt Alfred will be relieved to hear from you.'

'Yes, but what next? I can't believe you came all this way just to turn round and go back again.'

'No, I told you I am going to visit a relative in Moresdale.' She was stripping off her clothes as she spoke.

'Where's that?'

'I have yet to find out, but I do not think it is far.'

'You reckon Mr Linton is going to come all the way with us?'

'Not if I can help it.' She poured some of the hot water into a bowl and set about washing herself.

'Why not? He'd take us in his coach. Joe reckons he won't leave us 'til we get back to Barnet,' Betty said.

'Does he? Joe does not know everything, you know,' Louise replied tartly.

'I do not know why you are so set on going alone.'

'Because I am.'

'Then leave me 'ere. I'll stay with Joe and Mr Linton.'

'Betty, I cannot possibly do that. I am responsible for you. When we have been to Moresdale, then we will go home, but we will go together. Please do not make things any more difficult than they are already.' She threw the water into a slop bucket and turned to find a dress to wear, a blue-and-white striped silk, whose stomacher was decorated with a row of ribbon bows from the square neck to the pointed waist. Betty, still mutinous, washed and changed herself. They were just putting the finishing touches to their toilette when there was a knock at the door. Louise went to answer it.

'I am come to escort you to dinner,' Jonathan said, looking her up and down, appraising her. Every time he saw her he was taken afresh by how lovely she was, a loveliness that had no need of paint and powder. Now, if Dorothea Mantle were half as beautiful and spirited as this one, he might be tempted to obey his parents and pay court to her. He smiled at his own foolishness. 'Are you ready?'

Dinner was a noisy affair because the inn was full and everyone was trying to out-talk everyone else. The main topic of conversation was a daring robbery that had taken place on the city walls. York was a historic city, which had been occupied by the Vikings and the Romans before becoming an Archbishopric with a magnificent cathedral, called The Minster. It had also suffered at the hand of Cromwell's men in the Civil War. Its ancient ramparts, though decaying in places, still stood and afforded a pleasant walk from which to view the city and the surrounding countryside. The robber had attacked a young man out seeing the sights with his sweetheart and had threatened to throw him off the wall if he did not hand over his purse, sword and brown silk coat. The thief had put it on at once, it was said, leaving his own coat behind: a black stuff garment, green with age.

'There is a job for you,' Louise said to Jonathan. 'Catching the criminal will be far more rewarding than escorting me.'

'Why, my dear,' he said, 'I do believe you would be rid of me.'

'To be sure, I would not have you disappointed. I will bring you little reward, but the capture of a dangerous criminal would be another case altogether. You might even be able to buy yourself some fashionable clothes to match that fine carriage of yours.'

He laughed. 'So it would, but I am not one to change horses in mid-stream, you know. And no doubt the city's constables are on the man's trail. I have no interest in him.'

'Pity,' she said.

They were silent for some minutes, listening and not listening to the hum of conversation around them, pretending to concentrate on the food on their plates while Joe and Betty seemed to have plenty to talk about.

'I have booked rooms for tonight only,' Jonathan said, pushing his half-eaten food away. 'But if you wish to stay longer, I am sure it can be arranged.'

'Why would I wish to stay longer?' Louise queried.

'If your destination is close at hand, you might

need somewhere as a base, unless, of course, your relation invites to stay.'

'I am not sure about that.'

'Not sure your relative will invite you or not sure if the place is close at hand?'

'Both.'

'I see.' He paused, smiling at her in the knowing way of his, which made her hackles rise. 'But surely you know the name of the place?'

'Yes, of course I do. I simply do not yet know how to get there,' she admitted.

'Oh, that is simplicity itself,' he said, cheerfully. 'You get there with me in my carriage. I thought I had already made that clear, but it would make it easier if I knew where to tell Joe to go.'

'Mr Linton, how many more times must I tell you, that I do not require your services? If you are a thieftaker, then you would be better employed elsewhere.'

'First time I ever saw him bested by a woman,' Joe murmured to Betty.

'I heard that,' Jonathan told him. 'The lady has not bested me and I'll thank you to keep your opinions to yourself.'

Joe looked astonished. His master had never

snapped at him like that before. Miss Louise Vail had certainly got under his skin. 'I beg your pardon, my lord,' he said.

'My lord,' Louise echoed, looking sharply at Joe, whose face had turned scarlet, to Jonathan whose brows were drawn down in a frown. 'Did Mr Potton just address you as *my lord*?'

Jonathan shrugged. 'I believe he did and I shall have his entrails for it.'

'Who are you?' Louise whispered. 'You are not Jonathan Linton, are you?'

'For the purposes of this adventure, I am.'

'And who are you when you are not having adventures?'

He gave her a slight inclination of his head; doing more was impossible given they were sitting on a bench at a long refectory table. 'Viscount Jonathan Leinster, at your service, madam.'

'A Viscount!' Luke's teasing flew into her brain, followed swiftly by the memory of the conversation she had overheard between her father and mother about marrying a nobleman. And this particular nobleman was causing wave after wave of panic through her. She had heard Luke speak of him. His father was the Earl of

Chastonbury. Too close to home for comfort. Had he known all along who she was and why she was travelling? She had to shake him off.

He watched her changing expressions and had no difficulty in reading her thoughts. 'I am afraid so. But a name and a title make no difference. I am still the man you have come to know…'

'Do I know you? I think not. You are as much a stranger to me as you were the day we met,' she said, feeling stricken.

'Liar,' he murmured.

'You have had your fun, *my lord*, now let me be. I do not need you.' Angrily she scrambled off the bench on which she had been sitting and stormed from the room. He half-rose to follow her, but changed his mind and sat down again. She was truly the most exasperating woman he had ever come across.

'And don't you dare make another comment,' he told Joe. 'Go and arrange for the horses to be ready for tomorrow.'

Joe left with Betty in tow, and everyone else drifted away to amuse themselves for the rest of the evening. Jonathan called for brandy and sat on, brooding about a girl with the most amazing green-flecked eyes, who could make him feel so unsettled. He had never met anyone quite like her before. The young ladies with whom he usually associated were either daughters of his father's friends with whom he flirted lightly when occasion demanded or demi-reps with whom he dallied occasionally. Louise Vail was neither. He had to keep reminding himself she was not part of his world. Why then did he allow her to disturb him so?

Louise had asked the innkeeper to furnish her with writing materials before she went to her room, but she did not immediately begin her letter. It was not that she did not know what to write, though that was difficult enough, but the fact that she had been so deceived by Jonathan. She had come to rely on him, had let him dictate the pace at which she travelled, had accepted his gifts and admitted, if only to herself, that she liked him a lot and if it were not for this all-consuming mission to find her mother, she might have fallen in love with him. Might have? She sat on her bed trying to analyse how she felt, but all that did was make her more confused than ever. One thing she was not confused about was the need to keep him from knowing the real reason for her journey.

She gave a half-sigh, half-sob, and went over to sit at the table and write to her mama. She wrote about her journey as if it had been uneventful, that she had been delayed by taking a cold because the weather had been dreadful, but had been looked after by Mrs Slater, a travelling companion with whom she had become friendly. She even said she had made the acquaintance of Viscount Leinster who had business in Yorkshire. He had been very helpful in smoothing her path. Tomorrow she would go to Moresdale and then she would come home. She begged to be forgiven and prayed they would have her back, because she could not imagine life without them and her brothers.

She felt much better after she had written it and was just signing it when Betty came into the room. 'If you write a note for Alfred, I will seal this up and take it to the post,' she told her.

Half an hour later, she put a shawl about her shoulders and ventured out into the street. The air was fresh after the stuffy atmosphere of the inn and she breathed deeply as she walked, as much to steady herself as anything else. Having asked for directions, she walked briskly towards the Minster, whose tower she could see above the rooftops. Then she turned right and walked along a busy street, looking for the York tavern where the mails were collected each evening, so the proprietor of the Black Swan had told her. Having left her letter, she went on to the Minster and went inside.

It was a vast place, many times larger than her father's church, but its grandeur did not detract from its feeling of tranquillity. She wandered round it, reading the inscriptions and admiring the huge stained-glass window at the end of the choir and then knelt at the altar and prayed for divine guidance and forgiveness. She left feeling calmer in her mind, and made her way back to the Black Swan and Viscount Leinster. She would not let him overset her; she would be strong and resolute.

There were several people about, walking or riding in chairs, a young couple, a woman with a child in her arms and another clinging to her skirts, a gentleman riding home after a day out in the field, a beggar boy to whom she gave a penny, a chimney sweep with his brushes over his shoulder, two ladies and their escorts riding in an open carriage on the way to an evening's entertainment and a man with a short, untidy beard, leaning on a wall, smoking a dirty grey pipe. He wore a brown silk coat, which went ill with his grubby wool breeches, and seemed to be idly watching the people coming and going. He put his hand up to take the pipe from his mouth and Louise gasped. He had a finger and the tip of his thumb missing.

Chapter Seven

It could not be. The man had been sent under guard back to London. He should be there by now and safely locked up in Newgate. She was tempted to take to her heels, but forced herself to keep walking at the same pace as before. She was dressed in skirts, not breeches; her hair was arranged in curls and ringlets, not tied back in a queue, and she wore dainty shoes on her feet, not riding boots. He could not recognise her, could he? When he had last seen her she was, to all intents and purposes, Louis Smith.

It was only a few paces before she reached her destination and hurried inside in search of Jonathan, their quarrel forgotten for the moment. He had gone up to his room, she was told. Taking a deep breath, she climbed the stairs and knocked on his door, hoping he had not already retired. A moment later he was standing before her in breeches and stockings, but little else.

'Louise!' he exclaimed. 'To what do I owe the honour of this visit?'

'My lord,' she began and then stopped, all too aware of his state of undress, his muscular torso and wide shoulders. Not for the first time, she felt a surge of something strange flow through her, a tingling in her limbs and an almost irresistible urge to reach out and touch him, to feel his flesh and the tiny curls of hair that ran down from his throat to his midriff. It was shocking of her and she clenched her fists in the folds of her skirt to keep herself in check

'Jonathan,' he corrected her. 'We can hardly be formal under the circumstances.' Hearing footsteps, he looked past her, down the corridor towards the stairs. Someone was coming. 'You had better come in.' Taking her arm, he pulled her inside and shut the door before she could find her voice to protest.

'My lord!' She was standing so close to him, she could feel his warmth, could feel his breath on her cheek, smelling faintly of brandy, and began to tremble.

'Do you want half the world to know you visit

me in my room at night?' he queried with a smile, feeling the tension in her and wanting to lighten it. She had probably never seen a man's torso before. But it was too late to find his shirt.

'No, of course not. I would not have come, but I have just seen that man Jed Black, the one you said was safely on his way back to Newgate under guard, the one who swore revenge…'

He took her shoulders in his hands and looked down into her upturned face. The temptation to kiss her was almost overwhelming and he might have succumbed if she had been anyone but who she was. In spite of her independence, her spirit of adventure, her strength of character, she was an innocent, too distracted by what she had to tell him to realise the effect her presence in his room was having on him. It took all his self-control to speak lightly. 'My dear, are you sure you are not imagining things?'

She ignored the endearment; it was mere condescension and meant nothing. 'Of course I am sure. He has grown a beard and has changed his coat, but he could not disguise his missing finger and thumb.'

He was immediately attentive; this was no fancy on her part. 'Where did you see him?'

'In the street. He was standing on the corner, smoking a pipe. I am sure he was watching for us.' She slipped from his grasp and went to the window. 'He was on that corner, where he could see anyone who came in and out of here.'

He followed and looked over her shoulder to where she was pointing, but there was no one there. 'What were you doing out? Were you trying to give me the slip again?'

'No, certainly not.' She could feel his breath on the back of her neck as he leaned over her; it was like a tiny breeze, making her want to turn and fling herself into his arms. It was an effort of will to resist and keep her back to him. 'I was taking a letter to the post. It was still light and pleasant out, so I decided to go and visit the Minster. I saw him on my way back.'

'Do you think he recognised you?'

'No, he knows me as Lou Smith, doesn't he? And I gave no sign I had recognised him. But he will know you and Betty and Joe...'

'True,' he murmured, turning her gently to face him.

'What are we going to do?'

He smiled at her use of the pronoun. '*We* are going to do nothing. I suggest you go back to your room and leave everything to me.' He took her hand and led her to the door. 'I will see you in the morning. I think we have some serious talking to do, but it can wait until then.' He opened the door and looked along the corridor. 'All clear,' he added, putting her hand to his lips. 'Go now and do not worry. I will not let him harm you.'

'It was not me I was worried about,' she said. 'Not altogether.'

'Oh, my dear, I am flattered that you care.' It was said with a light laugh to cover his discomfiture. 'But I shall come to no harm. Now, go before someone sees you and jumps to quite the wrong conclusion.' He gave her a little push in the direction of her own room.

She sped along the corridor to her room, stripped off her gown and petticoats and flung herself on the bed, barely registering the fact that Betty was not there. Every time she tried to sever her connection with Jonathan Linton, or Viscount Leinster, or whatever he liked to call himself, something happened to draw them even closer. And tonight she had been especially close to him, his bare chest had been only inches from her face! He had the power to turn her insides to a quiv-ering jelly, simply by looking at her. Whatever would happen if he kissed her? He had gazed intently at her and, for a moment, she had half-expected he would, had braced herself for it, but then it had not happened. She did not know whether to be glad or disappointed. But he was a Viscount and she was…

For the hundredth time in the last two weeks, she asked herself who she was. The old Louise might have dreamed of catching the eye of a Viscount, but the Louise who travelled the road in search of an identity must put all such foolish thoughts from her. Tomorrow, she would go to Moresdale and she would perhaps learn the answer to the question that plagued her. But supposing she did not, supposing no one in Moresdale had ever heard of Catherine Fellowes? Supposing they had, but she had died and taken her secret to the grave? She would have to live the rest of her life not knowing. And who would marry her then?

Jonathan dressed hurriedly, pocketed his pistols, strapped on his sword belt and went in search of Joe. He found him in the corner of the parlour with Betty, who was giggling over something he had said. 'Madam, go to your mistress,' he said. 'She may have need of you.'

'She's not my mistress,' Betty grumbled. 'Though you'd never know it the way I'm treated. I only came with her to bear her company and have a little adventure.'

'Then pray bear her company now,' he said. 'And from now on, you are employed by me to look after her.'

'Seems to me, my lord,' Joe put in, 'the boot's on the other foot. Miss Vail be lookin' after Betty.'

'Whichever it is, they are neither of them making a very good fist of it.' He paused. 'Jed Black has got away again and he's in York.'

'He never is!'

'He is. You remember that robbery we were talking about at dinner? That was him. He is now wearing a brown silk coat and has grown a beard, but growing a new finger and thumb has been beyond him.'

'Are we going after him, my lord?'

'We are. He has threatened revenge and cannot be left loose.' He turned to Betty. 'Go up to your room and do not stir until I come to tell you it is safe to do so. Do you understand me?'

Terrified, she scuttled away, leaving Joe to follow Jonathan out into the street. It was dark now and though several of the buildings had flambeaux on the walls by their doors, casting a pool of light around them, much of the street was in darkness. 'Do you know where to look?' Joe asked.

'No, but he was watching the Black Swan, so I do not think he can be far away. I do not think he is aware we know of his presence, so for the moment we are simply out for a stroll.'

'How do you know all this, my lord?'

'Louise was out earlier this evening and saw him,' Jonathan said.

'Mayhap she imagined him. Women often see terrors where none exist.'

'Not this woman,' he said, with a chuckle. 'She is more likely *not* to see terrors that *do* exist. At any rate, she kept her head and did not draw attention to herself; as she was dressed in female garments, he probably did not recognise her. We shall make our way to the magistrate's house and ask him to let us have the services of a couple of reliable constables.'

'Then what? Do we take the devil back to

Newgate ourselves and make sure he gets there?'

'No. I imagine York has secure enough places to keep him out of harm's way. I will write to Lord Portman and he can come and take charge of him; it was his case, after all. I have other fish to fry.'

'Miss Louise Vail,' Joe stated.

'Yes.'

'What's so special about her?'

'Good question,' Jonathan said thoughtfully. 'She is special in so many ways, it is hard to enumerate them all. She is comely, for a start, brave and resourceful, intelligent and full of surprises. And not in the least cowed by greater strength or consequence...'

'She is also a parson's daughter.'

'So what is that to the point?'

Joe refrained from reminding him that Miss Vail was not a lady, not in the sense polite society meant it, and would definitely not be considered a suitable bride for a Viscount. Neither was she a woman he could dally with, not mistress material either. His lordship was perfectly able to think that out for himself. 'What I should like to know,' he said, ignoring the question, 'is what she is up to.'

Jonathan sighed. 'So would I, Joe, so would I.'

'Did her parents not tell you?'

'No. I fancy I was supposed to catch up with her and drag her back home without ever finding out.'

Joe laughed. 'And of course, being who you are, you could not do that.'

'No. Has Betty not dropped a hint?'

'Betty knows no more than we do, I swear it. All I have managed to winkle out of her is that Miss Vail is determined to find a long-lost relation and once that is done, she will go home. Seems a bit smoky to me. I reckon it's a lover.'

'She says not,' Jonathan said tersely.

'Well, she would, wouldn't she? It is most likely why she is so intent on slipping the leash.'

Jonathan did not like that idea and it was not only because he did not like to think Louise was a liar; there was more to it than that. He shook himself, unwilling to probe his own weakness where she was concerned. 'Let us get tonight's work over with and tomorrow might reveal all,' he said, turning into the drive of a considerable mansion and knocking on the door.

His name and the mention of the Society for the Discovery and Apprehending of Criminals was enough to gain them admittance and he was soon telling the magistrate all he knew of Mr Jed Black and soliciting his assistance. 'He is a slippery customer and no matter what we do, he has always managed to escape,' he explained. 'I would like two strong men, two sets of manacles and a heavy chain, and a secure vehicle to bring him to the prison. I am assuming you have strong walls and doors to your dungeons.'

'Yes, indeed. I will send for Fletcher and Maxwell. One is a butcher and the other a blacksmith, both big, muscular men. He will not escape from them. But, forgive me, do you know where he can be found?'

'Unfortunately not. He was seen in Coney Road earlier this evening and I imagine he is still in that area.'

The magistrate offered them some Flemish wine while the two constables were fetched and then all four set out to comb the roads and alleyways around the Black Swan. They did not find him there, but assuming he would have to find somewhere to stay, they began a systematic search of all the inns and taverns. They had almost given up when Joe spotted him, sitting in the parlour of the Star, playing cards.

'We cannot tackle him in there,' Jonathan said. 'Other people might be hurt. We need to lure him outside.'

'I'll do it,' Joe said and before he could be stopped had swaggered into the inn and ordered a pot of ale. Then he turned round and surveyed the company. Jed glanced up at him and then down at his cards, but then recognition dawned and he scrambled to his feet. 'Sorry, lads,' he said to the other gamesters, 'I've got some urgent business to attend to.'

Joe pretended shock at seeing him and took to his heels. Black followed. Joe dodged the startled onlookers and made for the street where Jonathan waited. Letting Joe pass him, Jonathan dropped his sword and flung himself at Black, bringing him to the ground. The man had no intention of allowing himself to be taken without a fight and he put up a good one. They rolled on the ground, trading blows, while Joe and the constables looked on, unable to help for fear of hurting their own man. By now a crowd had gathered and were taking sides. Jonathan thought he had the man, but he was slippery as an eel and managed to fetch a knife from his boot and before Jonathan realised his danger, he was hacking about right and left, cutting him about the face and arm. Jonathan tried to reach his sword, but could not grasp it.

It was then Joe intervened, grabbing the sword and holding it over the struggling men with both hands, ready to plunge it into the convict whenever the opportunity presented itself. 'I want him alive,' Jonathan gasped, rolling to one side, his strength spent. But so was Jed Black's. He tried to rise, but Joe felled him again with a punch. The constables rushed forward and fastened the manacles about his wrists and ankles, joining them with the chains they had brought with them.

Jonathan sat up, holding his hand over his bleeding arm. 'Whatever happens, do not take those chains off him,' he commanded. 'He's to be locked in the deepest dungeon you can find and watched night and day until someone comes to take him off your hands.' And then he slid back on to the cobbles, too weak to rise. Joe commandeered a passing chair and helped him into it.

'Stop fussing, man,' he said, asserting himself. ''Tis only a scratch.'

Nevertheless he allowed himself to be conveyed to the Black Swan with Joe running alongside. By the time they arrived, he had recovered sufficiently to walk into the inn and make his way slowly upstairs, while Joe went in search of bandages and brandy.

Louise was roused from a light sleep by a noise outside her room, a small sound as if someone were creeping past so as not to wake the sleeping guests, but it was too early for the servants to be stirring. Then she heard a rattle and an oath. Curious, she rose and padded over to the door and opened it a crack. Jonathan, candle in hand, was bending down to retrieve the sword he had dropped. As she watched, he straightened up and his features were lit by the flickering candle. He looked gaunt. Blood had run down his face from a cut on his forehead and there was a rough handkerchief tied about his upper arm over his shirt, which had been little use in stemming the flow of blood. He had a black eye and a livid bruise on his chin. His coat was slung over his shoulder, he had lost his hat and his hair was matted with blood. She ran out to him. 'Jonathan, what has happened to you?'

'It is nothing of any consequence.' Even in his weary state he became acutely aware that she was wearing nothing but a nightgown, a flimsy affair he remembered buying for her, and her hair was loose about her shoulders. Like that she was more than ever desirable. He gave her a weary smile, meant to reassure her. 'Go back to bed.'

'No, you need looking after.' She took his arm and pulled him into the room.

'Louise, what are you about?' he protested. Although he could easily have pulled himself away, he did not do so, but allowed her to push him on to a clothes chest, which stood at the foot of the bed. 'Have you no thought for your reputation?'

'I fancy my reputation is already past redemption,' she said. 'And I could not let you go, knowing you need help.' She went to the washstand where a jug of cold water stood in a bowl. Pouring some out, she dipped a cloth in it and began gently bathing his forehead. He suffered this without speaking, wincing only once when she dabbed too close to the cut 'We need some salve to put on it.' She turned and shook Betty. 'Wake up, Betty. Wake up!' Then, to Jonathan, 'I do believe she would sleep through an earth-quake.' She shook the girl again.

At last a tousled head surfaced from the heap of bedclothes. 'Wha's the matter?'

'The Viscount has been hurt. Go down and see if anyone is about. It must be nearly time for someone to be stirring. Ask for some salve for a cut and some clean cloths for bandages. Hurry up, before he starts bleeding again.'

Betty's eyes opened in astonishment when she saw Jonathan sitting in his shirt sleeves at the foot of the bed. 'What happened?'

'A slight fracas,' he said. 'Nothing serious.'

'Where? When? Is Joe hurt too?'

He smiled. 'Joe is indestructible. I left him going in search of brandy.'

She scrambled out of bed, clothed from head to toe in a long linen nightgown. She threw a cloak over it and disappeared.

'Now for the arm,' Louise said and began peel-ing away the makeshift bandage. It had stuck his shirt firmly to his skin. Carefully she wet it and, taking a pair of scissors from her portmanteau, cut the sleeve away and then took off the shirt, remembering with a wry smile that he had been like that not six hours before, but in very different circumstances. There was not time to think of that now; there was work to be done. The wound was ragged and deep. 'Was it a sword?' she asked.

'No, a knife. He had it in his boot.'

'I suppose you mean Jed Black.' She threw away the reddened bowl of water and poured a fresh one before continuing with her ministrations.

'Yes.' He smiled. 'You make a good nurse. Have you done this sort of thing before?'

'My brothers were always falling into scrapes and hurting themselves. I helped Mama to clean them up. She said it was as well to learn about such things. You never knew when the skill would come in useful.'

He laughed, though her gentle probing was hurting like hell. 'You never cease to amaze me.'

She ignored that. 'What happened?'

'We found him staying at the Star—'

'We being you and Joe?'

'Yes and two beefy constables. Joe lured him out, but he was wary, that one, and put up a fight. But we got him in the end.'

'Where is he now?'

'The constables have taken him, manacled hand and foot, to throw him into the deepest dungeons they can find.'

'And then, I suppose, you will escort him back to London,' she said quietly.

'Why, my dear, I do believe you would be sorry if I were to leave you to do that.'

'You did before,' she reminded him.

'And regretted it.'

'Because he escaped?'

'Yes, but also because you needed me and I was not there.'

'You feel responsible for me?'

'Yes.' He flinched because she was probing dirt out of the cut.

'Sorry, but it has to be done.' She tried to be more gentle. 'Why do you feel responsible for me? And do not give me that nonsense about being *in loco parentis*, I want to know the truth.'

'The truth, my dear Miss Vail, is that I do not know. It may be that I hate to see a young lady make a cake of herself, or it may be that, in spite of your courage and show of independence, you are vulnerable. I should hate to think anything bad happened to you when I could have prevented it.'

'Which is all very chivalrous, my lord, but—'

'Hell's bells, woman, what are you doing?' he yelled. 'That felt like a hot needle.'

'There is dirt in the cut and it must be got out. A knife, you say. The man must have been cutting up his dinner, or skinning a rabbit. Heaven knows what he used the implement for.'

She finished cleaning the wound and slipped into a dressing gown just as Betty returned with salve and bandages. She was closely followed by Joe with a bottle of brandy and a glass, and any further discussion was broken off. While Joe poured the spirit, Louise smeared the salve on the wounds and bound Jonathan's arm. 'That's the best I can do,' she said, standing back. 'I suggest you go to bed.'

He took the glass from Joe and knocked it back in a single swallow. 'And what will you be doing while I sleep? Creeping off to your rendezvous?'

'It is not a rendezvous,' she protested.

'You are not expected then?'

'No, I am not expected and for that reason, delaying my arrival yet again will not matter. I will not leave you until I know you are well and strong again.'

'Well and strong!' he exclaimed. 'What a deal of fuss about a little cut. Why, it is no worse than you gave me with your sword point.'

'It is far deeper and, I'll have you know, my sword was clean.'

'Come, my lord,' Joe said, bending to take his good arm and raise him to his feet. 'Miss Vail is right. You need to rest.'

He allowed himself to be led away. Louise set about tidying the room, throwing out the bloodied water and the cloths she had used to clean the wounds, picking up his shirt and the cut-up sleeve, holding it a minute, savouring the feel of it, still slightly warm from his body. She was beginning to worry that her feelings for him were growing stronger and that could not be allowed to happen, more especially since she had learned that he was a Viscount. There was no hope of a happy outcome there. She ought to take advantage of his indisposition and take herself off, but somehow she could not do it. She flung the shirt down beside the slop pail for the cleaning maids to clear away, and turned to dress, ready for the day ahead.

At noon, when Louise went to enquire how Jonathan was, a worried Joe told her his master had a fever and he had sent for a doctor. Alarmed, she pushed past him and went to the bed, where Jonathan lay drenched in sweat, his head moving from side to side. He was mumbling incoherently. Her heart went out to him.

She pulled up a chair beside the bed, fetched a bowl of cold water and a cloth and sat to bathe his forehead. 'Please God, do not let him die,' she prayed and then set about talking gently to him, about anything that came into her head. She had no idea if he heard or understood, but her voice seemed to calm him.

A doctor came and examined his wounds. The cut on his forehead was not deep and was beginning to heal, but the arm was another matter. 'There is a putrefaction there,' he said, after poking about in it and making Jonathan swear horribly. 'Clean it out and bind it up again. It is all that can be done. Your husband is young and strong, madam, so we must pray that will pull him through. My fee is a guinea.'

Joe, who had been hovering in the background, produced a guinea from Jonathan's purse and gave it to the man, who pocketed it and left. Louise, who had not corrected the doctor over her relationship with the patient, thought it was a guinea easily earned. The man had done nothing except confirm the rightness of what she herself had done.

She set about washing the wound out again. The surrounding tissue was inflamed and swollen. She did the best she could and bound it up again, then went back to bathing his face with cold water. Then she bathed his arms and hands and opened the neck of his nightshirt to cool his throat. That done, she sat and watched him.

His eyes were shut and she noted how long and thick his lashes were, how well shaped were his brows, how strong his chin, now sporting a day's stubble. His mouth was well shaped and firm; in all he was a very handsome man. He must be about twenty-five or -six, she surmised and still single. Not averse to marriage, he had said, simply cautious. His caution must be particularly deep-seated to have kept him unwed for so long, his requirements exceptionally difficult to fulfil. She wondered about those. His bride would have to be a lady of indisputable breeding, one of his own kind, and she was certainly not that. Even the daughter of a country parson would be far beneath him, let alone the daughter of a mismatch. He would probably expect a dowry, and no doubt required her to be beautiful and with no bad traits to be inherited by his offspring. One thing she was sure of: she did not qualify in a single instance.

He was thrashing from side to side, flinging off his covers, revealing a very short nightshirt rucked up round his thighs. Strong, firm thighs. Long, shapely calves. Hurriedly she covered him again and tried to soothe him. 'Hush, Jonathan,' she murmured. 'Hush, my dear. All will be well.' She looked across at Joe, who was pretending to be busy with something in the corner of the room. 'He will get well, won't he?'

Joe looked up and saw the anguish on her face. 'Course, Miss Vail. Constitution of an ox, he's got. When he comes to his senses, he'll need some nourishment. I'll see what there is to be had, shall I?'

He left the room, leaving her to resume her

watch on Jonathan. She fetched more water and changed the dressing on his arm again. He muttered something that sounded very like, 'Lou.'

'I'm here.' She did not know whether he heard her or not. 'Would you like a sip of water?'

She fetched water in a cup and sat on the bed to help lift his head so that he could drink. Then he lay back and went to sleep, with her hand in his. She dare not move for fear of disturbing him. 'Get well,' she commanded. 'Get well.' She lowered her head and brushed his lips with her own. It was only a featherlight pressure, but she fancied he smiled in his sleep.

It took three days before he became fully conscious, three days and nights of constant nursing, turn and turn about with Joe. One morning he opened his eyes to find her draped across his bed. He turned his head, wondering where he was and what she was doing there. It came to him that she had been sitting by his bed and fallen asleep across him. He reached out and took her chin in his hand, to turn her face to his. 'Oh, my dear, you really do have no sense of propriety, do you?'

His voice woke her and she scrambled up. 'Oh,

I did not mean to fall asleep. And you are awake. Oh, thank the Lord.'

Her eyes, still sleepy, were particularly seductive; the sharp green was softened to smoky sage and he pictured waking up beside her every morning and seeing that look. 'How long have you been there?' he asked, impatiently shaking the image from him.

It had been night when she had relieved Joe and come to sit with him. It was fully light now. 'I don't know.'

'All night?'

'Yes. You have been very ill.'

'How long?'

'Three days. This is the fourth.'

'I seem to remember something about a fight and a knife and you… Yes, you came…'

'Of course I came. Did you think I would abandon you?'

He smiled. 'I was in no case to think rationally, my dear, but I am heartily glad you did not.'

'How could I? It was no more than you did for me when I was sick.' She tried to sound offhand, but he was not deceived. If she had sat so long with him she could not keep awake, it was devotion above the call of duty or gratitude. It lifted his spirits.

He looked about him. 'Where is Joe?'

'I sent him to his bed. He will no doubt be here directly. He has been as worried as I have been.'

'Have you, my dear?'

Why did he keep calling her his dear? It was most upsetting; she could never be his dear anything, unless it was a nuisance. He would never have been wounded if it had not been for escorting and protecting her, and telling herself she had not asked him to made no difference. 'Everyone has been worried. You have been at death's door. Your arm…'

He looked at the neat bandage and tried to lift his arm and found it painful. 'I thought it was nothing but a scratch.'

'It became infected. If the putrefaction had set in, you might have lost it.'

He shuddered. 'Thank God for your nursing skills then. Once again I am indebted to you. I have no idea how to repay you.'

'You will repay me best by getting well and being your old good-natured self.'

He grinned. 'Was I a very bad patient?'

'You swore a lot when I changed your dressing.'

'Oh, dear, then I beg your pardon.'

'Granted.' She smiled.

'I'm devilish hungry.'

'Good. I will have some beef broth made up for you.'

'Broth! I don't want broth, I want a good big steak with potatoes and cabbage and a fruit pie to follow. And a pint of ale. Then I am going to get dressed.'

'But, my lord, you must not—'

'*Must* not, Louise? Do you presume to dictate to me what I may and may not do?'

'No, of course not. I was thinking of your welfare.'

'And I thank you for it. Now, be a good girl and go and see to your own *toilette*. You are looking delightfully tousled, but we do not want to cause a scandal, do we?'

She rose, her eyes full of tears. She had been dismissed and it hurt. After all she had done—sitting with him hour after hour, changing that messy dressing, holding his head so that he could take sips of water, praying for him constantly—he had turned her away. As she went out of the door she heard him shouting for Joe.

It was not ingratitude that made him send her away, just the opposite. He was afraid his gratitude might lead him into indiscretion. He felt physically weak and was afraid that weakness might extend to his mind and his heart, and that could not be allowed. He was immeasurably sorry if he had hurt her, but the sooner they returned to the old sparring relationship, the better for both of them. He had been commissioned to fetch her home to the vicarage and he would do well to remember that. If only she were plain and boring and not so enticingly beautiful and exhilarating to be with! If only… Joe entered the room and he thrust his thoughts from him.

It was difficult, but Louise tried not to think about him and went back to considering how she was to get to Moresdale. She changed into a yellow-and-cream striped gown with a quilted cream stomacher, with a huge yellow bow of ribbon hiding the top of her breasts, had Betty arrange her hair and went out to take the air with her friend in attendance.

'His lordship has recovered?' Betty asked,

as they made their way down Coney Road and turned towards the river with its wharfs and staithes, boats and sailing ships and barges. After all the recent rain, the water was high and lapping at the walls of the ancient friary.

'Yes, and is as infuriatingly superior as ever. He told me I looked tousled. Who would not be, sleeping in a chair?'

'Oh, I should not take any notice of that. His bark is worse than his bite, so Joe says. And he can be excused on account of being in pain.'

'No doubt you are right. I hope Jed Black does not escape again.'

'No, Joe went to see what they had done with him. He is in the Castle dungeons and according to Joe he'll never get out of there. And Lord Portman has been notified to come and take charge of him. He was the one who arrested him and had him convicted in the first place.'

'Who is Lord Portman?'

'He is a friend of the Viscount's and a member of the Piccadilly Gentleman's Club.'

'What is that? One of London's gaming hells?'

'No, it is a Club to solve crimes and arrest

criminals.' Betty giggled suddenly. 'Joe calls them "the grab 'em and nab 'em brigade".'

'So Lord Leinster *is* a thieftaker.'

'In a way.'

'So what does he want with me? It can't possibly be because I stole my brother's things.'

'Don't you know?'

'No, or I wouldn't ask.'

'It's as plain as the nose on your face, he's took a fancy to you.' Betty smiled.

'Nonsense. I do not believe it.' She did not want him taking a fancy to her; that could only mean one thing and it was not marriage. It made her feel uncomfortable and angry. Angry with him for thinking he could have her in that way, angry with herself for minding so much. 'Anyway, we shall be rid of him as soon as I find out where Moresdale is and how to get there.'

They turned back towards the centre of the city where most of the inns that serviced the coaches were to be found. It soon became apparent when she began to make enquiries that coaches did not go to Moresdale. ''Tis only a little village,' she was told. 'Don't go nowhere, except into the dales.'

'How far is it?'

The distance varied from ten miles to twenty, according to whom she asked. Even ten miles was a long way to walk, especially carrying a portmanteau. 'We ought to accept the Viscount's offer to take us,' Betty said.

'He is not yet ready to travel,' Louise said, looking for an excuse to go without him. 'And truly we ought to not put him to any more inconvenience. We will see if there is a carrier going that way.'

'The last time we went with a carrier, we got into no end of trouble,' Betty reminded her. 'I am not so sure I want to do that again.'

'It wasn't the carrier who caused the problem, it was the bargeman.'

There were carriers in plenty leaving York for all destinations, but none going to Moresdale in the immediate future. 'We wait until we have a load before setting off,' she was told. 'Come back later in the week.'

There was nothing for it but to go back to the Black Swan where they found Jonathan up and dressed and enjoying a hearty dinner with Joe. He had apparently decided he had had enough of being plain Mr Linton and was wearing a plum-coloured suit trimmed with white lace and silver buttons, had shaved and tied his hair back neatly, but he looked pale. His bruises were fading to yellow and the cut on his forehead was healing, but it would leave a little scar. And she could tell by the way he held his arm that it still caused him some pain. In spite of being hurt and annoyed with him, she could not help feeling sympathy. She stifled it at once. 'What are you doing up and dressed?' she demanded, as he rose to bow to her. 'Do you wish to be ill again?'

'I am enjoying my dinner and I never felt better.'

'Liar,' she said.

'Do you wish to fight another duel with me?' he asked, teasingly. 'I am afraid I cannot oblige at the moment, but later, if you were to repeat that slur on my character...'

'Of course I do not wish to fight a duel with you. What is the matter with you that you must always be fighting? I should have thought you had had enough of that.'

'Then do not call me a liar. Do you wish me to order dinner for you? The halibut is good and the pork chops very tasty. Or you could have boiled ham. Or chicken...'

'I'll take the ham, please, and some vegetables.'

He ascertained Betty's preference and beckoned the waiter, before sitting down heavily. He knew he was not yet up to full strength, but he did not want to give her an excuse for going on without him.

The waiter arrived promptly, soon followed by their meal, and Louise, who had not eaten much while she had been nursing Jonathan, ate with a hearty appetite.

'Where have you been this morning?' he asked, watching her eat. How could she be so infuriating one minute and so delectable the next?

'We went for a walk, to explore. I enquired about coaches for my onward journey—'

'There aren't any,' Betty put in.

'And no doubt you asked about carriers and barges and other forms of transport,' he queried, reminding them of their previous failed attempt to leave him behind. Why was it so necessary for them to be rid of him? He was determined to find out.

'Nothing before the end of the week,' the girl told him.

Louise looked daggers at Betty, who gazed back defiantly. Jonathan chuckled. 'Then you are stuck with me.'

She pushed her plate away, wondering how she could answer that. The trouble was that half of her wanted to be stuck with him, the other half knew how dangerous it was. He knew her name, the name she had used all her life, and she recalled Luke speaking of him once, saying he had met the Viscount at school; there was a chance that his lordship might connect her with Luke, but all that would tell him was that she was beneath him in the social order of things. If she also turned out to be a bastard, to have no known father and a mother who wanted to be rid of her at the first opportunity, then he would have such a disgust of her he would be glad to see the back of her. On the other hand, she could not help thinking of Betty's remark that he fancied her. She could not bear that, knowing where men's fancies took them when the object of the fancy was the lowest of the low. Betty would undoubtedly say she should be glad of his protection. But not Louise Vail. She had her pride. 'It is not far, we can walk,' she said.

'I think it is about time we had that little talk I spoke of,' he said, rising and holding out his hand to her. 'If you are not too fatigued, let us go for a stroll.'

She ignored the hand and they walked out of the inn side by side, but not touching. 'Now,' he said, deliberately taking her hand and tucking it under his arm. 'We will stop this to-ing and fro-ing and you will tell me exactly where you are going. You said you did not know if it was close, but it cannot be far if you propose to walk.'

She was tired of all the secrecy and bluster, too tired to hold out against him any longer. She wanted to know the truth about her parentage, but if her whole errand was a waste of time and she did not find her mother, if she remained as ignorant as she had been more than two weeks before and had to go home to Barnet, having him beside her might make it easier. And if she did discover she was born on the wrong side of the blanket, then he would know and drop her like a hot cake. That would hurt, but if that did turn out to be true, she would have to become used to slights and insults. 'Moresdale.'

'At last!'

'Do you know where it is?'

'Yes, it is a village in the Dales to the north-west of here.' He had discovered that for himself; it was one of the first things he had done on reaching York. 'But are you quite sure that is what you want? You can still change your mind and go back home. I am sure you will be welcomed with open arms.'

'How do you know that?'

'It would be an unfeeling mother who did not forgive her daughter, whatever she had done. I am sure if I had a daughter I would love her, no matter what scrape she fell into.' Mentally he added, Especially if she had a mother like you. But he did not say it aloud.

But instead of easing her mind, his words only stirred up her anxiety. Her real mother had not loved her even when, as far as she knew, she had done nothing to deserve being sent away. 'I have written to Mama to tell her that we have arrived safely in York. I said I had met you and you were looking after me. I said that to set her mind at rest, you understand, not because I wished for it.'

He chuckled. 'I understand.' He did not tell her he had written to the Reverend Vail and his wife from Doncaster, telling them he had found their daughter and her friend, Betty, and had appointed himself their escort, that he would stay with them and try to persuade Miss Vail to return home with him. 'So, having established that you have no wish to hurt your parents, will it not hurt them that you will not return home?'

'I have not refused to go home. I will go when I have completed my errand.'

'Then the sooner that is done the better, do you not think? I will take you to Moresdale and afterwards I will take you home. No more arguments.'

She gave a huge sigh. 'Very well. Since I cannot persuade you not to waste your time on me, I accept.'

He grinned. It felt like a battle won. He decided he would go along with whatever she wanted to do and he would not question her again. In time she might come to trust him enough to tell him everything.

Chapter Eight

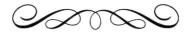

Moresdale was eighteen miles from York. Joe drove slowly, not only because the roads were little more than tracks once they left York behind, but so as not to jolt the Viscount, whose wound was still giving him pain. Not that he would have admitted it, certainly not in front of the ladies.

Louise was half-glad, half-sorry that they were going so slowly. The nearer they came to her final destination, the more nervous she felt. She had been telling herself that she wanted to know the truth, however unpalatable it was, but she was also afraid it would separate her for ever from the man who sat beside her, trying not to let her see that every jolt of the carriage sent pain shooting up his arm.

'Shall we stop and let you rest?' she asked him once when she saw him wince.

'Certainly not. We can rest when we get there.'

He paused. 'But tell me, will you go straight to your relative's house as soon as we arrive?'

'No. I have yet to find her exact whereabouts. I think I shall stay at an inn. I am sure there must be one in the village.'

He noted, with surprise, that it was a female she was going to see and in spite of his decision not to ask any more questions, he felt bound to ask one. 'What is the name of your relative, Louise?'

'Catherine Fellowes.'

It meant nothing to him. 'Then we go to the inn, book rooms and then ask for the house of a Miss—or Mrs—Fellowes, is that it?'

'No, I want to explore first. I want to find out about the village and what sort of person she is. I cannot go to her unprepared. Of course she may no longer live in Moresdale…'

She was being more mystifying than ever, but he realised, whoever Catherine Fellowes was, she held the key to Louise's happiness. 'I understand,' he said. But he did not.

Moresdale was situated in a valley between the folds of a hill. It was sheep-rearing country, judging by the numbers that dotted the slopes as they approached. Some even strayed on to the road and Joe was obliged to slow down even further so as not to run them down. On each side of the road, the hills rose to a craggy outline, with tumbled rocks and a narrow waterfall plummeting into a stream that ran alongside the road to join up with the River Swale on its way to the Ouse.

The village itself was only a cluster of cottages, a blacksmith's forge, a butcher, a small general store, an inn called the Moresdale Arms, and a church with its vicarage. The place seemed too small to contain so many people. It was crowded and there was obviously something happening on the village green. Men were marching about with planks of wood and tables, benches and chairs. Some were putting up flags and the women were decorating the houses. Children ran all over the place, getting in everyone's way.

Joe pulled the carriage up in a field gateway and they left it to walk. 'What's afoot?' Jonathan asked one beefy fellow, who was unhitching a cart loaded with planks and canvas.

'You must be strangers to ask that,' he said. 'We are getting ready for the annual sheep fair tomorrow. Famous it is. Draws crowds from all over.'

Jonathan thanked him and they moved on. It soon became apparent it was not only a sheep fair, there were to be side shows, stalls and refreshments. Louise began to wonder if it was a bad time to be asking about Catherine Fellowes; everyone was too busy to listen to her. Besides, she was suddenly afraid of asking.

'Where to now?' Jonathan asked. Somewhere along the road between York and Moresdale, she had stopped being the intrepid adventurer and become a young lady who had lost her way. She was quiet and withdrawn and very unsure of herself.

'Let us walk about a little. I want to get the feel of the place.'

Already she felt a certain familiarity with her surroundings, as if she had been here before. But of course she had; they had not moved to Barnet until she was five years old. What had caused her parents to move? Moresdale to Barnet was a huge step and not to be undertaken lightly. They arrived outside the church and stood looking at it for a moment. Her father—the Reverend Vail, she meant—must once have been the incumbent here. Her heart began to beat more quickly. 'Shall we go inside?' she asked.

Jonathan sent Joe and Betty to the inn to see about accommodation for them all. He knew this was a significant moment for Louise and the fewer who witnessed it the better. Taking her arm, he steered her through the lych gate and up the path, pretending not to notice that her steps slowed and she was almost stumbling. They entered the cool interior of a simple place of worship, genuflected and walked towards the altar side by side. He had a sudden vision of her walking up the aisle of a church towards him, both of them dressed in wedding finery, and hastily thrust it from him. He was having too many of these moments of foolish imagination just lately and they did not accord with his avowed intention not to tumble into marriage without a great deal of thought. And in view of his present situation, that was the last thing on his mind.

As they moved slowly towards the front of the church, Louise found herself back in a half-remembered past. She was a very little girl, holding tight to her mother's hand and flanked by her three brothers. They were making their way past the villagers already in their places, to the front pew to wait for her father to begin the service.

In the pew on the other side of the aisle was a very grand lady and gentleman with a little boy between them. The gentleman and the lady, who was wearing huge panniers to her shining gown and a white wig topped by a big hat with a sweeping feather, looked straight ahead and did not seem aware of the family on the other side of the aisle, but the little boy looked about him. He was a plump, handsome child, dressed in a blue coat and blue satin breeches. He had silver buckles on his shiny black shoes.

Louise, who was dressed in her Sunday best—a blue dimity dress and white cotton petticoats—stared at him and then giggled. He grinned back at her as if they were conspirators. His mother suddenly saw what he was about and spoke sharply to him. Obediently, he turned towards the front just as the Reverend entered the back of the church and came in procession up the aisle towards the altar to begin the service. She remembered the sound of her father's voice and the singing of the congregation, the kneeling in prayer and the sideways glances she made towards the gentleman, the lady and the little boy. Did she know his name? How well had she known him? Had they been playmates? She did not think so because they were obviously a family of some importance and the vicar and his family would be beneath them socially.

Jonathan felt her trembling grow stronger and wished with all his heart he could help her. Whatever it was that had sent her here it was not something joyful. She turned and started to hurry back to the open air. They were met at the door by a man in clerical garb.

'Good day,' he said, doffing his low-crowned hat. 'Do you find our little church interesting?'

'Yes, very interesting,' Jonathan answered for her. 'Is it very old?'

'Parts of it are. It was built by the first Earl of Moresdale when he came here in the time of Elizabeth. You will find memorials to all the family back to that time.' He waved his hands at the walls, which were heavily carved with tablets containing inscriptions and decorated with angels and wreaths. 'The men were great warriors. They were involved in the Civil War and in crushing the Jacobite Rebellion, only fifteen years ago. That was a bad time, a very bad time...'

Louise registered that fifteen years ago was the time her father had moved to Barnet and wondered if that could have any bearing on his decision, though half of her was still thinking about the service she had just remembered. She must have gone to dozens of such services from the time she was able to take her first steps, probably every Sunday, maybe twice on Sundays. Why had that particular one stuck in her memory?

'Sir,' she asked, plucking up her courage, 'do you know of a family called Fellowes?'

'To be sure I do. I thought you must know it too, since you showed such an interest in the church. Fellowes is the Earl's family name.'

Only Jonathan's hand under her elbow kept her upright. Somehow she found composure enough to thank him and walk out of the church into the sunshine and fresh air. Her mother had mentioned Catherine Fellows as if she knew her well and Louise had concluded the unknown lady was her mother. But had she been wrong in that? It was difficult to believe she came of that stock. On the other hand, it was just like the aristocracy to give away a child to save the family from disgrace. Her head was full of questions, questions she was afraid to ask. Could the family she had remembered seeing in church be the Earl and his wife? Then what was her connection with them and with the little boy? Where was he now? Did he know about her?

Jonathan, sticking close to her side, had only a hazy idea of what was going through her mind, but she had turned very pale and there was a strange faraway look in her expression that he found disturbing. She had been trying to keep whatever it was from him ever since he had come upon her, and Mrs Vail had been less than forthcoming, so what was the secret the family was hiding? A connection with the Earl of Moresdale, perhaps, but not one that could be acknowledged.

'The Dowager Countess will open the fair tomorrow,' the parson went on, unaware of Louise's tumbling thoughts. 'The Earl used to do it, but he has not resided at the Hall for some time. I believe he has business affairs that keep him in London. May I enquire your interest in the family?'

'I have heard my father speak of them,' Louise said, endeavouring to sound casual. 'He was the incumbent here many years ago. And as I was visiting York, I decided to take the opportunity to look round the village.'

'Apart from the church and Moresdale Hall,

there is little to see, though there are some fine walks in the hills, if you like walking.'

'We do, indeed,' Jonathan said, to help Louise compose herself. 'It is one of the reasons we came to the area.'

They said goodbye to the parson and left the church to return to the bustle of the preparations for the fair. 'You did not expect that, did you?' he queried.

'Expect what?'

'That your Catherine Fellowes was one of the aristocracy.'

'I do not know that she is. She may only be distantly related, a second cousin several times removed.'

'True. So how do you propose to find out?'

'Stay here awhile and see what transpires.'

'You do not feel inclined to pay a call on the Countess?'

'Certainly not. I should not be so presumptuous.'

'You are afraid,' he said bluntly.

She was saved from answering by Joe and Betty, who were making their way towards them, carefree and laughing.

'How did you fare at the inn?' Jonathan asked him.

'No room, my lord,' Joe said. 'Not for love nor money.'

'Oh, dear,' Louise said. 'I suppose we shall have to return to York.'

'But I want to come to the fair tomorrow,' Betty wailed. 'It's going to be a grand affair, with all manner of contests, bowling and races and a treasure hunt. Joe said he would enter them all.'

'Did he?' Jonathan asked, looking at Joe. 'You are assuming I shall not need you.'

'Will you, my lord?' he queried, head cocked to one side.

'No, but there is the matter of accommodation.'

'I noticed an inn in the last village we passed through,' Joe said. 'It's called the Shepherd's Crook. We could go back and try there.'

'Then let us go and see what they have to offer. If the accommodation is reasonable it would be better than going all the way back to York,' Jonathan declared.

The inn, three or four miles back along the road to York, was small but clean. Jonathan's title and the fat purse he proffered was enough to persuade the innkeeper to consult his wife in whispers about how they could be obliged. 'We can let you have two rooms, my lord,' he said, coming back to them while his wife disappeared in a flurry of petticoats. 'If you and your good lady would sit in the parlour and take a glass of something, I will have them prepared for you.' He ushered them into the parlour. 'What shall it be? I have ale, cognac, wine or cordial. We are always well stocked for the Moresdale Fair.'

Louise and Betty chose cordial and the men ale, and once they had been served the innkeeper, who told them his name was Jeremiah Winter, left them to themselves. 'Jonathan,' Louise whispered urgently, 'he called me your good lady.'

'I know.' He grinned at her.

'You must tell him at once that he is mistaken.'

'Mistaken? You mean you are not good, not a lady, or not mine?' he teased.

'Not *yours*. Not your wife.'

'But even if you are not my wife, you could still be my good lady.'

'I could not! How dare you suggest such a

thing? If you think that I agreed to your escort in order to become...' she floundered '...your good lady, then I am afraid you are under a misapprehension. I would like to repay your kindness, but I would never agree to that.'

He had spoken without thinking; it had not occurred to him she would jump to the wrong conclusion. 'I never meant to imply any such thing,' he said. 'Your company and the adventures you fall into have already repaid my small outlay. It is something I would not have missed for the world.'

'I think I hate you,' she said.

'Only *think*, Louise? You are not sure?'

'Well, I should like to, but you make it very difficult.'

He laughed aloud and, in spite of herself, she found her own lips twitching. 'Oh, you rise to the bait so prettily,' he said.

'I am not in the mood for jests,' she said sternly.

He straightened his face. 'Then I beg your pardon. We will be serious. Tell me how I may please you.'

'By explaining to the innkeeper that we are not married.'

'They might wonder at that. Shall I be your guardian again?' He had a way of looking at her closely and smiling that smile of his that made her melt inside. She must be strong, more especially since she had discovered he was a Viscount. Viscounts were way above her touch, as her papa had hinted to her mother during that fateful conversation. As if she could not have thought that out for herself!

'Say whatever you like, as long as they know I will not share a bedchamber with you.'

'Pity,' he said, with an exaggerated sigh.

'You are the outside of enough, Lord Leinster. And if you can find nothing else to do but tease, I shall take myself off.'

'Where to?'

'For a walk.' She rose and left the room. He followed, turning to Joe on the way. 'Tell the lady of the house we will be back shortly and will require supper.'

Once outside, he tucked her hand beneath his elbow and held it there. 'Let us walk together and I promise I will not tease you again.'

There was a steep slope at the back of the inn and a well-worn path meandered upwards. They took this, walking side by side in silence. The greeny, brown grass of the hills were picked out with patches of mauve and pinkish white heather, the white of the sheep and the dark grey of the craggy rocks that littered the hillside. Apart from the singing of a skylark, there was no sound, except their footsteps, crunching on the gravel.

'I am sorry I teased you,' he said at last. 'It was meant to make you smile, but I should have known better, when you are so worried.'

'Am I?'

'You know you are. In the last three weeks I have come to know you very well. I know all your moods: happy, mischievous, sad and worried, and at this moment you are worried. I would help you if I could.'

'I do not see how you can.'

'Try me. Whatever you tell me I will keep to myself.' There was no teasing in his voice now; it was gentle, caring. 'It does not take a genius to realise it is all to do with Catherine Fellowes. Who and what is she, Louise?'

She turned to face him. Keeping the truth from him was pointless. It was not as if they had a future together, whatever the outcome. And he had been so kind and helpful, rescuing her from her scrapes and buying her beautiful clothes, and keeping her company when she might have been lost, not to mention risking his life to arrest Jed Black. She might have said she would like to repay all he had done, but she knew she could not. He deserved her confidence. She took a deep breath. 'I think she is my mother.'

'Mother!' he exclaimed.

'Yes. I have only recently learned of it.'

So that was what she had overheard! 'Are you sure?'

'No, but I need to find out.'

'And your father?'

'I do not know who my father is. I am praying he is Catherine Fellowes's husband. Otherwise it means…' She could not go on.

'Oh, you poor dear,' he said, drawing her down beside him on a rock beside the path and putting his arm about her. He should have been shocked, but all he felt was a great tenderness towards her and a need to reassure her. 'Do you want to tell me about it? I might be able to help.'

'I don't see how you can, but you deserve to know the truth.' She went on to explain everything, how shocked she had been, how sad and angry both at the same time. 'I was sad to learn that the two people who brought me up from babyhood, whom I have loved and honoured all my life, are not my real parents, and very angry that they kept it from me all these years.'

'No doubt they had their reasons. Did you not think to ask them?'

'I might have done if they had been at home when I calmed down, but they must have gone out immediately after their discussion. There was no one in the house to talk to, so I hit upon the idea of trying to find Catherine Fellowes myself. I know it was impetuous and wrong of me, but once I had set out, there was no going back, and to be truthful, I did not want to. I want to understand why my real mother parted with me. What made her give me away? I cannot rest until I know,' she cried.

He did not comment, but it seemed to him that either Catherine Fellows was unmarried and had disgraced the family or she had been cuckolding her husband. Neither theory boded well for Louise's future. He knew many men openly had mistresses, his own father for one, and nothing was thought of it, but for a woman to take a lover and bear illegitimate children was another thing entirely. If Louise were the result of an illicit liaison, no man of consequence would have her for a wife. She must either content herself with marrying one of the lower orders or take her place in the *demi-monde*. Or remain a spinster all her life. He feared for her. 'Are you sure you still want to know? Would it not be better to remain in ignorance?'

'But one day, someone might want to marry me and how could I keep such a thing from my future husband? That's what Papa said to Mama and he was right. There should be no secrets in a marriage.'

'Is there someone?' he asked and held his breath for her answer, realising his own feelings for her had been growing in spite of himself, in spite of the impossibility of anything coming from it. He reminded himself, as he had been doing over and over again since her illness, when the madcap had become the vulnerable and delightful woman, that he was working on behalf of the Gentleman's Club and her family, and his own feelings should not come into it. But how could they not? She had found a secure place in his heart and he wanted her to be happy. He found himself wanting to know the truth as much as she did.

'No,' she told him with a sigh, knowing the only man who mattered to her was out of her reach. 'No one. It was speculation on Papa's part.'

He let his breath out in relief. 'Then we will unearth the mystery between us.'

'You mean to stay with me?'

'Of course. Do you think I would desert you now?'

'Why have you stayed with me so long?'

He hesitated. 'Since we are being honest with each other, I must admit that Luke asked me to.'

'Luke?' she queried in surprise. 'My brother?'

'Yes. He wanted me to see you safe.' He smiled suddenly. 'And that has been more of a task than I bargained for.'

Dear Luke. He was the best of brothers. But that meant… 'You knew who I was all along. You knew where I was going and why. You have been playing games with me, Lord Leinster.' Angrily, she jumped to her feet. 'You deceived me—'

'Hold hard,' he said, taking her hand and pulling her down beside him again. 'I have no more deceived you than you have me. I did not know who you were when we first met, you were dressed as a man, you remember, though I admit, I was puzzled.' And here he smiled. 'No man should have such wide, glorious eyes and long lashes, no man such a neat round *derrière* and pretty rosy lips. And to think I might have missed you if those highwaymen had not held up the coach at Baldock. I was sure you were far ahead of me.'

'We went to London to board the stage,' she said, trying to ignore his compliments and the warm, comforting feel of her hand in his.

'Why? It went through Barnet.'

'I did not want to board it where I might be recognised.'

'I see. So you thought it all out, planned it carefully.'

'Not carefully enough, if Luke could send you hotfoot after me. And I had no idea where Catherine Fellowes might be found. I should have asked you, should I not? You knew.'

'No, I did not. Believe me, Louise, Luke never mentioned Catherine Fellowes or your reasons for travelling. I do not think he knew. All he knew was that you had disappeared suddenly and he wanted you found. It was Mrs Vail who told me she thought you might be coming to

Moresdale and she did not tell me why. I was simply asked to follow you and bring you safely back to them.'

'Now you know as much as I do.'

'Which is little enough, but if you are sure you want to learn more, we will do it together. From now on, there need be no secrets from each other. I am here if you want me. And when the mystery is solved, I will take you back to Barnet because I know your family love you and want you home.'

'But they are not my real family.'

'Of course they are. I think they would be hurt to hear you say that. They have loved you all your life, they are more family than ever Catherine Fellowes is.'

'Yes, I know you are right. I am so confused and troubled.' She sighed.

'You could go home now, not wait to find Catherine Fellowes,' he said gently. 'It might cause you more grief than joy.'

'I know that. I do not expect her to fall on my neck, but I have to know. Don't you see, I must know.'

'And if she is not in Moresdale?'

'I will have to think again. But even if she is not, I believe the answers lie there.'

'Very well. Tomorrow we will go back to Moresdale and delve some more.' He stood up and held out his hand. She took it and he pulled her to her feet. 'Come, I am hungry. Let us hope Mrs Winter is a good cook.'

Mrs Winter was a very good cook. The dinner she produced was plain country fare, but well cooked and wholesome. There was soup, roast mutton, jugged hare, pigeon breasts served with broccoli, peas and green salad. And as she and Mr Winter joined them to eat, the conversation was of a general nature, most about the fair, the sheep farming and the different walks they could take into the countryside. The path they had ventured on earlier led over the brow of the hill to Moresdale, they were told, and the view from the top was worth the climb.

'Perhaps we will try it while we are here,' Jonathan said, as the table was cleared and a dish of blackberry tartlets and another of baked apples was put before them. Louise, having bared her soul, felt suddenly light-headed and did the meal full justice. Now that Jonathan was an ally and not a protagonist, they might do better. Two heads were better than one, when it came to solving riddles. But she knew that, at the end, they would part, perhaps never to see each other again, or perhaps to glimpse each other in the distance. She imagined him with a wife and family and then he would forget his little adventure with her, or if he did remember, he would not speak of it, would probably not even admit ever having known her. Her feeling of euphoria evaporated, leaving her miserable. She had to blink away her tears.

Jonathan was himself deep in thought. The tale she had told him had impressed itself on his brain, so that he found himself trying to think of ways in which she might have been mistaken, that the stigma of bastardy might be lifted from her. He wanted everything to come out right for her. And for him.

'You have had a long day,' Mrs Winter said, noticing the sudden withdrawal of the Viscount and his ward, as if they did not have the energy to continue the conversation. 'You must be very tired. When you have eaten sufficient, I will show you to your rooms.'

Louise knew at once that the bedchamber into which she was shown was that of their host and hostess. They had given it up for her and Betty because Jonathan had paid them well to do so. Jonathan was allocated a smaller room belonging to their son who was away serving an apprentice-ship with a neighbouring farmer. Joe was expected to sleep in the loft above the stables, which he said he did not mind at all. Louise wondered where Mr and Mrs Winter were to sleep.

She found out when, waking early, she dressed in a simple round gown in pale blue muslin laced at the front and without panniers, slipped into some sturdy shoes and went downstairs. They were fast asleep on the settles in the parlour. She silently withdrew and crept out of the back door.

The sun was a golden orb peeping over the summit of the hill. The sheep seemed hardly to have moved since the day before. The lark still sang. She supposed that would always be the same, whatever the outcome of her quest. The world would keep turning, people would be born and marry and die, just as if she had never been. It was humbling and yet somehow comforting. She wandered along the path she and Jonathan had taken the previous day, going over their conversation, the strange way they had met, the gambling and the duel. Had she really pretended to be a man and behaved in that unladylike manner? No wonder he laughed. It would have been funny if it were not so deadly serious.

Sighing, she sat down on the rock by the path and looked down at the roof of the Shepherd's Crook. It really did not deserve the name of inn—it was no more than a hedge tavern. Three weeks before she would never have considered staying in such a place. Indeed, she had never been inside an hotel, let alone an inn. Three weeks before... How her life had changed. And might change even further, when she found the elusive Catherine Fellowes. Jonathan had suggested going home, leaving the past buried, and though half of her wanted to do that, to have everything back to what it was, she knew that was not possible. You could not turn the clock back. And half of her could still hear that imagined voice saying, 'Come unto me.'

She stood up. The die was cast. Today was a new day, made for new discoveries.

Halfway down the hill, she met Jonathan coming towards her. He was dressed in country clothes, brown cloth coat and nankeen breeches.

He was hatless and his hair was tied back in a queue. 'You are up betimes,' he called as he approached. 'Could you not sleep?'

'The sun shining through the window woke me. It is a beautiful day.'

'Yes,' he agreed. She seemed more cheerful than she had been the day before. 'The fair will enjoy good weather. Will you come down to breakfast. Then we can go to Moresdale. That is, if you want to.'

'Yes, of course I do.'

He turned and they went down together.

Moresdale was a hive of activity as woven-willow hurdles were being made into pens for the sheep, which were being driven in from all over the hills. How the shepherds and their dogs managed to recognise their own and keep them separate, Louise had no idea. Already some of the stalls were set up and doing business, selling everything from ribbons, lace, stays, hats, buttons and buckles to cabbages, blueberries, books and pamphlets, puppies and kittens. There were flags and bunting everywhere.

At the other end of the village, on a relatively flat piece of land, the lines were being marked out for the races and the competitions. Bowling for a pig was likely to be a favourite with the crowd and competitions of strength such as hammer throwing and arm wrestling. There were also skittles, archery and bowls and races for the children and, the highlight of the day, a competition to decide the best sheepdog. Joe and Betty went off on their own, to investigate how to enter some of the competitions.

Jonathan and Louise, arm in arm, strolled among the crowds who were making their way to the open space where a dais had been set up. It had an archway of intertwined flowers and half-a-dozen chairs. This was where the dignitaries were gathering to open proceedings. Louise, with Jonathan in tow, pushed her way to the front of the crowd, determined to see as much as she could.

'I wonder how old the Dowager is,' Jonathan murmured.

'You think she might be Catherine Fellowes?'

'It is a possibility.'

'I prefer to think Catherine Fellowes has nothing to do with the Hall,' Louise said. 'A poor relation, perhaps, many times removed. I think of her as a sad person, someone who was forced into parting with her child, perhaps because she was too poor to keep her. Or perhaps she died in childbirth and her grieving husband could not bear to look at his child who was so like her mother.'

He did not point out that theory did not accord with her account of what she heard her father and mother saying—according to them, Catherine Fellowes was still alive. And so was her husband. If it comforted her to think that, who was he to say differently? He squeezed her hand in reassurance as a carriage drew up. It was easy to see it had once been a splendid affair, but now the gold paint had tarnished and the coat of arms on the door had faded. A driver in a fustian coat and woollen breeches sat on the box seat and on the step behind stood a giant of a man in blue-and-white livery, who looked about him, frowning at the crowds. As soon as the carriage stopped, he jumped down, opened the door, let down the step and held out his hand. It was grasped by a black gloved hand and that was followed by the lady herself.

She was tiny and this was emphasised by the width of her hoops and the tight lacing of her stays, all in a deep blue. Her white wig was piled high with rolls and curls and was topped by a tiny hat, perched at an angle on top of the creation. But the thing Louise noticed before all of that, was that she was very old and could not possibly be the Catherine Fellowes she sought.

Hanging on to the big man's arm, her ladyship proceeded in stately manner to the dais, mounted the steps and took her place on the largest chair. Her servant stood behind her, towering over her. She did not smile.

One of the men on the stage stood up to address the crowd, welcoming them to the fair and outlining the rules of the competitions that would take place after the more serious side of the business had been transacted. Then he bowed deferentially to the Countess and invited her to open the proceedings.

She stood up and came to the front of the dais and stood regally surveying the crowds. Her dark eyes swept her audience and came to rest on Louise. For a moment she appeared shocked as their glances met and held for several seconds, then she drew herself up and declared Moresdale Fair open in a firm voice that belied her age. This was followed by applause and cheers orchestrated by those on the dais. She accepted them without any sign of pleasure, turned to her servant and allowed him to lead her back to the carriage. The next minute it had disappeared in a cloud of dust.

'She might have stopped and looked round,' commented a woman, standing beside Louise. 'We spent hours and hours decorating the stalls and baking cakes and pies. I hoped she would taste one of mine. In't that just like the gentry, don't care a toss about us what works to keep them in their palaces.'

'It was almost as if she knew me,' Louise said to Jonathan, as they moved away. 'But she could not, could she? I was only five when I left here.'

'Perhaps you resemble your mother.' He, too, had seen that look. On her ladyship's face, it was not one of unalloyed joy.

'I never thought of that. There are so many questions I want to ask and they nearly all begin with why.'

'When do you propose asking these questions?' On the surface she was wide-eyed, like a child discovering something new, but he knew that beneath that façade she was afraid. And he shared her fear. The outcome of her investigation was important to her and because of that it was important to him too.

'Soon,' she said. 'When I have decided how to go about it.'

'Would you like me to do it for you?'

'Certainly not! Do you take me for a coward?'

'No,' he said, smiling. 'Never that. Obstinate and impulsive, if you like, but not cowardly.'

They spent some time going from one event to the next, watching the sheepdogs driving their flocks, listening to the bartering as flocks were sold and taking part in many of the competitions. He walked beside her, behaving in his usual cheerful way, pointing things out to her, commenting on what was happening, laughing at the antics of the people bowling for the pig, frowning at those who were encouraging a couple of cocks to fight. He tried his hand at archery, using a crossbow, and Louise, not to be outdone, entered herself. Drawing the bow was easier than a log bow, but she did not think it was as accurate. She squealed excitedly when she hit the centre of the target and scored better than Jonathan. He smiled, and let her enjoy her triumph. For a short while he had glimpsed the return of the madcap who had so attracted him and it did his heart good. But it was not to last.

They were looking at some ribbons on a stall when they heard someone mention the Dowager Countess and Louise pricked up her ears. 'She opened the Fair again this year,' a woman was saying. 'I don't know why the Earl leaves it to her. She's getting too old.'

'Too old to look after the Hall and that's a fact,' her companion added. 'I don't know why he don't come home and see to the place. It is getting more and more neglected.'

'Because no one will work up there, that's why,' a third put in. 'Except Hamish Mackay and he won't let anyone near her ladyship. It's my belief he's more than a servant. He says who comes and who goes. You can't get past him or those great dogs of his. They'll kill you on sight.'

'So, why don't the Earl come home?' the first insisted.

'How should I know? According to Hamish, he has business in London, which is no loss to Moresdale. A more bad-tempered man I have never met.'

'What about his wife?'

'No one ever sees her. Either she's shut up

in the house or she is in London too. It's the Dowager who looks after things in the village. What she says goes. She even takes the Earl's place as the presiding magistrate. Had young Timmins put in the stocks when his dog worried Farmer George's sheep and he's a simpleton and not above ten years old. Still, if it had been the Earl, he'd have had him strung up.'

The gossipers had no more to say on the subject of the occupants of the Hall and Louise and Jonathan wandered away. 'It does not sound like a happy place,' Jonathan murmured.

'No,' she said.

'What would you like to do now?'

'Let us find Joe and Betty. I am feeling guilty that I have allowed them to be alone together so much.'

'Joe would never compromise Betty. I think he is genuinely fond of her. You never know, they might decide to wed. Would you have any objection to that?'

'Me? It is not for me to say. She has an older brother; he would be the one to give his permission. But I have been sadly remiss in my duty towards her.'

'Then by all means, let us find them.' She was

prevaricating, he knew that, but he was a patient man; he had followed her so far, he could wait a little longer. In that time he might persuade her to let sleeping dogs lie and accompany him back to Barnet. And then they would part. The thought of that depressed him.

Joe was taking part in the arm wrestling, but he was up against a man with huge biceps and was soon eliminated. He grinned ruefully as he left the arena and rejoined Betty, who was standing beside the Viscount and Miss Vail.

'Bad luck, Joe,' Jonathan said. 'Try the races. I think you might have an advantage there.'

Joe and Betty were enjoying themselves hugely, but though Louise pretended to take an interest in everything, her mind was far away. How to get into the grounds of Moresdale Hall without being torn to pieces by the dogs was occupying her mind. And how to find her way into the presence of the Countess and what to say to her when she succeeded. She could not baldly state who she was and demand to know the whereabouts of Catherine Fellowes. She had to be more subtle than that. And if what she learned was not good news, how to tell Jonathan, Viscount Leinster.

He felt rather than heard the sob catch in her throat and turned to look down at her. There was a fixed smile on her face, but there was pain in her lovely eyes and now he knew the reason, he could feel her anxiety, as if it were a physical thing, a great lump of agony that would not go away. He wanted more than anything to relieve it. And perhaps there was something he could do. He had a title and some standing in the *haut monde*; surely they were not so far from civilisation here that it did not count for something. It would need some thought and he would say nothing to Louise. 'Have you seen enough?' he asked.

'Yes, I think so.'

'I have not,' Betty chimed in. 'And there is to be a country dance tonight on the green. We want to go to that, don't we, Joe?'

'We will come back for it,' Jonathan said. He tucked Louise's hand into the crook of his arm. 'Come, Louise, let us take a walk.'

Chapter Nine

'Where are we going?' she asked.

'Up that hill.' He pointed. 'I have a fancy to see the view.'

The slope was gentle at first, but grew steeper as they climbed. He held her hand, making sure she did not slip, though she was strong and healthy and easily able to make the ascent. Three-quarters of the way up, he stopped and turned. 'See,' he said.

She looked down at the village, nestling in the hollow, and could see the crowds and the flags and the sheep pens, quickly emptying as the animals were sold and taken away. But it was not the village he meant; he was pointing a little to the right, and then she saw it. The roof of a large house, heavily screened by trees. 'Moresdale Hall,' she said.

'I think so. I had hoped we might see more of it, but the trees are in the way.'

'It looks very big.'

'I expect it is. I have no doubt that when it was built it dominated the village, with clear views all round. A statement of the Earl's rank and wealth. I am surprised the trees have been allowed to grow and screen it so completely. Not only can the world not see it, it cannot see the world.'

'It does not tell us much, does it?'

'No, except perhaps the owner's wish for privacy,' he said thoughtfully.

'That is going to make it difficult to get inside.'

'You want to get inside?'

'Yes. I must speak to the Countess, but I am afraid she will not receive me.'

'Then we shall have to think of a strategy.'

'Jonathan,' she said slowly, 'I am grateful for your support, truly I am, but this is something I must do alone.'

'Of course, my dear. I understand.' There was a stray curl being blown across her face by the wind. He reached out and tucked it behind her ear. His touch made her go hot and cold, sending a shiver through her body from the top of her head to her toes. She must not let him see how it affected her, she must not. She turned away.

'Let us climb a little higher,' she said.

He sighed and followed. Touching her was not a good idea. It gave him ideas he should not have. She was a wholesome, innocent young lady for all her pretended worldliness, he did not doubt that, and as he liked to think he was an honourable man, he must curb his desire. Strenuous exercise might dampen it.

As they climbed higher the terrain became more rocky and they found they had to pick their way between outcrops of rock and huge boulders that looked as if some giant hand had flung them there. Just below the summit they had to negotiate a narrow path with a sheer drop on one side and a cliff face on the other. It was not especially narrow, but there was no room to walk side by side. He went first and turned to wait for her. She was halfway when she came to a stop, unable to move. She had suddenly become petrified.

Jonathan, waiting with his hand out towards her, was surprised; she had never shown fear before. 'Come,' he said gently, moving back towards her. There is no danger if you keep close to the cliff wall and do not go too near the edge.'

Still she could not move. She turned so that her back was against the cliff, her arms out to either side, hands spread against the rock face, frozen there like a frightened rabbit.

'Turn towards me, sweetheart,' he said, taking another step towards her. 'This way.' They could not go back because to do that he would have to pass her and he could not be sure she would not panic and both would hurtle to their deaths. 'Do not look down. Look at me.'

Slowly she turned her head to look at him. He was calm and resolute, his outstretched hand only inches from hers, if she could only bring herself to reach out for it. She could not speak. There were no words to express the terror she felt. He took another step towards her and grabbed her hand. 'Now turn slowly towards me,' he said. 'Give me your other hand.'

His voice was quietly reassuring. She half-turned, lifted her other arm and then he had both her hands in his. Slowly he took a step back-wards, taking her with him. And then another. And another. And then they were on a grassy plateau and she fell into his arms.

'It is all right, sweetheart, you are safe now,' he said, holding her close, so that her head was nestling in his shoulder. His heart was beating like a hammer. If she had panicked, thrust him from her, refused to take his hand and fallen, he did not know what he would have done. She was precious to him, so precious he could not bear to lose her. He loved her. It was not simply lustful desire for an attractive young woman, it went far deeper that that. It was a wish, a longing to nurture and protect, to have and to hold safe from all ills, to be as one, together facing the world, for always. She had established herself in the core of his being, became part of the man he was, the man he might become. It was a staggering revelation.

The strength of his feeling shook him and though his brain endeavoured to deny it, his heart would not. He stood holding her body close to his, fitting into his so effortlessly they could only have been made as a pair, and groaned inwardly. She was not mistress material, they had already established that. Neither was she suitable as a wife. It was a ridiculous notion, so why was he thinking it? Had he not vowed to think long and carefully about whom he should marry?

And what was there to consider about Louise Vail? As the daughter of a parson, she would not be considered a suitable bride for the heir to an earldom; as the product of an illicit union she would be ostracised and not received in polite society. Could love overcome those barriers?

The wind was strong up there on the peak and she was shivering. He put his arm about her and led her to the leeward side of a large boulder and drew her down beside him on the grass. 'Are you feeling better now?' he asked, keeping his arm about her shoulders.

'Yes, thank you.' Her voice was no more than a whisper. He had twice called her sweetheart. It meant nothing to him, of course, but to her it was breathtaking. Shattering. She loved him, had recognised the fact several days before, even as she realised nothing could come of it. He was a Viscount and Viscounts did not marry women like her. She was a nobody, more of a nobody that most, since she did not know who she really was, but here she was wishing and longing and knowing it could not be. If she were not shaking so much, she would get up and go back, but to do that she had to negotiate that ledge again. She shuddered at the prospect.

'You are cold.' He took off his coat and draped it round her shoulders, holding it there with his hand. 'Why were you so afraid? It did not occur to me you would be or I would not have taken you that way. The ledge was wide enough to walk along…'

'I know.' She paused, trying to put aside thoughts of an impossible love to try and answer him. 'I was perfectly happy about it until I reached the middle and then it was as if a giant hand came out and pushed against my chest, snatching my breath away. I could not go on. Something made me shake so much my legs would not support me and I was afraid of crumpling down and pitching over the edge. It was a strange sensation. It seemed to come from the air around me, not from something inside me. It was as if something or someone were holding me back, that going on was dangerous.' She paused and looked up at him. 'I am not making much sense, am I?'

'No.' Even talking nonsense, especially talking nonsense, she tore at his heart. This quest of hers was affecting her in so many ways. Affecting them both and that was not something he had bargained for when he set out.

'Must we go back that way?'

'No. Do you remember Mrs Winter said we could go over the summit from the inn to Moresdale? We can find our way back that way.'

'Was it a warning, do you think? A warning not to meddle with the past? Or the future?'

'Ghosts and ghouls and things that go bump in the night?' he queried, smiling at her. 'I would never have thought of you as someone given to flights of fancy like that. What has happened to the young stripling who led me such a dance all the way from Baldock to York? He feared nothing.'

'He was too stupid to feel fear, too stupid to know when he was well off.'

'You mean you want to go home to Barnet? We could, you know. We could leave this place to its secrets.'

'And then it would be fear that drove me away, fear of the truth.' She paused to look up at his dear face. He was looking down at her, his expression full of concern, and she wished it did not hurt so much. 'Papa always used to say, one should never be afraid of the truth. Perhaps that is why he thought I should be told it.'

She was not the only one afraid of the truth.

He feared it too. He was afraid it would hurt her, that she would find she was, in clerical parlance, baseborn. If she was hurt, so was he. How to mitigate that, he did not know. 'So, in spite of what you think are messages from goodness knows where, you will not give up?'

'No.'

He stood up and took her hand to help her to her feet. 'Then let us go back to the Shepherd's Crook, have some dinner and, if you feel up to it, dress up for the country dance, and see what tomorrow brings.'

It was a fair walk over the brow of the hill and down the other side and he was afraid he had tired her, but she seemed to have discovered an extra burst of energy from somewhere, which he correctly surmised was nervous in origin, though he said nothing. He knew that, when it was spent, she would flop with exhaustion.

Joe and Betty were already at the inn and wondering what had happened to them. They explained that they had decided to walk back over Moresdale Hill. Neither she nor Jonathan said anything about her sudden fright. They retired to their rooms to change ready for dinner and the evening's dance.

* * *

Louise wore the green silk dress Jonathan had bought in Doncaster which suited her so well, and Betty arranged her hair for her. She returned the service for Betty, who was dressed in pink-and-white stripes, decorated with pink bows. The girl chatted excitedly. She had never been to a dance before and her conversation was dotted with references to Joe. There was definitely a romance blossoming there and Louise found herself envying the girl her uncomplicated happiness.

They made their way down to the parlour where the men waited, also suitably dressed. Jonathan had reverted to being a Viscount, dressing in a plum-coloured suit of clothes, decorated with silver braid. His rose-coloured waistcoat was embroidered with silver thread and his matching breeches were held below the knee with rose-coloured ribbon. He wore white stockings and black shoes with silver buckles and high heels. Without a wig, his hair had been carefully arranged in curls on each side and the back held with a large black bow. Louise, giving him a deep curtsy, wondered why he had dressed himself up for a simple country dance.

Joe, though more plainly dressed, was smarter than they had ever seen him before, not quite the gentleman of course, but someone out to impress his lady love. They moved into the dining room where Mrs and Mrs Winter waited on them, before joining them at the table.

'Did you enjoy the fair?' Mrs Winter asked them.

'Yes, very much,' Louise said. 'There was so much going on.'

'It has been an annual event at Moresdale for as long as I can remember,' the woman went on. 'When I was young, it was always opened by the Earl and the Countess, her that is the Dowager now, of course. They would stop and visit every stall and talk to everybody. They even had a go at the skittles and bought things from the stalls. Sometimes they would come down in the evening and lead the dancing for a few minutes. People liked that. When the old Earl died, the new Earl and his wife kept up the custom for a few years, but that stopped when their little boy, Thomas, died. Only five years old, he was.'

'He died?' Louise echoed, recalling her sudden memory of the child between his parents when she visited the church. He had seemed about five years old. Was that why that particular scene had come back into her mind? It was the last time she had seen him before his death. She shivered.

'Yes. Tragedy it was. He wandered out of the grounds on his own and climbed Moresdale Hill.' She nodded her head in the direction of the slope behind the inn. 'He fell to his death off the ledge. You must have come by it if you came back that way.'

'Yes, we did,' Jonathan said, looking at Louise, who seemed to have been struck dumb. Her face had lost all its colour.

''Tis said the place is haunted by the child's ghost,' the landlady went on blithely, unaware of the disturbance she was causing. 'Can you wonder it sent his poor mama out of her mind?'

'No,' Louise whispered, perfectly prepared to believe in the ghost, for something had stopped her up on that ledge.

'What became of the Countess?' Jonathan asked.

'We were told she had to go away for her health's sake.'

'Hardly surprising,' Jonathan said.

'There was a rumour that she flung herself off that same cliff,' Mr Winter put in.

'Well, I do not believe that,' the good lady said, ignoring Louise's cry of distress. 'They would have had to bring the body down, same as they did when they found the little boy, and they couldn't do that without someone seeing it, not when the whole village was full of the boy's death. Besides, there was no funeral service, no gravestone. She didn't die. She's alive somewhere.'

'A recluse at the hall, perhaps,' Jonathan suggested.

'Recluse. Does that mean she don't go out much?'

'Something like that,' he said.

'Could be,' she agreed. 'It would account for the Dowager being the one to open the fair.'

'She didn't stay long,' Betty ventured.

'No, well, she's a bit strange too.'

'Where was the Earl when this happened?' Jonathan asked, reaching for Louise's hand beneath the tablecloth and giving it a squeeze of reassurance. 'He must have taken his son's death hard.'

'He was away in Scotland with his militia, fighting Bonnie Prince Charlie. Came back to find Thomas already cold in his grave. Until then he had been a reasonable sort of gentleman. It changed him.'

'Did…did they have other children?' Louise asked, her heart in her throat. She had stopped eating, knowing food would choke her.

'No, he was the only one and he came late. The apple of his father's eye.'

'How very sad.' It was hard to keep asking questions, but this was the nearest she had yet come to having any answered. 'Does that mean there is no heir?

'Don't seem to be.'

'Surely the Earl has brothers and sisters, cousins perhaps…' Louise was clutching at straws.

Mrs Winter shrugged. 'Not that I've heard of. That's not to say there aren't any. But if there are, they don't live hereabouts.'

'They would find the place sadly neglected,' Mr Winter said, helping himself to more meat pie. 'No one cares any more. Except Hamish Mackay. He's like a bodyguard. No one gets past him.'

Louise risked a glance at Jonathan. He smiled at her, trying to cheer her, but he knew what she was thinking, as plainly as if she had said it aloud. 'What is the Countess's given name?' he asked.

'The Dowager? Goodness knows, I don't.'

'No, I meant the young Countess.'

'Don't know that I recall it. Something beginning with C. Caroline…Charlotte… No, I remember now, it's Catherine.' She paused. 'You are not eating. Have some more meat pie.'

Unable to speak, Louise mutely shook her head. Jonathan declined politely. 'It was delicious,' he said. 'But we will not be able to dance if we eat any more.'

Louise did not feel at all like dancing. She wanted to go away on her own and think. She had come to Moresdale to discover the truth. Had she learned some of it today or was it all a smokescreen? She excused herself and left the table, wandering out of the inn to stand staring up at the hill. Over the brow of that, lying in the next valley, was Moresdale.

Jonathan joined her. 'Joe is harnessing the horses,' he said, standing beside her, but not touching her. She seemed brittle, fragile as precious china, ready to break.

'I cannot go.'

'Yes, you can. If you stay here, you will only brood and brooding will not help.'

'The Countess's name is Catherine,' she said dully.

'Is is a common enough name. And Mrs Winter said they had no more children.'

'How can she know that? It would be easy enough to conceal a birth in a secluded place like the Hall.'

'But, Louise, why would she want to?'

'I do not know, do I?'

'But if my calculations are correct, the little boy was the same age as you. Unless you were twins, you could not be her child.'

'Twins?'

'Yes, but unlikely, wouldn't you say? Keeping one child and giving away the other, especially when they had no others, is hard to credit. No, sweetheart, I think you are barking up the wrong tree,' he said.

'Do you really think so?' There was faint hope in her voice.

'Yes.' He took her hand. 'Come, let us go to the dance with Joe and Betty. We cannot spoil their evening and it *will* spoil it if we do not go.'

'You can still go.'

'Not without you. I stay by your side whatever happens.'

She gave a mirthless laugh. 'You may come to regret that.'

He grinned. 'Perhaps. But not tonight.'

She allowed herself to be drawn back to the inn, where Betty and Joe waited. 'Hurry up,' Betty said. 'I don't want to miss any of it.'

Joe offered her his arm, making her giggle. Jonathan and Louise followed them out to the carriage, which Joe was to drive. In her finery Betty could not climb up beside him, which she would have liked to do, and so got in with Jonathan and Louise, leaving them unable to continue their discussion, even had they wanted to. There seemed nothing more to say. The mystery was as deep as ever it was.

'Did you find your relation?' Betty asked Louise as they bowled along.

'Not yet. Tomorrow, perhaps.'

'The crowds will leave tomorrow. It will be easier.'

'Yes,' Louise agreed.

If Betty thought she was being particularly unforthcoming, she did not comment; she was becoming used to her friend's secretiveness. Nor did it occur to her to connect Louise's search for her relative with the story they had heard over dinner.

The dance was to be held on the green, there being no hall large enough in the village. Lanterns had been strung all round it and a dais constructed of straw bales on which a fiddler and a piper played. Everyone was dressed in their best, though Jonathan attracted some stares, being a cut above everyone else on the social scale. He did not seem to mind and pulled Louise into the dancing with boyish enthusiasm. 'Tonight we enjoy ourselves,' he murmured in her ear. 'Tonight is for us. We will let tomorrow take care of itself.'

He was as good as his word. The dance was a boisterous affair, with no ceremony whatsoever, and in the end Louise began to relax a little. Whatever was to be would be and he was right—tomorrow was time enough to think of what to do next. Determinedly she put her worries to one side to make the most of the music and the revelry, the starry moonlit night and the plentiful supply of ale and punch, the feel of his hands holding hers as they danced, his smiling countenance as he looked down at her, knowing it would be gone tomorrow, like dandelion seed on a puff of wind, only to be recalled with poignant nostalgia in later years.

It was gone midnight when they tumbled into the carriage for the return journey. Joe had partaken liberally and the ride was not without its bumps, but the horses seemed to know the way to their stables and they arrived without mishap.

Leaving Joe to put the horses away and take himself off to his own bed in the loft above them, the other three crept past the parlour where they knew Mr and Mrs Winter were sleeping and made their way as silently as possible up the stairs to their rooms, not bothering with candles. Betty went into their room, leaving Jonathan and Louise standing together on the landing facing each other, reluctant to say goodnight.

The window was uncurtained and the landing was half-lit with moonlight. They did not speak for several seconds, simply stood and searched each other's faces. In the moonlight they were pale, but their eyes were bright, hers more than his, because they were filling with tears. This love of hers could never have a happy outcome and yet she could not bear to part from him. 'Thank you for tonight,' she whispered at last. 'I shall always remember it.'

'The pleasure was all mine.'

'It is tomorrow already,' she said.

'Yes, you could say that.'

'Goodnight, Jonathan.'

'Goodnight, my love.' He reached out and cupped her face in his hands and bent to kiss her lips. And then he was gone along the corridor to his own room.

She turned and went into her own room and undressed, flinging her clothes off anyhow and scrambling in beside Betty, where she lay sleepless, trying not to let her bed mate hear her crying.

In spite of the late night, she woke early. Betty still slept and would do until noon, Louise guessed. She crept from the bed, washed and dressed in the blue muslin. Brushing her hair and tying it back, she put on a wide-brimmed straw hat and tied it beneath her chin with a blue ribbon. Then she crept from the room, down the stairs and out of the house. She had told Jonathan this was something she had to do alone and she had meant it.

The sun was barely up, but she had a long walk ahead of her and set out resolutely. Unwilling to go past that fearful cliff on the hill path, she took the road to Moresdale. People were busy in the village when she arrived, dismantling the stalls and taking down the dais and the decorations. She did not linger, but carried on past the green and up the lane to Moresdale Hall. Following a high wall, she came upon the entrance gates quite suddenly. They were closed. Beside them was a small door in the wall, meant for pedestrians. Taking her courage in her hands, she pushed this open and ventured inside.

Before her was a narrow drive hung over so closely by trees it was like a dark tunnel. There were trees everywhere, growing so densely they barely allowed the light to filter through. Beneath them the underground was dense with brambles, elder and young saplings. She shivered and took a few paces forwards. Somewhere ahead of her was the house, but what she meant to do when she reached it, she had not decided. She ought to think about it, rehearse what she would say. She could not say outright, 'I believe I am your granddaughter.' Besides, it might not be true. Jonathan could be right. Did she want it to be true? She was ambivalent about that. It might be the end of her search, but did she want to be related to so tragic a family? Had little Thomas's ghost been warning her not to go on? But could she go back to Chipping Barnet not knowing? Could she resume her old life, as if she had never made this fateful journey? She knew she could not. She took a deep breath and went on, though she could not see the house.

There would servants, butler, footmen, parlourmaids and that giant of a man she had seen at the Fair, Hamish Mackay, Mrs Winter had called him. She would have to get past them to reach the Countess. Was it the Dowager she wanted or her daughter-in-law? But if rumour were to be believed, the younger woman was not there. Unless she was being held prisoner. Her imagination ran wild.

She heard them first, the baying of dogs, and then they were in front of her, six huge wolfhounds, standing in the road, blocking her path, barking furiously. There was no passing them and nowhere to go but backwards. Something told her that it would be fatal to run. She forced herself to stand still. For several seconds they stared at each other. She ventured a tiny step backwards and they came forwards barking again. She stopped.

The big man appeared suddenly behind them. He was not in livery today, but in a cloth coat, leather breeches and sturdy boots. He held a shotgun at the ready. 'What are you doing here?' he demanded, calling the dogs to heel.

'I was out walking. I thought the house might be interesting.' It was the first thing that came into her head. 'I thought the Countess might allow me to view it.'

'She will not.'

'Then I will not trouble her. If you would call off the dogs, I will take my leave.'

'You were at the Fair yesterday,' he said, ignoring her request. 'I saw you there.'

'Yes.'

'Stranger here, are you?'

'Not exactly.' She was keeping a wary eye on the dogs in case they decided to disobey their master. They looked as though they would like to eat her alive. 'I lived in Moresdale as a little girl.'

'What brought you back?'

'I was staying in York and decided I would come and see if I remembered it.'

'And do you?'

'Only faintly.'

'Tell me your name,' he ordered.

'Louise Vail.'

'Ahh.' It was a long drawn-out sound, as if the name meant something to him.

'You know the name?' she asked.

''Twas the parson's name. Long time ago now.'

'Yes.'

He called the dogs to his side and ordered them to sit. 'You can go now,' he said. 'Turn round and walk slowly. I advise you not to run. Shut the gate behind you.'

She obeyed, forcing herself to walk steadily and not look back, though the hair on the back of her neck prickled uncomfortably. 'Do not come back,' he called after her. 'I might not be on hand to control the hounds next time.'

She reached the gate, slipped through it and shut it behind her, then she sank to the grass on the side of the road. Her legs were shaking so much she could not walk another step until she had recovered.

Five minutes later she stood up and made her way down the hill to the village. She was not sure what to do next. Jonathan had been right; she needed a strategy. More than that, she needed him. He seemed to be the pivot of her existence. Whenever she was in trouble, she wished for him.

Her wish was granted because she saw him making his way towards her, once again dressed as Jonathan Linton.

'Where have you been?' he demanded, his anxiety making him sound angry.

'To Moresdale Hall.'

'And?'

'And nothing. I could not get past the dogs. Six huge wolfhounds, nearly as tall as I am.'

'Louise, you foolish, foolish girl. You could have been killed.'

She shuddered. 'That big servant who attended the Countess yesterday came and called them off. He questioned me, asked me my name. He knew it too.'

'Did you mention Catherine Fellowes?'

'No. I wanted to see the Countess and ask her. But I could see that was useless and so I left. He told me not to go back. He was almost as menacing as the hounds.'

As they stood talking, the Countess's carriage

bowled past them with the old retainer on the back step. The curtains were drawn and they could not see inside it.

'The Dowager,' she said. 'We could go back and try to get in, while she is out.'

'I thought you wanted to speak to her. I cannot see any reason to risk those dogs, which have undoubtedly been left wandering loose, when there is nothing to see and no one to answer your questions.'

'The Countess. Catherine.'

'She might not be there and if the Earl is in residence and is as ill tempered as he is rumoured to be, you will get no welcome, especially if you are his wife's daughter and not his,' he pointed out.

She did not like to be reminded of that. 'What makes you think I might be?' she demanded crossly. 'Yesterday you were doing your best to persuade me I am not related at all, though perhaps that was only to get me to go to the dance.'

'I was only trying to be logical, though in the state you are in logic is beyond you.'

'You would be in a state if you were me. I do

not know who I am, and it is not kind of you to remind me.'

'Do not fly into the boughs over it, I was simply pointing out—'

'I know what you were pointing out. You do not need to remind me that I am a bastard, unacceptable in polite circles. I am under no illusions.'

'Louise…' he began and stopped.

'I do not know why you stay with me.' She laughed suddenly. 'Oh, but I do.'

'Do you?' he asked softly.

'Yes, Luke asked you to and no doubt he had to pay dearly for the services of one of the famous Piccadilly Gentlemen's Club. You see, I know its name. I wish he had not wasted his money.'

'Wasted it?' he asked, angry himself now and not inclined to tell her he had received no payment and would ask for none. 'Your brother loved you enough to ask for our help in finding you and keeping you safe. Do you throw that love back in his face?'

'He is not my brother,' she said flatly.

'And now you disown him. I am ashamed of you, Louise Vail.'

'I know that! I am not fit company for a

Viscount, so I will relieve you of the burden of it.' She turned on her heel and ran across the green, going she knew not where.

Jonathan watched her go and cursed himself for his clumsiness. They had no proof she was not legitimate and he should not have brought the subject up. She was hurt, confused and angry and all he had done was add to her feelings of being an outcast. He did not care who she was, what secrets were hidden in her past, who had been her mother or who had fathered her. She was a person in her own right, brave, spirited, resourceful and lovable. And he loved her. He had not told her so, but perhaps he should. But where was that love leading? To marriage? What had happened to his vow to think very carefully?

Thinking did not help. There was every reason to reject the idea. He made himself list them. She might be, probably was, illegitimate and, even if she were not, she had been adopted and brought up by a parson who had no pedigree that he was aware of, and it was an unconventional upbringing at that, more like a boy's than a girl's. She would bring no dowry, no prestige to his household. Neither society nor his parents would accept her. Reasons enough, his head told him, but it made no difference. Reason did not come into it, when his heart was engaged.

He could not tell her how he felt, not while she had this bee in her bonnet about her birth. The sooner that mystery was solved the better. On the other hand, if she were to think he had delayed proposing until he knew there was no taint of illegitimacy about her, she would turn him down on the spot, and he could not blame her. He had to do something to bring the whole matter to a conclusion. After all, he told himself with a wry smile, was it not one of the aims of the society to solve mysteries? It was time to visit the Dowager.

Louise had disappeared towards the York road and he assumed she was returning to the Shepherd's Crook. He ran after her, falling into step beside her. She knew he was there, but did not acknowledge it. If she could stay angry with him, then she could perhaps bear his presence without bursting into tears.

It had all gone so terribly wrong. Finding her mother had seemed such a simple thing to do when she first thought of it, almost an adventure, with reunion at the end and a return to the vicarage, if not exactly in triumph, at least with satisfaction. How very different it had turned out. The journey had been far from straightforward, made bearable only by the presence of Jonathan. While she had thought he was simply Jonathan Linton, she had enjoyed his company, playing cards, even duelling, because that had been no more than play, but as soon as she knew of his title, she realised the intrepid adventurer could be no more and life suddenly became very serious. What on earth had possessed Luke to ask him to look after her?

'I suppose you will keep up this silence until I apologise,' he said.

'What have you to apologise for? You stated nothing but the truth.'

'We cannot know that.'

'It is too late to retract. Words said cannot be unsaid.'

'I wish to God they could.' He paused and took her arm, bringing her round to face him. 'Louise, I am sorry. I should not have said what I did. It makes not a jot of difference to me who you are. I love you.'

'You *love* me?' she echoed.

'Yes. I thought you must have guessed.'

'Why? Because you kissed me? Kisses mean

nothing. No doubt you kiss your mistress,' she retorted, thinking that's what he wanted her to become.

'No!' he almost shouted it. And then he took her face in his hands and put his lips to hers in a kiss that was searing in its intensity.

She stood passively, determined not to react, though it was taking every bit of will-power she possessed. If it had been a tender kiss, she could not have succeeded, but it was hard and demanding, the kiss of a man used to having his own way and not liking it when he was thwarted. Realising he had compounded his error, he drew back, his breath coming in jerky gasps. 'Oh, God, Louise, I am so very, very sorry. Please forgive me.'

She did not answer, but turned away and began walking quickly down the road, almost stumbling in her haste. He followed a few paces behind her. Once at the inn, she went up to her room and slammed the door behind her. He stood outside a moment, then turned away. She heard him go and collapsed on the bed in a paroxysm of weeping. And the person she wanted most at the moment was her mama, far away in Chipping Barnet.

Chapter Ten

She did not leave her room any more that day. No one came to her. What Jonathan told everybody she had no idea, probably that she had the headache. And that was true enough. Her head whirred and thumped, her thoughts tying themselves into knots as she tried to make sense of what had happened. She wished she had never come on this ill-fated expedition. It had been ill thought out and unkind to her mama and papa and her brothers, especially Luke. She had never meant to reject them, never meant to hurt them. If Mama were to walk through that door now, she would fling herself at her and beg forgiveness, cry in her arms as she had done when hurt as a child, and be comforted.

Here there was no comfort, not even from Jonathan. He had kissed her, said he loved her, but he could say things like that to a mistress, his *jolie femme*, and probably mean them at the time. Young gentlemen did. She was not his *jolie femme*, not his anything. And her heart was breaking. Compared to that, her curiosity about her birth dwindled almost to nothing.

She emerged from her room next morning, pale, bleary-eyed with weeping, but resolute. She went down to breakfast some time after Betty. The girl had been inordinately cheerful. She had not seemed to notice how quiet Louise was as she chatted away in her usual inconsequential way about the fair and the dancing and how clever Joe was. By the time Louise had dressed and made her way to the dining parlour, Betty and Joe had finished their meal and gone out to feed and water the horses. Jonathan was still sitting at the table, an empty plate and an empty cup in front of him. He appeared to be brooding.

She sat down opposite him and began slowly spreading butter on a piece of bread. He looked across at her, trying to gauge her mood. Was she still angry with him? He smiled. 'Good morning, Louise.'

'I want to go home,' she said flatly.

'Home?' he asked in surprise. 'You mean Chipping Barnet?'

'I have no other home. You did say you would take me, though if you would rather not...' She left the end of the sentence in the air.

'Of course I will take you. Have I not said so all along? Does that mean you are not proceeding with your enquiries?'

'There does not seem much point in going on, does there?'

'None at all,' he said cheerfully. 'I do not care one jot who you are, who gave you birth, it is all one to me.'

'I know that.'

'You misunderstand. Let me finish. I do not care because that is all in the past and my concern is for the future, for your happiness and incidentally mine, which is inextricably linked with it.' He reached out and put his hand over hers. 'I love you, Louise Vail. You are everything to me, the air I breathe, my sustenance, never out of my thoughts. My head and my heart are yours and without you, they will shrivel and die. I realised that when you were stuck on that ledge. I imagined you tumbling over, dying on the rocks and I knew, whoever you were or whatever you were, I could not live without you.'

His words were so tenderly uttered, they set the tears running down her face again, silent tears of despair. She should have been happy, overjoyed at his declaration, but she knew how foolish that would be. She must harden her heart and not be swayed. 'You want me for your mistress,' she said flatly. 'You want to set me up somewhere discreet and visit me when you can spare the time from your wife and family.' The tears dried up, her emotion a spent force. 'I will tell you here and now, I will not have it. If I have to die a wrinkled old maid, then so be it.'

He had known when all that unnatural energy was used up, she would be exhausted and listless and that was exactly as she appeared. He could have wept for her. But what she was saying was far from what he had meant. 'No, you are not listening to me. I want you for my wife. I need no one else.'

She stared at him, uncomprehending. 'I do not understand.'

'I cannot put it any plainer, but I have been clumsy and careless of your sensibilities. Of course you wish to have it done properly, every young lady does. Let me make amends.' He sank to his knees at her feet, and took both her hands in his. 'Miss Vail, I love you, I can think of nothing that would give me greater happiness than you should become my wife. Will you do me the inestimable honour of consenting to marry me?'

She stared at him, her lovely eyes expressing her delight, then just as quickly a veil came over them, shutting out the pleasure, as the true implications of what he had said came to her. 'You can't mean that.'

'But I do.' She did love him; he had seen it fleetingly in those speaking eyes, and he would not allow her to deny it. 'I would not have said it otherwise. And you love me too, don't you?'

'It is impossible, you know that. Madness.'

'Why is it impossible? Are you saying you do not love me?'

'I...' She could not go on, could not deny it. She sighed. 'That is not the point.'

'Of course it is. If we love each other what is there to stand in our way? I am single and you are single, there is no impediment that I can think of.'

'I can think of dozens.'

'Name one.'

'You do not know who I am. Even I do not. You are a Viscount. You must marry one of your own kind. If you married me, society would condemn you. We would be ostracised. Your family would never accept me, especially when they learned the truth about my birth. I would not want to be the cause of rift between you and your parents.'

He had told himself the same thing a hundred times, but it made no difference. 'Society can go hang and my parents will learn to love you as I do. Princess or pauper, I want to marry you and the only person who could prevent that is you. I love you. I beg you to consider becoming my wife.'

'But we met less than four weeks ago and part of that time I was pretending to be a man...'

'And a very fetching man you made, my darling. But it makes no difference. I could no more have stopped myself falling in love with you than stopped breathing. Tell me you feel the same.' He looked up at her from his position on his knees, searching her face. 'Tell me.'

'It is impossible,' she said again, shaking her head.

'Even if you find out you are not ill born? Would that make a difference?'

'I do not think so. In any case, I have come to the conclusion that no other explanation is possible. All I want to do is go home.' She smiled wanly. 'Do get up, Jonathan, you will dirty your breeches.'

He scrambled up and pulled up a chair to sit beside her and take her hand. 'Listen to me, sweetheart. We will go home whenever you are ready, back to the vicarage where you will tell the good people who have raised you that you are going to marry me and become Viscountess Leinster. And until that happens you are Louise Vail and your home will be with the Reverend and Mrs Vail, your mother and father.'

'You will change your mind,' she said. 'As soon as we get back to civilisation, you will see how foolish you are being.'

'I shall not.'

'I shall not hold you to it.'

He gave up for the moment. He still had one card up his sleeve. But at least she now knew how he felt, knew it had nothing to do with what she was, with her birth, and everything to do with who she was now, and they had two hundred miles of travel for him to persuade her to think about it.

She was already thinking about it. All those miles behind her and nothing achieved except a great deal more heartache, all those miles ahead of her in the company of the dearest of all men, all of them exquisite torture. But she did not think she could undertake them with only Betty for company. The intrepid madcap had vanished, somewhere around Doncaster.

'If you can be ready we will set off tomorrow, after breakfast,' he said. 'I will alert Joe to have the carriage and horses ready.'

'Not today?'

'It is nearly noon. A little late to make a start.'

'We could go as far as York.'

He sighed and stood up. 'So we could. Perhaps you should start packing then. I shall go and find Joe. Goodness knows where he and Betty have got to.'

He left her climbing the stairs and went out to the stables, hoping Joe had taken Betty off somewhere that would delay their departure for an hour or two. He had hoped the summons from Moresdale Hall would have come by now. He had not bargained on Louise suddenly abandoning everything and demanding to be taken home. He was not sure whether to be glad or sorry. Would she change her mind again?

He was halfway across the yard when he saw the Countess's coach stop in the road and Hamish jump down. He walked over to meet him.

'The Countess would like Miss Vail to call on her,' the big man said. 'I have brought the carriage.'

'I will fetch her.' He left Hamish in the yard while he went inside to find Louise.

She had heard the coach pull up and looked out of the window, expecting it to be Jonathan's carriage with Joe on the box, ready to start their journey, annoyed with Betty for leaving her to do all the packing. She was so immersed in her conversation with Jonathan, the pleasure at his declaration, followed swiftly by a return to sanity, that she did not consider Joe could not have harnessed the horses so quickly. When she saw who it was her heart began to thump uncomfortably in her breast.

She ventured out on to the landing. Jonathan was just mounting the stairs. He looked up. 'The Dowager Countess wishes to see you,' he said.

'I…I can't go.'

'Of course you can. It is what you have wanted all along. I will go with you, if you like.'

'No,' she said, suddenly resolute. 'I will go alone. Oh, but I must change my dress and arrange my hair. I cannot go like this.' She looked down at the simple muslin.

'Wear the green,' he said. 'Shall I fetch Betty to do your hair?'

'No, I can manage it. Will you ask Mr Mackay if he would mind waiting a few minutes?'

She went back into her room and stood in the middle of the floor, gazing into space, trying to still the shaking of her limbs. Her ladyship had sent for her. That must mean she knew who she was, knew where she was staying. And why. She might be going to find out the truth at last. On the other hand, she might be told to go away and stop probing what did not concern her.

She moved at last, dragged the green dress from her portmanteau where she had folded it not five minutes before, shook it out and put it on, fumbling with the lacing on her stays. She was struggling with them when there was a light knock at the door and Jonathan entered. He strode across to her, took the laces from her hands and deftly tied them for her, before fastening her bodice and draping a gauze kerchief round her neck, tucking the ends into her décolletage. She shivered as his fingers touched her bare skin, felt the prickling sensation go right down her body where it lodged somewhere in her groin. Seemingly unaware of what he had done, he picked up her hair brush. 'Sit down,' he commanded. 'You will be all day if someone does not take you in hand.'

She was too bewildered to do anything but obey. He stood behind her and brushed her hair in long steady strokes. 'I shall do this often when we are married,' he said calmly.

She did not answer, but the brush strokes were soothing her, which is what he had intended. He stopped. Taking a handful of hair, he twisted it up on top of her head. 'How do you hold it there?'

She laughed suddenly and took over herself, putting pins and combs into the creation and setting a wide-brimmed hat at an angle on top, tying it with green ribbon. 'Beautiful,' he murmured from behind her. Then he bent and kissed the back of her neck. She stood up and faced him, her neck still feeling the pressure of his lips. She tried and failed to ignore it. 'Will I do?'

'You will more than do. Now, off you go. I shall be here when you return.'

He opened the door and ushered her down the stairs and out to the carriage where he handed her in with all the aplomb of a courtier. He shut the door, Hamish sprang up on to the step, the driver flicked the reins and they were away. Jonathan watched the vehicle until it disappeared around a bend in the road, then he went inside to try to contain his impatience for her return by making plans and writing letters.

So much for his determination to think carefully before venturing into marriage, he told himself wryly. When you fell in love, wholeheartedly and without reservation, all the thinking in the world would not avail you. But it was a wonderful, pleasurable feeling, or it would be if she would only see how right it was. Even when she agreed, and he prayed she would, they would still have obstacles to overcome—she had been right about that—but they would be overcome, on that he was determined

The carriage turned into the open gates of Moresdale Hall and stopped while Hamish went back to shut them again, then they proceeded up the gloomy tunnel of trees, until they reached the house. Louise sat forwards to catch a first glimpse of it. It had an imposing frontage of stone, probably quarried locally. It had a round tower at each end and a balustrade running along the roof from one to the other. Climbing plants had been allowed to run riot over it walls so that they almost blocked the windows. The paint on these was flaking. A space had been cleared in front of the door for the carriage to be able to turn round, but the rest of the garden was a wilderness of overgrown plants, twining round each other, choking each other, the strongest forcing out the weakest. It had once been a lovely house, Louise concluded, and felt sorry that it should be so neglected.

The carriage stopped outside the door. Hamish Mackay jumped down to hand her out of the carriage. His expression was immutable, showing no sign of the antagonism he had shown when they met before. Neither was it welcoming. He went before her and opened the heavy door. There was no sign of a footman. 'Please follow me.'

He led her down a corridor, past several shut doors, and up a wide carved oak staircase to a galleried upper floor. Louise looked upwards.

The well of the stairs went up two more floor to a domed roof, beautifully carved, though hung with cobwebs. Her guide stopped outside a door and knocked gently.

'You may come in.'

He pushed the door open and ushered Louise before him into a small sitting room where the Dowager sat near the window. The room was at the side of the building facing south and there were no trees close to the house on that side, because it was bathed in sunshine: a light, airy, comfortable room. It was the first thing Louise noticed as she moved forwards and curtsied to the old lady.

She did not realise the big man was still behind her until her ladyship spoke to him. 'Ask Jane to bring us some tea and cakes, Hamish.' Then she turned to Louise and pointed to a stool at her feet. 'Sit down, child, where I can see you.'

Louise obeyed and waited, surreptitiously taking in the old lady's appearance. She wore a purple silk gown with wide panniers, its bodice fastened to a pink quilted stomacher. Its neck and sleeves were trimmed with lace. The voluminous gown somehow made her look even smaller than she was, though she sat regally upright. Her face was lined, but her pale blue eyes were bright and intelligent. Louise guessed they missed nothing of what went on around her.

'So, you are Louise Vail,' she said at last, looking her up and down, her gaze coming to rest on Louise's face.

'Yes, my lady.'

'I should have known you anywhere. You have that look about you. And the eyes—yes, the eyes give you away. Tell me about yourself. Have you had a happy childhood?'

Louise was full of questions herself, but endeavoured to answer politely. She told of her contented childhood, her parents and brothers, her schooling and how she helped her mother with parish duties. She paused awkwardly when it came to speaking of the reason for her arrival in Moresdale. She was given a reprieve by the arrival of a maidservant with a tea tray containing a caddy, a teapot, a boiling kettle and two cups on saucers.

The Dowager sent the maid away and busied herself making the tea. Louise watched her silently, trying to gather her thoughts, wondering if the old lady would ever get around to telling her why she had sent for her. Only when she had poured the tea and handed a cup to Louise, did she speak.

'I knew who you were the minute I set eyes on you when I arrived to open the fair,' she said. 'It was as if the young Catherine was back among us. I am old and the shock took my breath away. I could not stay and wander round the stalls as I meant to do. I asked Hamish to bring me home.'

'I did not mean to upset you,' Louise murmured, taking a sip of tea to calm herself.

'Oh, but I believe you did. I was sure you had come to cause trouble…'

'No, my lady, I protest. That was never my intention.'

'I wanted you to go away, I did not want to speak to you. I told my man that if you called he was not to admit you.'

'Yes. I could not get past him and the dogs.'

'He is a good and loyal servant and always concerned for my welfare.' She smiled suddenly. 'I think he has always been a little in love with me and I am afraid I take advantage of that.'

'What made you change your mind—about seeing me, I mean?'

'Why, that pleasant young gentleman who came

to see me and persuaded me that you meant no harm, you were simply searching for the truth.'

'Young gentleman?' Louise queried. 'Do you mean Viscount Leinster?'

'Yes. He came and requested an interview yesterday afternoon. Oh, I knew he was in the village; someone as consequential as he is could not fail to be noticed. I could hardly turn away a Viscount, especially one whose family is as old as our own.'

'So you know why I came to Moresdale?' Louise said, vowing to have words with Jonathan when she saw him. He had no business to go behind her back, especially when she had told him she had to deal with her problem herself. She discounted the fact that she had signally failed to do so.

'Yes, I do.' The Countess paused. 'But I am not at all sure good will come of satisfying your curiosity.'

'It is not just curiosity,' Louise protested, refusing to be cowed. 'It is wanting to know who I am, who gave me birth, why I was given away. That is something I cannot understand.'

'And what do you hope to gain by having such information?'

'Gain?' she queried, mystified. 'Knowledge, I suppose.'

'Knowledge is power.'

'Oh, no, my lady, you misunderstand me. I am not seeking power, not asking for anything. I do not want money or consequence. I simply need to know…' She stopped. She could not bring herself to mention her fear that she was illegitimate.

'What have you been told? I gather from Viscount Leinster that you have only recently been made aware that you were adopted.'

'Yes.'

'It must have come as a shock.' She picked up a plate of little cakes. 'Do have one. Jane is a very good cook and rarely has the opportunity to display her talent.'

Louise shook her head. 'They look delicious, my lady, but I am not at all hungry.'

'Naturally you want to know the story,' the old lady went on, putting the plate down again.

'Please.'

'You cannot see Catherine. She is not here. And I do not think I could allow it, if she were. She is not well, you see.'

'But she is my mother?'

'Oh, yes.'

'I heard a rumour…'

'That she committed suicide? Yes, I have heard it. There is nothing that goes on in the village that I do not hear about. The vicar and Hamish between them keep me well informed. She is in a sanatorium. And do not look so shocked, she is not mad, not in the sense that some would have us believe. Her illness is entirely due to what happened to Thomas.'

'I am very sorry. I have a memory of seeing the little boy once, in church, when my father was the incumbent. I must have been about five years old, the same age as he was.'

'To the day,' the old lady added, her eyes taking on a faraway look as if she was back in that time and place.

'We were twins?'

'Bless you, no.' She paused and drained the tea from her cup before going on. 'I see I shall have to tell you the whole story.'

Louise, who was more confused than ever, simply nodded.

'I was not living here at the time,' she said. 'Or I would never have allowed it to happen. I learned it later, much later, when Thomas died so tragically. I came to the funeral and stayed to help Catherine because she did not seem able to pull herself together. And Augustus, that's my son, the Earl, was even more affected and he took himself off to London, unable to bear his loss.'

'I am sorry,' Louise murmured. 'It must have been a dreadful time for everyone.'

'Yes, everyone. The vicar and his wife and the whole village were brought down by it. Thomas was a popular little boy. Now, do not interrupt me again, or I shall never get it done.'

Louise sat obediently and listened, the rapidly cooling tea forgotten.

'Catherine had been trying for a baby ever since she mar-ried. She desperately wanted to be a mother and of course Augustus was anxious for a son and heir. She had miscarriage after miscarriage, but no live babies. Every time she lost one, and there were boys among them, she wept uncontrollably for days. I am afraid my son blamed her; he said she must be doing something wrong, it was obviously not his fault because she had managed to conceive. Each time he called in the best doctors who kept close watch on what she was doing. They made her rest, did not allow her to pick up so much as a teapot. But still the babies died, sometimes very early in the pregnancy, but twice she carried to full term, only for the infant to be born dead.

'Their marriage, begun so happily, was falling apart. Augustus spent more and more time away from home, and when he did return, he was so frustrated, their relationship became one of duty, no more. He felt it was his duty to continue to try for an heir and it was her duty to succumb, but she was becoming frail with the constant pregnancies that came to nothing.' She held up her hand, when it seemed that Louise was about to interrupt. 'You can understand my son. It is important for a man of his rank to have an heir. He talked of divorcing her and marrying someone who could give him the son he so badly wanted. And that was breaking Catherine's heart.

'Her pregnancies became fewer and further apart, but just when it seemed that her fertility was coming to an end and she was resigned to being childless and divorced, she became *enceinte* again. Everyone prayed she would take it to term and that it would be a boy. Augustus did not hold out much hope of it, but Catherine grew and was surprisingly well. The child kicked within her and suddenly she started to hope again. It was calculated that it was due to be born in the second week of January. Augustus stayed at home, intending to be in the house when the baby was born. Late in November, he had an urgent summons to London to do with his East India stocks and shares. He said he had to go, but he would be back in time for the birth and he trusted that this time she would be delivered of a live son. The consequences of not doing so, Catherine knew full well.

'That winter of 1739 to 40 was bitterly cold,' the Countess went on, after taking a sip of tea. 'The temperature did not rise above freezing the whole way through from December to February. The night of the twenty-ninth of December was particularly bad. There was a hard frost and a violent easterly gale, and then heavy snow, which drifted into great piles wherever it came against a solid object. The hills became blanketed in white, the roads were impassable. We knew Augustus could not get back, nor could the doctors he had engaged get through from York when Catherine went into early labour on the last day of the year. They could not even get a message to a wet nurse. The servants had to clear a path down to the village and fetch Mrs Hurst, the village handywoman

'The child, a healthy girl, was born on the first of January 1740. When Catherine realised she had borne a live child, heard it cry quite lustily, she was beside herself with joy. But then she was told it was a girl and she did not want to believe it, would not believe it, until Mrs Hurst put the infant in her arms. Then she pushed it away and wept so much she made herself ill. She knew that when her husband returned, he would be angry, and she had come to fear his anger. Mrs Hurst could not pacify her.

'In the middle of all this, a message arrived from the village that the midwife was needed at the vicarage. Mrs Vail, the vicar's wife, was about to give birth. Mrs Hurst left Catherine in the care of a maidservant and hurried back to the village.

'Catherine told me afterwards how miserable she had been, all her joy at giving birth to a live baby blown away and how resentful she felt of Mrs Vail who had three sons already and was longing for a little girl. She said as much to Mrs Hurst.' The old lady, thirsty from talking so much, sipped cold tea before going on. 'Mrs Vail had another boy, her fourth—'

'*What*?' Louise interrupted her.

'Yes.' There was a long pause. 'If I had been there I would never have allowed it,' she said again, almost to herself this time. 'If Augustus had got back in time, it would not have happened. If the doctors had arrived from York, they would have noted the circumstances of the birth and it could not have been done. As it was, Mrs Hurst persuaded Mrs Vail to exchange the babies. How she did it, I do not know, except that Mrs Vail so wanted a little girl. It was done with the best of intentions. The vicar himself was not at home at the time; he was attending the deathbed of a parishioner in an outlying part of the village and could not get back because of the snow. No one need ever know.

'Mrs Hurst bundled the baby boy up in warm blankets and brought him here to the Hall and then took the little girl to Mrs Vail. No one knew anything of this except the two mothers, the midwife and the maidservant.'

'I can't believe it!' Louise said, as the implication of what the Countess had said sank into her brain. 'Are you telling me…?'

'That you were that baby girl? Yes, I am.'

It was shocking, truly dreadful. Louise could not credit it. But why would her ladyship lie? She had not wanted to tell her at all. It was some time before she could speak. 'You mean I am the lawful daughter of the Earl of Moresdale and his wife?'

'Yes.' The old lady gave a twisted smile. 'You might have difficulty proving it. Mrs Hurst is long dead and the maid was paid a fortune to keep her mouth shut. I believe she left and went to serve a family going to live on the Continent. And it would mean denouncing the dear lady who has brought you up. Do you want to do that to her?'

'No, of course I do not. I never would.' She was beginning to regret telling Jonathan not to accompany her. She would have given anything at that moment to be able to reach out for his hand and derive comfort from it. 'But that is not the end of the story, is it?'

'No. Do you wish me to go on?'

'Yes, please.'

'My son returned as soon as the roads were cleared and he was ecstatic with joy to find his wife with a beautiful son. He was christened Thomas and the whole village rejoiced.'

'I wonder what Mama was thinking at that time?' Louise said aloud. 'And Papa.'

'I cannot speak for them, you will have to ask them yourself. But as far as I know they were happy with their daughter, as my son was with his heir. He doted on him. They became a completely happy family. The child thrived… Both children did. Until…' Her eyes clouded over and she felt reluctant to go on.

'Until?' Louise prompted.

'Until Thomas died in a tragic accident at the age of five. Augustus went out of his mind with grief. He blamed Catherine and, though he is my son, I must be honest and say he treated her cruelly. She was convinced it was a visitation of God for her deception. She became wild and hysterical and took to drinking to ease her pain. Augustus sent for me to try to calm her and I came at once. I have never left since.'

'Poor Mama,' Louise murmured, but she was not thinking of the Countess when she said it. The vicarage must have been a very unhappy place at that time too because she did not think her mother would ever be able to forget she had given birth to the little boy.

'Catherine went up Moresdale Hill and stood poised to jump off where Thomas had fallen to his death, but Hamish, who always accompanied me wherever I went, followed her and dragged her to safety and carried her home. It was then she told me the story. She was determined to confess all to her husband; she wanted to try and take you back. I begged her not to do so. It would not mend anything; Augustus would undoubtedly punish her and reject you, and it would ruin other lives too. You could not be uprooted from a loving family to come and live here. This place was dark and cold with unimaginable grief; you would have been miserable. The deed had been done, it could not be undone. I told her she must never breathe a word of it to a living soul.'

'Mama and Papa left Moresdale about that time,' Louise said.

'Yes. I advised the vicar to leave. Catherine had become used to seeing you about the village with your mama and I was afraid she might break down and grab you back.'

'Does the Earl know the truth now?'

'No. He never did and I pray he never will.'

'What happened to the Countess?' The woman was her mother, but she could not bring herself to call her that.

'She never really recovered her wits and began to drink more and more; guilt and misery and the strain of carrying that secret were too much for her. She had to be confined for her own safety. My son was afraid she might harm herself and he thought she would be better somewhere where she could be kept safe and where the peace and quiet would help her recover. Unfortunately that seems not to have happened, according to my son.'

'Poor lady.' Louise was entirely absorbed in the story.

'My son resides in London and rarely comes to Moresdale,' the old lady went on. 'I am left here alone to moulder away along with the building, trying to keep up appearances.' She paused and reached out to put a hand on Louise's arm. 'Now you know it all, I beg of you do not cause trouble or you may find yourself declared mad and in the same situation as Catherine.'

'I would not dream of it.' It was all too much to take in. She was relieved to know she was not illegitimate, that she was in fact the daughter of an Earl and his Countess, but as the old lady pointed out, it was a secret that could not be told. 'Does Viscount Leinster know?'

'No. His purpose in coming to me was to persuade me to see you. He asked no questions. Whether you tell him or not is up to you, but I beg of you, do not let it become common knowledge. No good can come of it.' The old lady was exhausted from telling her tale, but she managed a wan smile. 'I believe he wants to marry you.'

'He says he does.'

'What about you?'

'I love him dearly but he will be making a huge sacrifice to marry me and I cannot allow him to do it.'

'I think you should let him be the judge of that. As your grandmother, I give you my blessing.'

'Grandmother,' Louise repeated in wonder. 'So you are. I never thought of that.'

'Grandmother for a day only. You must go away and never come back,' the old lady insisted.

'I am sorry for that. I am glad I met you. I only wish I could have met the Countess.'

'It is for the best, child. Meeting you would throw her back into the abyss.'

Louise sat on, unable to take it all in. She found

herself thinking of her adopted mother and how she must have felt at losing her son in that horrible way and yet she had still looked after Louise and loved her as a daughter. Never, in all the years, had Louise ever felt unwanted.

'Now I am tired…' It was a clear dismissal.

As Louise rose to go, Hamish returned. Louise was surprised; the old lady had not rung a bell and perhaps the servant had been listening at the door. Louise hoped he was as discreet and faithful as the Countess believed him to be. He walked over to the Countess and bent to whisper something in her ear. He seemed agitated, which he had never been before, and he glanced at Louise as he spoke.

Listening, the old lady looked shocked. She was shaking as she rose and picked up a walking stick, but her voice, when she spoke, was steady. 'I have to go. Hamish will take you back.'

'There is no need. I can easily walk. I need to think.'

'Very well. Hamish, wait two minutes after I have gone, then take Miss Vail to the gate, then come back to me.'

'Yes, my lady.' He looked doubtful. 'You will be all right?'

'Of course I will. You are too fussy. Goodbye, Miss Vail.' She walked slowly out of the room.

Although Louise rose, ready to leave, Hamish obeyed his employer to the letter and stood, doing nothing but allow the two minutes to pass. Then he said, 'Follow me, Miss Vail.'

He took her back along the corridor and down the stairs, walking slowly and sedately with Louise behind him in a dream. It must surely be a dream? It was too bizarre to be real. Never in her wildest imagination, and there had been theories enough, had she imagined anything like this.

They were on the ground floor, passing the closed doors, but one was not properly shut and the dowager's voice drifted out to her. 'Catherine, what are you doing here? Does Augustus know?'

And then she heard the quiet reply, 'He is dead, Mama. Of a heart attack. It is all over. I am free.'

Louise stumbled and would have stopped, but Hamish turned and glared at her, waiting for her to keep up with him. She could not turn aside; he would have physically stopped her if she had. He took her down the drive under its dark canopy of trees, to the gate, watched her pass through, then shut it after her. She was alone on the road.

Slowly, on leaden feet, she began to walk down the hill to the village, trying to think what the revelation could mean to her. Everything had changed and yet nothing had. She had asked how a mother could give away a child, meaning herself, but she had not been the only one given away. There was Thomas. She wondered what would have happened had he grown up and then learned the truth. What would the Earl have done? What would her parents have done? When had Papa learned the truth? Knowing how close they were, she sup-posed her mother could not keep it from him. How had he reacted? He was a parson, committed to the truth. He would have been appalled. But he had ultimately accepted the situation and been a good father to her. She was still the adopted daughter of the Reverend Vail and his wife, still too lowly to be considered a suitable wife for Viscount Leinster. Knowing she came of noble birth could make no difference, because it could not be told.

Her steps quickened and then became faster and faster until she was running, tumbling down the hill, almost falling over her own feet. Her hat fell off down her back and the pins came out of her hair, so that it tumbled about her shoulders.

The village green was deserted except for some children playing with a mongrel dog. She sped across it and into the church where she sank on to her knees at the back and prayed as she had never prayed before. She prayed for understanding, for the humility to accept what she had learned about herself, for the strength to go back to Chipping Barnet and face her mother, for the courage to reject Jonathan if he asked her to marry him again.

Chapter Eleven

Jonathan, leaning against a tree idly watching the children, saw her mad dash and followed her. He stood at the back of the church watching her prostrate herself and his heart went out to her. Whatever she had learned had not filled her with joy; it was up to him to convince her it did not matter. He waited patiently until she crossed herself and rose to her feet. She turned and saw him.

He smiled, holding out both hands to her. She hesitated and then walked slowly towards him. She did not return his smile, nor did she take his hands. 'Was it so very bad?' he asked quietly, dropping his arms to his side.

She did not answer that. 'You asked the Countess to see me. You went behind my back. Did you think she would tell you the truth and not me?'

'No. I did not ask for explanations. I asked her to consider talking to you because I knew how important it was to you. You vowed not to give up and go home until you had spoken to her.'

'I changed my mind.'

'I did not know you were going to do that yesterday when I spoke to her.'

'No, but all the same…' She stopped; it was unfair of her to take her unhappiness out on him. 'Oh, it does not matter now.'

'What happened? What did she say?'

'I cannot tell you.'

'Then do not. It does not make the slightest difference to me.'

She gave a harsh laugh. 'Oh, it is not what you think.'

'What, then?'

'It is not who I am or what I am that has upset me so much as what they did, the way they ordered their children's lives, as if they were animals to be bartered and not human beings. I find that impossible to comprehend.'

He pulled her down beside him into a pew. 'Who are they?'

'The Countess and my adoptive mother, and the nurse too…'

In spite of himself, he was intrigued. 'I think now you have started, you had better go on.' It was said quietly, but it was an instruction none the less, almost an order. 'I will not tell another soul unless you give me leave.'

'The Dowager said it was up to me whether I told you, but she does not want it noised abroad. Too many people would be hurt.'

'I am listening. I will say nothing.'

Bit by bit he dragged the story out of her, prompting her when she stumbled. At first she was dry-eyed, but as she related how the babies were changed, the tears began to flow. He put his arm about her shoulders and held her close, kissing the top of her head. She hardly seemed to notice, so involved was she in her tale. In any case he did not know what to say. He was almost as surprised as she had been and was too concerned with how she must be feeling to analyse his own reaction. It was a minute or two before he felt the relief of learning she was not a bastard. She was a true-born gentlewoman, and his marriage to her would be acceptable—more than acceptable, would be received with joy and satisfaction among relations and friends—but this was quickly followed by the realisation that the truth could not be made public. For one brief second, his heart sank, but it was only a tiny pause before he realised it did not make a jot of difference to him. He would marry her regardless.

He was tempted to repeat his proposal, but she was still too full of her interview with the Dowager and what she had been told to listen to what he had to say. It could keep. 'Are you ready to go home now?' he asked.

'Yes.' She looked up at him and smiled wanly through her tears. 'There is so much I want to ask Mama. About Thomas and why she agreed to the exchange. He lived for five years, five years when she would often have seen him about the village with the Countess or his nurses and certainly in church every Sunday. How could she bear it?'

'She had you.'

'Yes, and I suppose the same applied to the Countess—she had Thomas. At least at first. I am finding it very difficult to grasp any of it.'

'I can understand that, but it was done and there is no undoing it.' He paused. 'You do not want to try and undo it, do you?'

'No, it is much too late. It was too late on the

day I was born. It was certainly too late when Thomas died. Poor little boy.'

'He wasn't poor, Louise. He had everything a child could wish for and his death was a tragic accident, due perhaps to his adventurous nature and the negligence of those who should have been looking after him.'

'Yes, you are right, but I think I had the best of the bargain, don't you?'

'Undoubtedly,' he said, standing up and taking her hand to pull her to her feet. 'Let us go back to the Shepherd's Crook. Tomorrow we begin our journey south. It is too late to make a start tonight.'

Hand in hand they left the church and walked towards the gate. They were halfway when he led her off the path and across the grass to a monument, which he had seen earlier while waiting for her. He did not speak, but stopped in front of it. It was elaborately carved with cherubs and wreaths. Louise read the inscription. 'In loving and abiding memory of Thomas Augustus Fellowes, Viscount Thirsk, only son of the Earl and Countess of Moresdale, taken to rest on the 10th of March 1745, aged 5 years. RIP.'

'Better that he never knew,' she murmured, crossing herself. 'We must leave him in peace.'

Together they turned and walked away.

After supper that evening, Betty went with Joe to help look after the horses, though how much of that she did and how much time was spent watching him work and then enjoying his kisses in the room above, no one but they knew. It was still daylight and the air was balmy; Jonathan took Louise for a walk up the hill behind the inn.

They stopped and sat on the rock where they had rested before when she told him the true reason for her journey. So much had happened, it was impossible to believe it was only three evenings ago. And the wonder of it was he had not condemned her, nor her parents, nor the Countess. But he was not the one in turmoil, not any more. His doubts had been resolved.

'Darling,' he said, taking both her hands in his. 'Yesterday when I asked you to marry me, I did not know the truth, but I wanted you to know how I felt about you no matter what you discovered. Today I feel no different. I am still determined to make you my wife.'

'Even if you cannot tell your parents who I really am?'

'Louise, I am twenty-five years old and of independent means. I am perfectly able to choose a wife for myself and the wife I have chosen is you. And I am convinced when they meet you and get to know you, they will love you as I do.' He took her in his arms and kissed her tenderly, starting with her forehead and then her nose and then her cheeks, one at a time, and then her lips. It was nothing like his previous kisses, the one short, with no pressure to speak of, the other fierce and demanding. These kisses were gentle but persuasive. He put all his love, all his hopes, all his passion into them, murmuring her name, telling her how much he adored her, until she really began to believe it.

'Oh, Jonathan, do you think it is possible?'

'Possible?' He laughed, playing with her fingers. 'More than possible. A certainty.'

She was still doubtful. Nothing had really changed. She was still Louise Vail, still, according to the world, the daughter of a parson. 'I am afraid…'

'Afraid, Louise? You, my intrepid adversary, are afraid? What is there to be afraid of? Do you think my love will not last?' He paused. 'Shall I tell you something?'

'Go on.'

'No one would think it to look at them, but my parents' marriage has been far from happy. My father has had a string of mistresses and my mother has had lovers. And my sister is married to a brute who beats her and yet she will not leave him. Marriage should not be like that. It put me off and I vowed to think long and hard before venturing into it.' He gave her a rueful grin. 'And what do I do? In the space of a se'nnight, I fall headlong in love with a madcap of a girl who is half-convinced she should have been a man.'

'I am not,' she protested. 'I never thought that!'

'That is just as well, for you are far too beautiful to be a boy and you have curves where boys should not have curves.' He stroked his finger down over her cheek, down her throat and across the top of her stays, sending shivers of delight through her body. 'But that is by the bye. What I am trying to say is that, when it came to it, I did not need to think because I knew. I knew as night follows day that no other woman would do for me. It is you or no one.'

She laughed. 'Oh, Jonathan, I should hate to condemn you to the life of a lonely bachelor.'

His eyes lit up. 'Is that a yes? You do love me and you will marry me?'

'Yes, I do love you and I will marry you.'

He let out a huge breath of relief. 'Thank the good Lord. I do not know what I would have done if you had refused me again.'

He put his arm about her shoulder and with his other hand took her chin and turned her face towards him. He had never seen those extraordinary eyes look so bright. He bent to kiss her lips. She put her arms about his neck and kissed him back, finding it hard to believe it would all come right for her. There were still questions she needed to ask, but the answers were back in Chipping Barnet. And it did not matter now. She had Jonathan and she would soon have a new name, one which was truly hers.

'If we are going to spend another week or more travelling together, I am going to find it almost impossible to maintain even a pretence of being a gentleman,' he told her, when he stopped for breath. 'For the sake of your reputation and my sanity, we ought to be married first.'

'But how can we do that? There is a new law

about having one's intention to marry read out in church for three consecutive weeks before the ceremony.'

'I know that, but a special licence can be obtained from a bishop. York has an archbishop. If he agrees to marry us, no one dare say anything against it.'

'But I always wanted my father to marry me, and my family all about me. And my friends. I do not want it to be a hole-in-the-corner affair...'

'I understand, my darling. We can have a quiet ceremony in York to make it all legal and then have another service and a wedding breakfast when we get back and invite everyone. We can write and tell our respective parents so that they know what is happening.'

She laughed. 'And give them time to get over the shock before we arrive.'

'If you like.' He did not say how much of a shock it was going to be to his parents; it would only spoil her joy. And there was no need. Once they had established their own household and everyone realised how well he had chosen and how happy they were, Louise would be accepted and loved, he was sure of that. 'We can take our time going back, make it a wedding trip to remember. All those places we visited on the way up will seem very different when we go back as husband and wife. Viscount Leinster and his Viscountess.'

She laughed suddenly and joyfully. 'I will wager the Piccadilly Gentleman's Club did not expect you to marry the object of your investigation when they sent you after me.'

He laughed too. 'That is only because they did not know you. I will invite them to our celebration and you will meet them all. You will like them, I know.'

'If they are all like you, I am sure I shall.'

'Come, sweetheart,' he said, 'the evening is growing chill. Back to the Shepherd's Crook for our last night.'

They met Joe and Betty crossing the yard and went into the inn together. Jonathan called for a bottle of their best wine and some glasses. 'We have something to celebrate,' he told their host. 'Will you join us?'

The drinks were poured and Jonathan raised his glass. 'You may congratulate me. Miss Vail has consented to become my wife…'

'I thought you were the lady's guardian,' Mrs Winter said, half-disapproving.

'There is no law that says a guardian may not wed his ward, Mrs Winter. We are both single and not so far apart in age and the guardianship was only temporary while Miss Vail was travelling. Her parents asked it of me.'

The good lady smiled broadly. 'No doubt they guessed the outcome.' She raised her own glass. 'I drink to you both. May you always be as happy as you are today.'

'I am sure I shall be.' He looked at Louise, smiling conspiratorially. 'We intend to marry in York, the day after tomorrow.'

There were congratulations and toasts and much laughter, culminating in the news that Joe had proposed to Betty and been accepted. She could not wait to go back to Chipping Barnet to tell Alfred and arrange her own wedding.

'We shall make a start tomorrow,' Jonathan said.

Tomorrow they were leaving Moresdale, probably for ever, but Louise would remember it for so many reasons. The astonishing revelations, the sadness at what she had learned, Moresdale Hall and the church, the memory of the little boy and his grave, still so large in her mind, but in years to come it would be remembered as the place where Jonathan had proposed and a whole new chapter in her life had begun. Her only regret was that she had to leave without meeting the mother who had given her birth. But she must respect what the Dowager had told her and not make her presence felt.

She went to bed and fell asleep with Jonathan's kisses tasting sweet on her lips.

She was woken by the sun shining through the window of her room and the birds twittering in the eaves. It was a moment or two before she recalled the events of the day before and went over them in her mind, every word the Countess had told her, Jonathan's understanding and his proposal. Had she really accepted him? She slipped from her bed, leaving Betty snoring as usual, dressed quickly in her blue gown, tied a hat over her loosely brushed hair and went downstairs. No one was about and there was still some time before they had to leave.

For some reason she could not explain, she felt drawn back to Moresdale and a last look at the village, nestling in its valley. She would go there once more before she left, and then she would go home and make her peace with her mother. The past could not be undone and she had so much to look forward to. Could Jonathan really obtain a licence to marry at once? She smiled as she walked; he seemed able to get his own way in most things.

As she drew near the village, she heard the church bell tolling a single mournful note and saw little groups of people gathering to talk in whispers. At the gate to the churchyard she met the vicar. 'What is happening?' she asked him.

'The Earl of Moresdale is dead,' he said. 'He died over a week ago and has already been buried in London, but the news has only just reached the village. It is a sad day for Moresdale and no heir to take over.'

'I am sorry.'

'I am going to the Hall to offer my condolences to his wife and mother and arrange a service in his memory.'

She watched as he tipped his hat to her and hurried off towards the Hall, while the mourning bell still tolled. It was hard to comprehend that the Earl of Moresdale was her true father. She had never known him and did not feel the loss. But she could not help recalling Catherine's voice saying, 'He is dead, Mama. It is all over. I am free.' It had held a note of quiet relief, as if the death meant that she could leave wherever she had been confined and come home.

Still musing, she was not paying attention to where her feet were taking her and was surprised to find herself on the path on Moresdale Hill and climbing. She did not want to go back to the Shepherd's Crook that way—it meant passing the place where Thomas had fallen to his death. Thomas Vail as he really was. In spite of that she felt drawn to the spot and continued upwards. She had almost reached it when she met a lone figure coming towards her. It was a woman in her mid-fifties, perhaps a little older, dressed in a black cloak with a hood pulled over her hair, but what Louise could see of it was a rich chestnut brown, rather like her own. She was thin and very pale.

The path was narrow at that point and as they passed, they both paused to look at each other. Hazel eyes, flecked with green, looked into hazel eyes flecked with green. There was a quiet moment of recognition between them, the exchange of a faint smile, and then they passed each other and went on without speaking. To have done so would have opened floodgates of emotion, and upset everyone: Catherine's fragile mental health and Louise's adoptive parents' good name. Better to let the matter rest.

Louise carried on to the ledge. There was no detaining hand today; it was calm, the slight breeze cool on her cheeks. She stood and looked down at the drop, unafraid now. It was about fifty feet. She looked up at the sky, a clear cobalt blue, with two or three fluffy white clouds floating by. 'You are up there, aren't you, Thomas?' she murmured. 'Looking down at me and wondering… I may not have known you well in life, but I feel as though I know you now. May you rest in peace.' She turned and retraced her steps. There was no sign of the Countess; she probably knew another way to reach the Hall from the hill. Louise surmised she had also been paying her last respects to the child she had nurtured. She hoped she could be at peace now.

Back in the village, she met Jonathan who had heard the bell tolling as he set out to look for her. He had heard the news about the Earl, but having heard Louise's account of what happened at the Hall the day before, he was not surprised. 'I thought I might find you here,' he said.

'Have all your goodbyes been said? You are not planning to stay?'

Full of her encounter with her mother, she smiled. 'No, I am not planning to stay. Let us go home.' Delighted, he hugged her and they walked back to where Joe and Betty were waiting with the carriage, ready to depart.

It took ten days to return to the vicarage, ten days in which the Viscount and his new Viscountess enjoyed every minute. They retraced some of the steps they had taken on the way, visited Mr and Mrs Slater to tell them their news, explored the countryside, planned how many children they might have, all of whom, boys and girls, would be loved and nurtured. 'My father's estate includes a house and a small parcel of land some five miles distant, which has always been the home of the heir,' he told her. 'I have never used it, but now I think I must take an interest in the running of the estate. My father has been urging me to do so, for some time. Would you like that?'

'Whatever makes you happy will make me happy,' she said. 'But what about the Gentleman's Club? Shall you go on with that?'

'I can do both. James does. And they are re-cruiting others all the time. When there are more to take over, I can retire and spend my time with my family.'

'Is that what you want?'

'More than anything. But I should still like to be involved with law and order.'

'You could take your seat in the Lords and use your experience and influence there.'

'Yes, I could. But there is no hurry. I want to enjoy married life first.'

As they drew nearer Chipping Barnet, Louise became quiet, wondering what her mama and papa would have to say to her. 'I am nervous as a kitten,' she told Jonathan, lying in bed in his arms the morning after their last night on the road. She was contented and sated after a night of lovemaking, which was all she had ever dreamed lovemaking would be. Jonathan was gentle and caring, drawing her on to the heights of ecstasy, an explosive coming together that left her full of wonder and drowsy contentment. She could not have been happier. Except for that one little cloud. 'Will they forgive me? Will they condemn us?'

'Yes, to the first and, no, to the second,' he

said, springing out of bed. 'Come, sweetheart, the vicarage first and then Chaston Hall.'

'I am dreading meeting your parents. They will undoubtedly disapprove of me.'

He thought that was highly likely but he would not, for the world, have said so. 'Of course they will not. They have been telling me for years to find myself a wife and, now I have, they will be pleased.'

'Pleased with a vicar's daughter?'

'Why not?'

'Rank and family are important to them. Now if I had been—'

'Louise, we promised ourselves we would not think of that. You are you and all I want in a wife. Only…'

'Only what?' she asked, in alarm.

He laughed 'Do not, I beg you, tell them you dressed as a man and fought a duel with me. You will give them apoplexy.'

And on that happy note, they set out on the last few miles of their journey, arriving at the vicarage in the early afternoon.

The whole family was there to greet them: Papa, Mama and all three brothers, Matthew and Mark with their children, and Luke given a day's holiday from his new curacy. Louise did not wait for the carriage door to be opened, but flung it open herself and jumped down, running to hug each one in turn. Jonathan followed her and stood quietly waiting until she should notice him again. 'Forgive me,' she said over and over again to each of them and was assured they did.

When she had embraced everyone, she turned and held out her hand to Jonathan, and he came quickly to her side. 'Mama, Papa, everyone, this is Jonathan, Viscount Leinster. My husband.'

Everyone made elaborate bows to him, which were reciprocated, and bade each other 'How do you do?' and then they all went inside where a sumptuous spread was laid out in the dining room. 'Come and eat,' Mrs Vail said, as Joe disappeared with Betty to find Alfred. 'Tell us all your news.'

Much of what had happened they would not recount, and it was evident only her mother and father and Luke knew the real reason for her sudden departure and it was put down as a sudden desire to see the place of her birth. She blessed them for their discretion and concentrated on the places she visited on the way, her stay with

Mrs Slater, the Moresdale Fair and Jonathan's proposal and her acceptance. 'The archbishop married us himself,' Louise said. 'Joe and Betty witnessed it.'

This led to talk of their plans for a second ceremony in the church and a wedding breakfast and the arrangements were discussed. 'Then we are going to live in Barnet,' Louise told everyone. 'And Jonathan is going to stay with the Piccadilly Gentleman's Club. At least to start with.'

It was later when Louise was alone with her mother in her old bedchamber, sitting together on the bed, that they talked about the reason for her journey. 'I am so very, very sorry I dashed off like that,' Louise said, hugging her. 'It must have broken your heart to be treated so badly.'

'I was hurt at first, but then I asked myself what I would have done if I had been you and I had to admit I might have done the same.'

'I didn't mean to eavesdrop,' Louise said. 'The window was open and I could not help hearing. I was so shocked, I didn't know what to do. I wanted to talk to you, but you had gone out and then I felt angry that you had kept the truth from me. You were always telling me what a madcap I was, and in this I proved you right, didn't I? Mad and impetuous. Please forgive me.'

'Of course I do.' Elizabeth paused. 'I did not like to ask in front of everyone else, but did you see Catherine? What did she tell you?'

'I only had one glimpse of her and we did not speak. I had an interview with the Dowager. She told me everything.'

'Then it is I should be asking forgiveness. I should not have kept the truth from you. I denied you your birthright.'

'Let us not apportion blame, Mama. I could not have been more loved and protected. I have not missed anything. Poor little Thomas had the worst of it.'

'Yes. I grieved for him, Louise, I really did, but I had the consolation of other sons and I had you. Catherine had nothing.'

'But why did you agree to the exchange in the first place?'

Elizabeth sighed. 'I cannot really explain why I did,' she said. 'I suppose I was still suffering the after-effects of the birth and not thinking clearly. And I had so wanted a daughter. The midwife was very persuasive and I knew Catherine would suffer dreadfully at the hands of her husband and so would you for not being the son he wanted. I regretted it the next day, but it was too late then. Your papa came back from attending his parishioner and he was so delighted with his daughter I could not bring myself to tell him what I had done.'

'When did he find out?' Louise supposed her mother was in the same situation as the Countess. The deed had been done; confession and changing back again was simply not possible.

'When Thomas died.' She stopped speaking, gathering her strength to go on. 'I was inconsolable, it was impossible to hide my distress, and your papa knew something was wrong, so I confessed what we had done and that Thomas had been his son.'

'He must have been shocked.'

'That was the least of it. He would not speak to me for days and spent hours on his knees in the church, but in the end he realised nothing could be gained by revealing the truth. Thomas was dead. He had always thought of you as his daughter and that would not change. He said he did not think the Earl would acknowledge you and it was best to leave him to his grief over

Thomas. But we could not stay in Moresdale, so he took the living at Chipping Barnet, telling everyone it was a preferment and being near London was more convenient to launch the boys into careers.'

'According to the Dowager, I am very like the Countess when she was my age.'

'Yes, you are.'

'Did you know her well?'

'Oh, yes, she is my cousin, our mothers were sisters, daughters of the Earl of Sheffield.'

'An Earl!' Louise exclaimed. 'You mean you are the granddaughter of an Earl?'

'Yes.'

'Oh, Mama!' Louise exclaimed. 'I never knew that. Why has it never been mentioned in the family?'

'My marriage to your father was frowned upon by my family and they cut me off and because talking about it might upset your dear papa, I never brought it up. The only person who did not condemn us was Catherine. It was she who persuaded her husband to give your papa the living at Moresdale. We were very close then. She envied me my strong sons and when we were both expecting at the same time we would talk about our plans for our children. She badly wanted a son for the Earl's sake and I wanted a daughter to make my family complete, so you see the exchange was not perhaps as cold-blooded as it sounds. We were all family. But your papa wanted you to be told, because he wanted you to make a good marriage to fulfil your birthright and as the daughter of an Earl, you could almost take your pick of the eligible bachelors. By refusing to let him do it, I was denying you the opportunity. And for that I beg your pardon.'

Louise laughed and hugged her mother. 'I found my eligible bachelor for myself, so you denied me nothing. I had a happy childhood, which the Dowager felt I would not have had at Moresdale Hall and now I have Jonathan. What more could I possibly want?' She stopped. 'I promised the Dowager I would not reveal anything about being the Earl's daughter to anyone but Jonathan, even though it would make it easier for me to be accepted by his parents. He said it did not matter in the least, but there is no secret about who you are, is there?'

'No, but Lady Chastonbury knows it anyway. I guessed she might be a stickler for protocol, so when I received your letter saying you and Lord

Leinster were going to be married, I had your father drive me over to call on her. She was stiff-rumped at first, angry with her son and inclined to think you had inveigled him into marrying in haste so that she would have no opportunity to voice her disapproval and bring an end to the liaison.' She laughed suddenly. 'I can be haughty when I choose, you know, and I met her formality with my own and told her the Earl of Sheffield's title was senior to the Earl of Chastonbury's, which her husband confirmed and after that she was all sweetness. You go to Chaston Hall with your husband, Louise, and you hold your head up. Be proud. Show her you are more than a fitting bride for her son.'

'Oh, Mama, I will. And I thank you from the bottom of my heart.'

'Whatever for? Being a mother?'

'Yes, exactly that. For being my mother.'

They hugged each other again and cried together. 'I am glad I went,' Louise said. 'But even more glad to be home again. And now beside two parents and three brothers, I have Jonathan who has proved himself to be a man in a million and one I shall love to the end of my days. If it had not been for him, I would never have got there and back in one piece.'

They stayed at the vicarage that night and next morning went to Chaston Hall where Louise was welcomed warmly. 'It is time Jonathan settled down,' his mother told her. 'And I hope it means the end of his thieftaking.'

'Jonathan will do what he thinks is right,' Louise answered firmly, recalling her mother's advice to be proud and show she was a fitting wife for Jonathan.

Her ladyship looked startled for a moment, then smiled. 'You'll do, my dear.'

Louise went on to speak of their plans for another ceremony to bless the wedding and a wedding breakfast to which everyone would be invited, an idea that had her ladyship's enthusiastic support. 'Have the feast here,' she said. 'We have acres of room. And it will please me to arrange it.'

And so it came about. Louise went to her father's church in a dress of pale lime brocade with dome-shaped hoops over which swathes of tulle were looped up to the waist. The quilted stays were embroidered in gold and laced with gold ribbon. Her hair was combed back in loose waves from a centre parting into a knot on top of her head from which ringlets fell about her ears. She wore the tiniest creation of a hat on top of that.

Jonathan was in a full-skirted cream satin coat with deep embroidered cuffs. His long waistcoat was of the same material heavily embroidered with gold-and-silver lace, with a long row of silver buttons. In honour of the occasion he wore a full-bottomed wig tied at the back with a huge black bow.

All Louise's relations came, except the Dowager Countess of Moresdale, who said she was too old to make the journey, but she did send a gift of a set of silver cutlery from her and her daughter-in-law. Her brothers brought their families and Jonathan's sister and cousins came and so did the members of the Piccadilly Gentleman's Club, cheerful and teasing.

'I do not know about being an organisation for dealing with criminals,' Harry said afterwards, smiling at Louise who was standing beside Jonathan in the great reception room at Chaston Hall, her arm linked in his. 'But it seems to me to have more to do with matchmaking. It has already been instrumental in finding wives for three of its members. James, Sam and now Jonathan.'

'And Joe,' Louise added. 'I know he is not strictly a member, but he played his part well.'

'And you will be next, Harry,' Sir Ashley put in. 'You have been a widower long enough.'

'Or perhaps you,' Harry retorted. It was nearly five years since his wife had died in childbirth, after only a year of marriage. Sometimes it was difficult to believe he had ever been married at all.

'Not me. I am a bachelor and a bachelor I will remain. I do not have a great estate waiting on my heir.'

'You'll see,' Jonathan put in, laughing. 'One day you will find yourself in love and all your intentions will fly out of the window. And a good thing too. Marriage is something I can heartily recommend.' He turned and smiled down at his wife. 'With the right woman of course.'

And so the celebrations continued until it was time for the happy couple to leave for their new home and their new life together.

* * * * *

HISTORICAL

Large Print

PRACTICAL WIDOW TO PASSIONATE MISTRESS
Louise Allen

Desperate to reunite with her sisters, Meg finds passage to England as injured soldier Major Ross Brandon's temporary housekeeper. Dangerously irresistible, Ross's dark, searching eyes warn Meg that it would be wrong to fall for him… But soon sensible Meg is tempted to move from servants' quarters to the master's bedroom!

MAJOR WESTHAVEN'S UNWILLING WARD
Emily Bascom

Spirited Lily is horrified by her reaction to her new guardian, Major Daniel Westhaven. He's insufferably arrogant – yet she can't help longing for his touch! Brooding Daniel intends to swiftly fulfil his promise and find trouble-some Lily a husband. Yet she brings light into his dark life – and into his even darker heart…

HER BANISHED LORD
Carol Townend

Hugh Duclair, Count de Freyncourt, has been accused of sedition, stripped of his title and banished. Proud Hugh vows to clear his name! Childhood friend Lady Aude de Crèvecoeur offers her help – after all, turbulent times call for passionate measures…

 MILLS & BOON®

HISTORICAL

Large Print

THE EARL'S RUNAWAY BRIDE
Sarah Mallory

Five years ago, Felicity's dashing husband disappeared into war-torn Spain. Discovering a dark secret, she had fled to England. Still haunted by memories of their passionate wedding night, Felicity is just about to come face to face with her commanding husband – back to claim his runaway bride!

THE WAYWARD DEBUTANTE
Sarah Elliott

Eleanor Sinclair loathes stuffy ballrooms packed with fretful mothers and husband-hunting girls. Craving escape, she dons a wig and disappears – *unchaperoned!* – to the theatre. There she catches the eye of James Bentley, a handsome devil. His game of seduction imperils Eleanor's disguise – and tempts her to forsake all honour…

THE LAIRD'S CAPTIVE WIFE
Joanna Fulford

Taken prisoner by Norman invaders, Lady Ashlynn's salvation takes an unexpected form. Scottish warlord Black Iain may be fierce, yet Ashlynn feels strangely safe in his arms… Iain wants only to be free of the rebellious, enticing Ashlynn. But then a decree from the King commands Iain to make his beautiful captive his *wife*!

 MILLS & BOON

HISTORICAL

Large Print

RAKE BEYOND REDEMPTION
Anne O'Brien

Alexander Ellerdine is instantly captivated by Marie-Claude's dauntless spirit – but, as a smuggler, Zan has nothing to offer such a woman. Marie-Claude is determined to unravel the mystery of her brooding rescuer. The integrity in his eyes indicates he's a gentleman…but the secrets and rumours say that he's a rake beyond redemption…

A THOROUGHLY COMPROMISED LADY
Bronwyn Scott

Has Incomparable Dulci Wycroft finally met her match? Jack, Viscount Wainsbridge, is an irresistible mystery. His dangerous work leaves no space for love – yet Dulci's sinfully innocent curves are impossibly tempting. Then Dulci and Jack are thrown together on a journey far from Society's whispers – and free of all constraints…

IN THE MASTER'S BED
Blythe Gifford

To live the life of independence she craves, Jane de Weston disguises herself as a young man. When Duncan discovers the truth he knows he should send her away – but Jane brings light into the dark corners of his heart. Instead, he decides to teach his willing pupil the exquisite pleasures of being a woman…

MILLS & BOON

HISTORICAL

Large Print

VICAR'S DAUGHTER TO VISCOUNT'S LADY
Louise Allen

Stunned by the death of her lover, pregnant Arabella Shelley is horrified when his brother, the inscrutable Viscount Hadleigh, demands she marry him instead! As Bella struggles with a new, luxurious lifestyle, and her scandalous desire for her stranger-husband, will she find a love that matches the passion of their marriage bed?

CHIVALROUS RAKE, SCANDALOUS LADY
Mary Brendan

Beautiful recluse Miss Jemma Bailey has spent years trying to forget her passionate, scandalous response to Marcus Speer's seductive touch. But Marcus has returned and this time he won't let Jemma go until he's exacted revenge for her debutante flirtation – he'll bed her rather than wed her! Though soon this isn't nearly enough…

THE LORD'S FORCED BRIDE
Anne Herries

A handsome stranger fighting in a town square mesmerises youthful Catherine. His shirt off, skin glistening with sweat – he's all man! But meeting him again in the opulent Royal Court, Catherine finds he is Andrew, Earl of Gifford, and bad blood runs between their families. He is also the lord she'll soon be forced to wed!

MILLS & BOON